WAITING TO VANISH

Also by Ann Hood

SOMEWHERE OFF THE COAST OF MAINE

Bantam New Fiction is devoted to novels with contemporary concerns. Publishing some of the most exciting voices at work today, these titles are available wherever quality trade paperbacks are sold.

BANTAM NEW FICTION

WAITING TO VANISH

Ann Hood

BANTAM BOOKS
TORONTO • NEW YORK • LONDON • SYDNEY • AUCKLAND

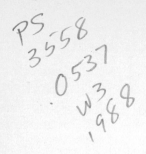

WAITING TO VANISH
A Bantam Book / July 1988

Grateful acknowledgment is made to reprint the following excerpts: "It's Only a Paper Moon" by Harold Arlen & E. Y. Harburg. Copyright 1933 by Warner Bros Music & Chappell & Co., Inc. Copyright renewed, International copyright secured. All rights reserved. Used by permission. "Yesterday," words and music by John Lennon and Paul McCartney. Copyright © 1965 NORTHERN SONGS LIMITED. All rights for U.S., Canada and Mexico controlled and administered by BLACKWOOD MUSIC INC. Under license from ATV MUSIC (MACLEN). All rights reserved. International copyright secured. Used by permission. "By the Beautiful Sea," words by Harold R. Atteridge, music by Harry Carroll. Copyright 1914 Shapiro Bernstein & Co., New York. Copyright renewed. Used by permission.

Library of Congress Cataloging-in-Publication Data

Hood, Ann, 1956–
  Waiting to vanish.

  (Bantam new fiction)
  I. Title.
PS3558.0537W3 1988   813'.54   87-47900
ISBN 0-553-34521-4

Published simultaneously in the United States and Canada

PRINTED IN THE UNITED STATES OF AMERICA

SEM   0 9 8 7 6 5 4 3 2 1

For Melissa

ACKNOWLEDGMENTS

A special thanks to my parents, Bob Reiss, Gail Hochman, and especially Deb Futter.

CHAPTER ONE

Mackenzie kept telling herself that if the family had stuck together after Alexander died, it would be different. Easier somehow.

Jason suggested that things do not just fall apart like that. "There must have been a crack in the structure already," he'd said. "Your brother's death was just the catalyst."

She had found his theory too ridiculous to be taken even a little seriously. Mackenzie carried an image of her family in which they were all in Rhode Island together in the big white Victorian house that her great-grandfather had built. She imagined them around the Queen Anne table, with cranberry candles in the just-polished candlesticks and, teetering in the center of the table, an angel that Alexander had made from dough in a long-ago art class. The food was familiar and comforting. And everyone was smiling. It wasn't a real moment, but rather a combination of many moments, all true in some way. The curl of her mother's auburn hair; the sound of her father clearing his throat, a habit of his; how Alexander squinted when he concentrated. Daisy, her brother's ex-wife, wasn't in it, although their son, Sam, usually was. And Grammie's sternness, her sense of manners and protocol, hovered somewhere off center. But what dominated this montage were Mackenzie's feelings of love, of rightness in that house.

"Sorry, Sigmund," she'd told Jason, "your theory doesn't hold for the Porters."

Gently he had reminded her that in the stories she'd told him she had often mentioned her mother's moodiness, her father's silence.

"Those are personality traits," she'd said. "Don't distort them."

Now she and Jason were in her apartment on Bedford Street. He had suggested a matinee, brunch at the NoHo Star, the Klee show at the Museum of Modern Art. But the day was cold and wet, and Mackenzie had said it was a day to stay home. Besides, Jason was leaving in a few days for a small town upstate where the new play he'd written was going to be performed as a workshop production. So they stayed in and made love while an old Tarzan movie played on television with the sound turned off.

Jason lay sprawled on the sofa bed. The couch itself was covered in a happy chintz, pinks and vivid reds. The sheets were scattered with tiny yellow roses. "Let's go to the flower garden," Jason had whispered earlier as he urged her toward the couch.

Mackenzie had turned the one bedroom into her darkroom. Her landlord had told her that Washington Irving had once lived in the apartment. And Dylan Thomas. Though not together, of course, he'd added. She loved the slightly sloping floors, the careful fleur-de-lis pattern carved into the moldings along the ceilings. If she was working late at night in the darkroom, snores rose through the floorboards from the apartment below. Now classical music drifted up. Mozart.

"Are you awake?" she whispered to Jason.

"Trying," he said.

She wrapped herself in her old kimono and curled up on the window seat to look out. The right sleeve of the kimono had faded in spots from pale peach to, surprisingly, lemon yellow. The wind rattled the windows and something halfway between rain and snow fell. Mackenzie tested herself. She focused on a wreath hanging on a door directly across the street. It was fastened with a big red and green plaid bow.

"This is silly," she mumbled.

Behind her Jason stirred, yawned.

"Tarzan is *still* on?" he said.

In two weeks, she thought, this will be over. I will have gotten through Christmas.

"Have you thought about my idea?" he asked. "To spend Christmas upstate with me?"

The night before Mackenzie and Jason had gone to a Christmas party at *Travel Horizons,* where Mackenzie worked as a free-lance photographer. But halfway through the evening, her own false cheer and strained enthusiasm had gotten to her. The art director, Margot, was telling Mackenzie about her holiday plans. "We're driving to Connecticut this year and spending the whole week there. John says he's going to cut down a tree and everything." "That sounds fabulous," Mackenzie had said, smiling and nodding, feeling awful. Across the small room, Jason was helping someone get a fire started in the fireplace. "I'm trying to think of something really corny to do for John," Margot was saying. "Like knit a scarf." She was wearing red Christmas tree ornaments as earrings. It was too much.

Mackenzie knew she could not smile or say "fabulous" one more time so she left, practically ran out the door and down the hall that smelled like an Indian restaurant.

Mackenzie had spent the next few hours walking the tangled streets behind her building, trying to get lost. On a corner she passed a little boy giving away kittens. "Take one," he told her. "I have to drown the leftovers." When she got home, Jason was in her apartment, pacing the uneven floors.

"You are not alone," he had shouted at her. "Do you hear me?"

"Everyone can hear you," she'd said.

Now Jason was saying, "You'll come to Poughkeepsie. We'll spend Christmas together. Egg nog. 'Silent Night.' The works."

Mackenzie pressed her fingertips against the window, as if to stop it from shaking.

"Mackenzie?" Jason said.

She turned to face him. On the television, Tarzan comforted a frightened Jane.

"I don't know," she said.

He tried to make his voice light. "I hope it's Poughkeepsie that's the deterrent and not me."

Mackenzie studied the tip of her long ponytail. Out of the sun, her pale blonde hair had darkened to the color of beach sand. Lately she'd picked up an old habit of hers from her teens, searching the bottom of her hair for split ends.

"Of course it's not you," she said.

She tried to picture herself on a train speeding up the Hudson toward Jason, tried to imagine what kind of Christmas they would have together. She thought of old barns, deep snow, a bed covered with quilts. She would bring him winter things for gifts. Fur-lined gloves. Irish whiskey. A sled. Last year she had given her nephew, Sam, a sled.

Its runners were a glossy red. Her mother had painted "Rosebud" in curly letters across the top. Stop, Mackenzie told herself. Stop thinking about it.

She watched as Jason pulled on his jeans and walked over to the coffee table littered with Chinese food containers. She had made that table from an old lobster trap, and it filled her with memories of home in Rhode Island, of trips to the ocean and clambakes in their backyard.

"Have you ever noticed that it used to snow more when we were kids?" Mackenzie said. Her grandmother used to say that if you wanted to avoid an argument, talk about the weather.

"Greenhouse effect," Jason said. He seemed relieved to change the subject too. "Someday New York will be as hot as Florida. Everything's shifting."

"You mean people will flock to the Rockaways for suntans in winter?" she said, and forced a smile. It felt stiff on her face.

"Hey," he said.

Behind them, Tarzan gripped a long vine and started to swing through the trees. If the sound were on they would hear his famous yell. Instead, a Mozart concerto swelled beneath them.

"I'm trying not to focus on this damn holiday," she said. "But it's so pervasive. They even pipe Christmas music into elevators."

"What do you say we run away somewhere that doesn't have Christmas?" he said, trying for a real smile. "Jerusalem? Beijing? Teheran?"

"Don't tempt me," she said.

And then, inexplicably, she was gripped with sadness. She moved back to the window and looked down on Bedford Street. The wind turned a woman's umbrella inside out.

"Rain in December," Mackenzie said. "It's ridiculous."

"I have a great idea. A swell idea. You'll come up with me tomorrow instead of waiting until Christmas. I bet you can get some great photographs of the country. Trees laden with snow. Very rustic."

She shook her head. "You'll be working on the play," she said. She heard herself, a slight whine in her voice. She had been doing well, or at least better, before all of this holiday cheer had been forced on her. For a month now she had been filled again with grief. With an incredible ache. This was the first Christmas without Alexander. She longed for even the mechanical good cheer of her mother. But Cal had left, had just packed up Alexander's old car and driven off. "I've had enough," she had said. As if the rest of them hadn't. Cal's sister, Hope, got postcards from her, from national monuments and landmarks all over the country. Messageless postcards with her initials at the bottom. Mackenzie and her father hadn't even gotten those.

Mackenzie had made halfhearted efforts to get through until New Year's. She had bought Christmas cards of a smiling Empire State Building holding hands with the Statue of Liberty, but they remained in their boxes somewhere amid the pile of unopened cards she'd received. She'd brought home a small tree that sat on the kitchen table bare until Jason suggested they decorate it. He had strung unraveled typewriter ribbon like an inky garland, and had hung broken pencils from its branches. Finally Mackenzie had joined him. She looped film into the shape of a star and placed it on top.

Now she turned to Jason.

"I can't get through this," she said. "I mean, how much is a person supposed to take? I'm tired of reading about survivors. People stranded in the Andes and wiped out in wars."

"You'll come with me," he said.

"Everybody has found a way to get through this. My mother takes off for who knows where. My father becomes a shoplifter. A kleptomaniac, for God's sake. Everyone is acting out and I'm the one trying to get through this holiday alone. Me and Alexander's ghost."

"It's worse around this time of year," he said, then shrugged, knowing the sentiment sounded empty. "Hey," he said, smiling, "you can teach me how to ski. We'll make s'mores. You know, I've never had a s'more."

"It just doesn't seem right," she said.

At Thanksgiving her father had invited her for a turkey dinner at Oakdale, the rehabilitation center where he was living. But she couldn't bear the thought of eating there, surrounded by abused women, pyromaniacs, and sad old men. She couldn't bear to admit that her own father, that Jams, was one of those troubled people. "He's lashing out by taking other people's things," his doctor had told her. "It's not uncommon." "You mean it's common?" Mackenzie had said, finding it hard to believe that mourners everywhere were thieves. "I mean it's not unheard of," the doctor said coldly. Still, Mackenzie could not grasp the comparison between Alexander's death and stealing a box of staples.

She hadn't joined Jams at Oakdale. He had called her the next day. "Turkey loaf," he'd said sadly. "It's a good thing you missed it. *Canned* cranberries. They tasted like Jell-O." She had wanted to shout at him. Ask him what he was doing there. They could have been home together, gotten through this first Thanksgiving without Alexander, if he hadn't checked himself in there. But she hadn't said anything at all. Even when he confessed to her that he'd stolen a loaf of pumpkin bread from the kitchen, she remained silent. "I didn't even eat it," he'd said. "I just threw it away."

As if he could read her mind, Jason said, "Thanksgiving would have been easier if you had come to Louisville for the play competition with me."

"What? And watched that redheaded vixen chase after you?" Mackenzie laughed.

"Kyle is a baby. Besides, anyone can tell that I'm hopelessly in love with a blonde vixen."

Once, a photo assignment had kept Mackenzie in India over Thanksgiving, and all the Americans had banded together for a makeshift dinner—roasted lamb instead of turkey, fried bananas, and basmati rice. When she'd called home, Sam, then four years old, had said, "Are you in a teepee? Are you wearing feathers?" Alexander had laughed on the extension. "I'm trying to teach him to say Native American," he'd said.

It will be like India, Mackenzie had thought. She'd have an orphan's Thanksgiving and invite everyone she knew who had no place to go. She would buy Indian corn and pumpkins for decorations. But everyone she called had someplace to go. Dinners with second cousins, maiden aunts, ex-boyfriends. Anything not to be alone. "Volunteer at a shelter for the homeless," her friend Beth had suggested. Beth was flying off to Bimini for the long weekend. "I did that one year and it really helped me put everything in perspective." "I don't think my perspective is off," Mackenzie had said. "Last year I had a normal Thanksgiving. I fought with my mother for being too cynical. My brother and I smoked a joint in the garage and trashed his ex-wife. And Sam spilled the entire plate of stuffing in my father's lap. That is a normal Thanksgiving. That's all I want." "I don't know," Beth had said. "I'd rather go to Bimini."

Mackenzie had spent the day alone in the St. Mark's Cinema and watched *East of Eden* and *Rebel Without a Cause* over and over, crying, thinking that Alexander had looked like a dark blonde version of James Dean. Her dinner was two falafels on Macdougal Street, where she cried at the black and white posters of early Simon and Garfunkel. Everything around her seemed representative of lost things, of sadness. The empty streets, the smell of espresso, the old man urinating in the corner—all of it made her more and more lonely. Finally she'd sat on a bench in Washington Square Park, tucked her legs under her, and willed herself to disappear from New York, from her sadness.

"No," Mackenzie said out loud.

"No?"

"I'm going to have a terrific Christmas. I'll drive down to Maryland and get Sam and we'll do something wonderful. Stay at the Plaza, maybe. Go to Radio City."

"Mackenzie," he said, "I want us to be together. We can be a family. We can."

She turned to him, her eyes a deep jade. "I have a family," she said. "Don't ever say I don't."

They stood in an angry silence until he said, softly, "I want you to do whatever you have to do to work this out. If it means not coming upstate with me, all right. But, please, work it out."

Work it out. She had tried so hard to do just that. When Alexander had first died, she had written letters to anyone she thought might be remotely responsible for his death. Meteorological societies. The telephone company. His landlord. Her brother had been in his apartment in Boston, talking to Sam on the telephone, when lightning struck and electrocuted him. "Dear sir," she'd written in letter after letter, "you've killed my brother." She cited faulty wiring, sloppy installation, whatever applied.

After a while, she stopped writing and grew intro-spective. She'd sat on the beach and watched the waves, studied the patterns with which they rose and fell. Then

9

she had tried to escape through Jason somehow. What now?

Alexander's ex-wife, Daisy, had spent the summer calling from Maryland and shouting at whoever answered the telephone. Sam had stopped talking altogether. "He won't say a word," Daisy would shriek into the phone. "What am I supposed to do?" Each of the Porters held the receiver lightly in their hands, slightly away from their ears, like the deadly weapon it had become to them. Mackenzie had imagined that Daisy had no fear of it, however, that she gripped it tightly, clutched it, unafraid of what it might do. "That woman," Cal said after each time Daisy called. "Why did Alexander ever marry her in the first place?" Mackenzie had always been sure it was because she was so different, so unlike the Porters. Right after Sam was born, Alexander had said to Mackenzie, "Isn't Daisy incredible? We were on the dance floor until her contractions were ten minutes apart." His voice had been filled with amazement.

"Maybe what I need," Mackenzie said to Jason, "is to go back home. Recreate an old-fashioned Porter Christmas." He sat with his back to her. Tarzan had ended and now Abbott and Costello ran through a crowded outdoor market full of camels and Arabs in headdresses.

Her words seemed hollow. Impossible. She imagined, as she often did, her mother somewhere, living a different life. In Chicago or Miami or Des Moines. Writing poetry, sending blank postcards. Mackenzie wondered if there could be a "Porter Christmas" without her mother's carefully wrapped packages and special plum pudding with brandy sauce.

She kneeled down in front of Jason. His eyes behind his wire-rimmed glasses were as brown as Hershey's kisses.

"Maybe it will help Sam," she said. "Going back to Rhode Island." Last Christmas he rode the new sled all

10

day in the backyard. He'd also gotten Ralph Lauren sweaters the colors of sherbert and a box of paints. Alexander had marked off Sam's height, the tiny pencil mark even with Alexander's when he had been six. At night they'd all played Twister, and had fallen together in a woolly heap in front of the tree.

"Maybe," Jason said, "it will help you."

His eyes softened, now the chocolate a melted brown.

Mackenzie climbed onto the couch beside him. He wrapped his arms around her.

"I love you," he said. "Do what you have to do so we can get on with our lives. With us."

Her mind filled with scattered images, the smell of pine and bayberry, her mother's staccato laugh, Alexander in a dark green sweater, smiling. She shook her head to rattle the images, to shake them up, or to make them go away.

"Even I'm tired of it," she said. "Only half living."

She felt his breath on her neck. His tight brown curls tickled her cheek.

He said, "I love you." His voice was a whisper. He said, "It's all right."

CHAPTER TWO

Jason sat at a rickety table in the Holiday bar drinking a draft beer.

Sometimes he and Mackenzie met there at the end of the day to decide what to do about dinner. An Indian place over on Sixth Street? Chinese delivered? Or, if it was still early enough, maybe they could get a table at The Great Jones Cafe. As he sat here alone now, Jason's heart skipped a beat every time the door opened, as if it might be her coming in.

When he'd wait for her, he would stumble out of his apartment as if from a cave, his head fuzzy with ideas, and make his way down First Avenue. He always arrived first, like an anxious teenager on a first date. Then Mackenzie would come in, her camera bag slung over her shoulder, and she would talk about her day. Her day was like a collage, images of the city and its streets and occupants.

"I saw a man," she'd say, "and he was singing opera in the middle of the street, stopping traffic. He wore a tuxedo and his voice was really beautiful. The sun," and here she'd use her hands to demonstrate, "circled his head like a halo."

She talked about her freelance work too. Book jacket photographs and pictures of the downtown art scene, in black and white, for a new magazine. But her own project was photographs of doorways. She roamed the city looking for them. She was out at dawn or in blinding rain, or to catch the light between the buildings so the shaft would shine on a particular door.

Just last month—no, only three weeks ago—they had spent a snowy morning in bed at Jason's apartment. They drank espresso that he made from a noisy machine that spit coffee and steam at him as it brewed. They had newspapers from different cities, which they bought at a newsstand on St. Mark's Place. Every Sunday they got the *Times* and the Los Angeles and San Francisco papers and then one they'd never read before. *The Cleveland Plain Dealer* or the *Miami Tribune*.

Suddenly, right at noon, as the bells on the Ukrainian church down the block rang, the sun burst out.

Mackenzie jumped up, ran to the window.

"The light," she said. "And the snow. It's perfect."

He had looked up from an LA travel piece on Tahiti. "What?" he said.

In her bag she carried a small blue notebook with pages of addresses. Doorways she had seen with notes of what would make the shot perfect—a purple cast to the sky, autumn, night. She flipped through it now.

"Somewhere. Perry Street, I think. Or Barrow. There's this doorway made of stone and the stone has flecks of gold through it. Here it is. Barrow."

She'd looked at him and her eyes were flashing with excitement.

"Against the snow," she said, "and with this bright light, it will look like the Piazza San Marco in Venice."

Jason laughed.

"You'll see," she said.

She pulled on black tights and a loose fisherman's sweater that hung to her knees.

"Don't go," he said.

He held up an untouched newspaper.

"Remember Cleveland," he said.

"I only hope they haven't shoveled yet. I want the snow to reflect upward."

He watched her hands pushing upward at the air as she talked. She was, he thought, the most lovely woman he had known.

"Listen," he said, "stay here and marry me and we'll run off to Tahiti. What do you say?"

"I'll bring back pastries," she said. "Babka."

She'd wrapped her hair in a bright blue beret and draped his long black and white scarf around her neck.

When Jason saw the picture, it was as she'd said. The tiny flecks of gold blazed in the sunlight. The snow, heaped against the door, sparkled like sugar.

"Mackenzie," he said, studying the photograph, "you really should have a show. You have enough in this series, easily."

She shook her head hard. "I have too much to do," she said.

And so the photographs remained scattered through her apartment, all glorious doorways. Wrought iron cast in shadow. Peeling paint in Bermuda blue. Smudged brass ornamentation. In one, the door was slightly ajar. In the distance, a bare bulb burned. The late afternoon sun cast a sinister shadow, slashed across it.

Jason finished his beer and ordered a second.

He wanted her back. She had put everything on hold since Alexander died. And now she had this idea that she could put all the pieces of her family back together again.

He had met her before Alexander had died. Jason had won a grant for his play *The Year of Peace and Love*. Part of the prize was to have it performed at a play festival at the Kennedy Center. A mutual friend had suggested he call Mackenzie while he was in Washington. Later, she told him that she had expected an overaged hippie with straggly hair and a Grateful Dead T-shirt. "I was," she said, "pleasantly surprised."

It was two days before she left for her trip to New Zealand. Her assignment was a photographic essay on the country's unique natural beauty. Her apartment was littered with clothes—"It's winter there," she'd explained as she moved sweaters off a chair—and maps that marked waterfalls, forests, and mountains.

The thing that had struck him immediately was her energy. It radiated from her, lit her face. She had shown him the maps, explained the route she'd take through New Zealand.

"I'm renting a camper," she said. And she'd smiled at him. "It's a real wilderness trek."

It was then that he noticed she was beautiful too.

Her apartment was small. Framed prints leaned against an exposed brick wall.

"I haven't even had time to hang those," she said. "I just got back from Indonesia."

"A real jet setter," he said.

But he was thinking, How will I get to know her better if she's gone so much?

"I'm afraid so," she said. "It's hell on relationships."

A cat peered down at him from the top shelf of a bookcase. Another rocked gently in a chair.

"Does that mean you're . . ." he struggled for a word.

"Unattached?" she said.

He nodded.

"Very."

He felt relieved.

They ate at a cafe called After Words that sat behind a busy bookstore.

"I have a confession," Jason told her. "I *am* an old hippie."

"Really?"

"I wake up and wonder what has happened. I mean, the younger generation has become apathetic and materialistic. They all want to make a million bucks." He shook his head sadly.

"Whose fault is that?" Mackenzie said.

"Don't tell me it's ours."

"Whose, then?"

The lights came on, bright, and they looked around, startled. The restaurant was empty.

"Politics make me crazy," he said.

"They are too apathetic out there," Mackenzie said. "It's good to see someone so impassioned."

He leaned over then and kissed her.

Their waiter sat nearby, refilling ketchup bottles.

"Just my luck," he said. "I get the table that decides to fall in love."

"I think that's our cue," Mackenzie said.

They left the restaurant and wandered for hours down the streets hidden by Connecticut Avenue, past brownstones and all-night 7-Elevens. He invited her to go with him to see his play performed the next night.

After he left her at her apartment, Jason worried that he'd sounded too cynical, too pompous and self-righteous. He went over their conversation again and again. She had smiled. She had agreed with him. She had kissed him. Oh please, he thought, like me.

He knew he came on strong. His last girlfriend, Amanda, had accused him of being too intense. When he listened he frowned, or closed his eyes. He hunched over, like an old man, Amanda used to say.

"I'm terrible at parties," he had told Mackenzie. "I can't make small talk at all."

"Oh, God," she'd said, "I'm a master at it. It was something we learned as children. Always remember the person's name to whom you're speaking, and use it in the conversation. Avoid talking about politics and religion. And sex, of course."

"Wait," he'd laughed. "Should I take notes?"

Amanda had moved out to Los Angeles and he had gone with her. They had met at Yale, where he studied playwrighting and she studied acting. She became a television commercial actress. Her face was plain enough and pretty enough to fit any role—a housewife shining floors, a college student reaching out to touch someone, a daughter comparing douches with her mother.

His only play there had bombed.

"Mr. Fine," a critic wrote, "wake up! It's the 1980s, not 1969. Say good-bye to that burdensome decade, or at least keep it to yourself."

"You and Los Angeles," Amanda had told him, "are oxymoronic."

He'd moved back to New York. Amanda's face still filled his TV screen. She chewed Dentyne and rid her hair of dandruff. Every few months she sent him something. A crate of kiwis. "See, darling," she'd written, "we can do anything out here. Almost." Another time she sent him Mickey Mouse ears with his name sewn on the back. "A thinking cap?" her note had said.

Amanda had been happy as a television commercial star. She was satisfied with everything, just as it was.

"What exactly do you want?" she would ask him. "A revolution?"

"But you must want more than to sell toothpaste on TV," he'd insist. "How about a bigger apartment? Or a starring role in a movie?"

"Well," she'd said, reluctantly, "maybe I'd like a house or something in the mountains." Then she'd wrinkled her nose. "But when would I go there? And how would I get there? No, that would be a waste. Never mind."

After that first date with Mackenzie, Jason had worried all day. Had he been, again, too intense?

He remembered the way he'd raged when Reagan was reelected.

"So what, Jason?" Amanda had said.

"This country," he had shouted, "is going down the tubes and all you're doing is getting a suntan."

Mackenzie, at least, had seemed interested. But then again, she'd said herself that she was a master of small talk, an expert on etiquette.

The first thing he did when he picked her up for the play was apologize.

"For what?" she said.

"I really went on last night. And on and on."

"I liked it," she said. And she touched the side of his face, softly.

His anxiety left him in one sudden rush.

As they started to leave, the telephone rang.

"I shouldn't get this," she said, "but my machine's broken."

He nodded, stood in the doorway as she spoke.

"I can't talk," she said into the telephone. "I am literally out the door." She laughed. "I will have a good trip. Don't run off with this Lydia before I get back. I'll bring you something really exotic."

"My brother," she explained to Jason. "We're like this."

She held up two fingers, crossed together.

It was the last time Mackenzie spoke to Alexander.

Jason was already back in New York when she left for New Zealand via Los Angeles the next night. He sent a dozen yellow roses to her hotel in LA with a note. "I tried to match the color of your hair," he wrote. "This was as close as I could come. A poor second."

He was totally and completely full of her, and he had spent fifteen minutes on the telephone with the florist describing the exact tint of gold he wanted in the roses. Her hair, when he'd touched it, had seemed like that of a fairy princess.

When she called him from Los Angeles to thank him, her voice sounded small and far away.

"That's because I am far away," she said, laughing.

But he imagined her as a pinpoint of light, receding from him, growing smaller and fainter.

"I want postcards," he told her. "Lots of them."

The postcards never came.

A few hours after they spoke, she got the news about Alexander. Months later, Mackenzie told Jason that she had tried to call her Aunt Hope, to ask her to pick her up at Logan, but she couldn't remember the number. On the plane ride east, she'd wandered into first class, where an elaborate meal was being served from carts. A flight attendant stood in the aisle, carving a chateaubriand. Another poured wine from a crystal decanter.

"I need . . ." Mackenzie had said loudly.

But then she forgot what exactly it was that she needed. A bathroom? For Alexander to be home and alive when she got there? Help?

Businessmen stared up at her.

"Miss," the flight attendant carving the roast said, "you'll have to go back to your seat now."

The fork pierced the meat and Mackenzie watched blood trickle out.

She realized then that she hadn't even asked what had happened. Aunt Hope had called, had told her to hurry so she'd catch the last flight back that evening. Otherwise she'd have to wait until the next day. Alexander, Mackenzie thought, dead? This was impossible.

"Miss," the flight attendant said again.

And then Mackenzie started to cry. To sob.

"I hadn't cried until then," Mackenzie told Jason.

But he learned all of this later.

When there was no word from New Zealand, he was sure he had scared her off. Perhaps, he thought, the roses were a bad idea. Or the note. He called her number in Washington and a recording told him it had been disconnected. At the magazine a receptionist said, "There's no Mackenzie Porter on my list."

He pictured a plane crash. He imagined the rented camper toppling over a mountainside. He thought of those waterfalls swallowing her up, her golden hair floating like some kind of magical seaweed, stuck with twigs and pebbles.

Amanda sent him a bright yellow poster with an orange peace sign on it.

"Peace is back!" she wrote. "You are a trendsetter, dear!"

He threw it away.

Finally, he rented a car and drove to Rhode Island, a state he'd never been to before, a state that as a child growing up in Chicago he'd assumed was an extension of New York. He knew it was a crazy thing to do, but it didn't matter. When she'd called from LA he had wanted to ask her if she believed in love at almost first sight. Now he wished he had.

It was July and hot and the air conditioning in the car didn't work. Or at least he couldn't get it to work. He knew he should practice what to say to her parents when he got there but his mind felt like cotton. What am I doing? he thought as he passed New Haven. He still had a friend or two there. He should turn around and take that exit and stop by to see them. But he continued north, remembering her golden hair.

He thought of the play he was writing, *Still Looking for Paul McCartney*. Three women in New York, products of the sixties, holding on to some idealized vision of the man they wanted. "Remember," one of them says, "watching Paul McCartney on *The Ed Sullivan Show*? Remember the way he made you swoon?" "He was," the second one says, "so perfect." "Sure," the third woman laughs, "then we grow up and find out he was dropping acid like candy."

He thought of the play all the way to the Porters' front door. So that when Mrs. Porter opened it, Jason looked confused, the way he looked after he wrote all day, as if he were a foreigner and didn't understand the language. As if his spaceship had just landed.

"Yes?" she said.

He remembered thinking she looked weary.

He squinted at her, damned himself for not making a plan.

"Are you here to save my soul?" she said.

The house was large and white, the doorway framed in red.

"Soul . . ." he said.

"Jehovah's Witness? Mormon? What?"

He shook his head, unable to grasp what she was saying.

22

"It certainly needs saving," she said, as if to someone else.

"Has something happened to Mackenzie?" he blurted. She frowned.

"Not directly," Cal said. "Something has happened—" she paused.

He thought she might cry.

"—to all of us," she finished softly.

And then Mackenzie was in front of him. Her skin was tanned to the color of copper, a dirty penny.

"I can't believe this," she said. "You found me."

She stepped outside, around her mother, whose eyes were heavy and downcast.

The air was still.

Mackenzie wore red and white paisley boxer shorts and a loose T-shirt. He saw the outline of her breasts.

"I thought maybe you had drowned," he said.

Seeing her here in front of him, it sounded silly. He thought of his image, her golden hair, tangled and floating.

"It's my brother," she said, staring past him. "Alexander." She doubled over slightly at the name, as if it wounded her to say it.

They drove to the ocean and she spoke in a calm voice. She told him about her nephew, Sam, how he'd stopped talking, how he'd sat holding the telephone, screaming, as her brother lay on the other end. "It was lightning," she said. "An electrical storm. The phone was a conductor. As children we weren't allowed to take baths or answer the phone during storms. He knew better."

They ate stuffed quahogs and clamcakes and chowder and drank a pitcher of Narragansett Beer.

In the same controlled voice, like a sleepwalker, Mackenzie had said, "No one is coping. They're all falling apart."

She took him for a walk along the seawall. It was

beautiful. The food was salty on his tongue, the ocean stretched ahead of them like a hand.

When they got back to the Porters', the house was dark.

"My mother always used to leave a light on for us when we were out," Mackenzie said.

"I have to have you in my life," he said.

He thought this sounded dramatic, and inappropriate beside her grief.

But she smiled, and nodded.

"I've thought of you," she said, "but it's been as if time has disappeared."

A month later she moved to New York.

Jason knew that somehow Mackenzie had to give in to her grief. She kept holding back, keeping it at arm's length. This mission she was on, taking Sam to Rhode Island for Christmas, was an effort to retrieve what had been lost. But the old structure could not be revived. Wasn't that, after all, the very nature of death?

He told her they could get married and build a home together.

"Your image of home," he'd told her, "is precious and beautiful. But it's gone."

"No," she'd said.

He knew that for her to admit that was to accept Alexander's death. To marry him and start a life together was to turn her back on her brother.

Jason ordered another beer.

Kyle O'Day walked through the door.

She was over an hour late for their meeting. As she moved toward him, Jason's gut ached for Mackenzie.

"Dance class," Kyle said as she sat down.

Her red hair hung loose and fell around her in gentle ripples. She had a pouty mouth that she painted in a clear gloss that smelled like bubble gum.

He wanted her to disappear. Or to metamorphose into Mackenzie. Mackenzie opening her bag and laying out photographs of doorways. He imagined them there before him—brick against wood, or a bright green one decked in flowers.

"God," Kyle said, and rolled her eyes. "Dance. Voice. Scene study. I hardly have time to breathe. Really."

She lit up a clove cigarette.

"Want one?" She held the crumpled red packet toward him.

Jason shook his head.

"The thing I wanted to focus on," he said, "is that the role you're playing—"

"Tracy."

"Yes. The role of Tracy is someone older, but still childlike. That's why she can really hold Paul McCartney as some idol. Ideal."

She nodded.

"I'm not sure you have a grasp," he said, "of who Tracy is. Or rather, where she's coming from."

"Well," Kyle said, "personally I would fall for George. I mean, me, Kyle O'Day. I would like George. He was all dark and mysterious, right?"

Her voice was breathless and quick.

"Since Tracy's crush on Paul, that is to say, since she was a child, a lot has happened," Jason said. His nose tickled from all the sweet smells. Clove. Bubble gum. "She was thrown into a world of questioning. Rebellion. The Vietnam War. Drugs. Free sex."

"Blah, blah, blah."

He frowned.

"Listen," Kyle said, "I know."

She puffed on her clove cigarette for effect.

"I was at Woodstock," she said.

"Kyle."

"I was."

"In 1969 you were, what? Five years old?"

"Three." She smiled. "I was one of those naked little kids playing in the mud. I'm even in a magazine picture. All dirty, holding a flower."

His frown deepened as he listened.

"I'll show you the picture sometime," she said. "My parents were into all that. God, my brother may have even been conceived there. That just blows my mother away. They even named him Arlo, for some—"

"I know," Jason said.

"Right. Now my father works for Donald Trump. My mother thinks it's disgusting, that my dad's this big real estate mogul. He says he laughs all the way to the bank."

"What do you say?"

Kyle shrugged. "It sure beats fucking in a pile of mud while Jimi Hendrix blows his mind on stage."

They stared at each other.

He wished she'd disappear.

"No offense," she said.

Jason finished his beer.

He closed his eyes while Kyle talked about the character. He imagined Mackenzie, driving south toward Maryland and Sam, and tried to will her back to him.

CHAPTER THREE

Sometimes Sam liked to lie in bed with all the lights off. Even the clown lamp, with its soft-colored balloons. He lay there and tried to erase every thought from his head. He pretended his mind was a blackboard, and imagined a hand wiping it clean. Swoosh. Swoosh. Then nothing.

His mother hated when he went in there and did that.

She'd open the door and right away turn on the lights. Every one of them.

"Sam," she'd say, "what exactly are you doing? Sit up. Sit up, right now."

Before his father had died, Sam would never have done anything like that, like lying in bed in the dark. He would draw instead. Big pictures with lots of yellow and blue in them. Pictures full of smiling fish, and a big round happy sun. His father had had one of them framed and he'd hung it in his living room in Boston, like it was real

27

art. That picture had a rainbow, and tall flowers that looked like lollipops, and green green grass.

He knew that his mother was afraid he was crazy. He had heard her telling her best friend, Allison. She had said, "Can little boys lose their minds?" Allison had said, "Yes. Look at Sybil. She went crazy when she was just a little girl." Sam didn't know Sybil, or any crazy children. He wasn't worried anyway, because he knew that he was sad, not crazy.

His mother called him Mr. Turtle. She tried to laugh when she said it but her voice sounded nervous, the way it sounded when she talked to Grandma Cal when she used to call. Another time, he'd heard his mother say to Allison, "He's like a shell." Even though she'd said it like it was a bad thing to be, it had made Sam think of the ocean and seashells and the tiny animals who lived in them and he liked the idea of it. He was a shell. His father had told him stories about seashells. They were like marble palaces to the sea animals, he'd said. So when Sam had heard his mother say that, he'd smiled, and curled himself into a tight ball, like a sea scallop in its fan-shaped palace.

Sometimes, after his mother came in and turned on all the lights, she'd say, "Let's read."

The truth was, he didn't like books so much anymore. Instead, he liked to try to remember the stories that his father had told him. Looking at books just mixed him up.

She'd pull out a Curious George book from the shelf. The one about the hats. The pictures used to make him laugh. All those funny hats piled on that little monkey's head.

"Look how funny Curious George looks with all those hats," she'd say.

Sam would look, just to make her happy. But it didn't

28

seem funny to him anymore. Instead, he'd try to remember. Had his father ever told him a story about a monkey? Or was it just a book? When he couldn't remember exactly, he'd slam the Curious George book closed and bang it with his fist.

Once, after he did that, his mother shouted, "You are impossible and I am tired of you. Do you hear me?"

Sam had rolled himself up tight. He thought of a story his father used to tell about an island that disappeared and he pretended to be there, a sea scallop in a purple shell on the island of Atlantis.

Daisy stood in the doorway of Sam's room, gritting her teeth so hard they almost hurt. Looking at her little boy curled up like this, in the dark, should make her feel sympathy, she thought. Or sadness. But all it did was make her angry.

"All right, Mr. Turtle," she said, not even trying to make her voice sound cheerful. "Mackenzie will be here any minute and I want you ready to go. Got it?"

Sam didn't budge.

"Good," she said, as if he had answered.

She turned on the overhead light, then waited for a reaction from him. When she got none, she left.

In the living room, she piled magazines, shoes, toys— whatever was laying around—and threw it all into the closet. She wanted order. She wanted Mackenzie to see that Daisy's life was going swell. When Alexander had moved out on her a couple of years ago, Daisy had thought she'd fall apart. She'd imagined the Porters in their big house, nodding at each other, feeling self-righteous, thinking Daisy Bloom had lost after all. She was going to show Mackenzie that she hadn't lost. She had made money as a cosmetics company sales rep. She'd bought this condo. She'd even won a pale pink Cadillac for being the top saleswoman in her district last year. All without being Mrs. Alexander Porter.

Daisy was only seventeen when she'd first met Alexander. She had just graduated from high school, despite all the teachers' threats that she'd never make it. Even though everyone around her was going to college, or into the Navy, or getting married, Daisy felt that she was going to leave them all behind. She had big plans. She was tall enough and skinny enough to be a model. When she looked in the mirror, she didn't see that her hair was too brassy or her teeth too crooked on the bottom. Instead, she'd imagine herself taking the train to New York and marching into the Eileen Ford Agency where Eileen Ford herself would gasp. People were always telling Daisy that she resembled Goldie Hawn. Same shaggy hair and blue eyes as round as Frisbees.

She used to always talk about becoming a model. Before school ended, she used to cut classes and take off to the beach with whatever boy she liked at the time. Maybe someone with a new Camaro, or an old boyfriend home on leave. They would drink a bottle of Riunite Lambrusco and smoke dope and Daisy would talk about being a model. "You need to be tall and skinny and beautiful," she'd say. Then she'd undress for them. "Am I beautiful?" she'd ask. Even now she sometimes thought about those days at the beach, about all those boys who believed in her, who believed that Eileen Ford would hire her as a model, that she'd make five hundred dollars a day and be on the cover of *Glamour* magazine. She still could remember the hairless chests and faded jeans they all seemed to have, and the taste of the too-sweet wine mixed with smoke, their eager hands and tongues on her. Their names had all faded in her mind. Instead, she recalled a sea horse tattoo, an appendectomy scar, a gold stud earring. "Beats algebra," she always said afterward.

It was her standard line, rehearsed like her Goldie Hawn giggle and the particular way she rolled her eyes. At home she practiced walking with a book on her head. But nobody ever saw that.

All that summer after graduation she worked at Jordan Marsh and saved her money to pay a photographer for her portfolio pictures. She wrote to Eileen Ford, and got a form letter that said she needed a picture in formal wear, one in jeans, and one in a bathing suit. The photographer posed her in front of a screen with a sunset painted on it. He was short and fat with a goatee. He smelled like garlic. For almost an hour she posed in her bright orange bikini in front of that fake sunset. Finally she'd said, "Can I change now?" His beard had grown damp and there were big circles of sweat under his arms and on his back. "Why don't you touch yourself?" he'd said. He reached over and slipped his moist hand into her bikini bottom. "Touch yourself here," he said. She didn't move. He had three hundred dollars of hers. He whispered, "I know Eileen Ford. I've sent girls to her. Mona Grant. You know Mona Grant?" He reached over and unsnapped her bikini bra. Her breasts fell out and the top dangled around her neck by its thin straps. "Do you really know Eileen Ford?" she'd said. "Really?" Later, he'd laughed. "Kid," he told her, "you need to see a dentist. And your nose is too long. But your body's pretty good." He gave her his card. "I do movies too. You want to work for me, give me a call." "Fuck you," she'd said, and left.

When she met Alexander, she told him that she had been to New York and that the Eileen Ford Agency had sent her to a photographer who told her modeling was a terrible business. "He thought I'd be a good actress," she'd said, "but I wanted to do more with my life." Alexander had been impressed. He used to introduce her as a former model sometimes. He was the first guy to take her on real dates. To open the car door for her and pay for her dinner. The first time she walked into the Porter house, she had felt like a princess entering a castle. And then Mackenzie had come in, and Daisy had known that here was the real princess.

"Not anymore," Daisy said out loud.

She looked around her living room, pleased.

But a few minutes later when Mackenzie arrived, Daisy felt embarrassed by the room. The gray suede couch that she'd paid a fortune for looked tacky. The two glossy prints of large pink flowers seemed cheap, tasteless. And the balloon curtains on the window seemed funereal suddenly, like the satin interior of a coffin.

"Nice," Mackenzie said politely.

Daisy shrugged. She thought about how long it had taken her to pick those prints out, how unsure she'd been about the curtains.

"How's Sam doing?" Mackenzie asked.

"Fine, considering he still refuses to talk. It's enough to drive you crazy. You'll see."

"Well, Daisy," Mackenzie said, "he's had a terrible trauma. We all have."

Daisy noticed that Mackenzie's eyes were a murky green instead of their usual bright turquoise.

The room seemed to grow more and more shabby the longer Mackenzie stood there in her brightly striped sweater and shiny blonde hair. Daisy had an impulse to move things around, rearrange everything so that it might look better. She thought of the house she'd grown up in.

The Bloom house was square and brick. Every house on the street was identical, and people added shutters or awnings or porches to make theirs stand out. But the Bloom house remained untouched, until its plainness was what made it, finally, different from the others. The night their father left, Daisy and her sister, Iris, were eating potato chips, dipping them into a mixture of Lipton's dried onion soup and sour cream, and watching *Petticoat Junction* in the kitchen on a nine-inch-screen TV. Their mother, Donna, watched *Peyton Place* on the big television in the living room.

"Oops," their father said, and he patted his shirt pocket. "I'm out of cigs. You need anything, Donna?"

"You can pick up some soda," she said, "if you're going to Cumberland Farms."

She didn't look at him, just stared at the television. The room, as Daisy remembered it, had been cast in a smoky blue light.

He had walked out without anyone looking up. Iris and Daisy stared at the tiny screen, watched Billie-Jo, Bobbie-Jo, and Betty-Jo, as their father walked out forever. "One woman's garbage is another's dessert," Donna had said in explanation. Their mother had dozens of sayings, one for any occasion that could pop up. "To each his own." "If you spit in the air, it comes back in your face."

After their father left, Donna stopped cooking. Sometimes, late at night, she'd make a pot of spaghetti or a pot roast and they'd eat it whenever the mood struck them. Most of the time, they each threw their own meal together and ate it wherever they happened to be. Unwashed dishes could be found anywhere, as they were left beside the bathtub or on top of a bureau or chair. Every couple of months, when there were no more clean dishes, the three of them would go on a search mission to unearth all the used plates. They would wash them in the bathtub and then start over. "If you're hungry," Donna used to say, "make a little something."

When Daisy first started to date Alexander, she'd come home and scream, "They eat real meals there. They all sit together and eat. Roast beef. Mashed potatoes.

33

String beans." She redecorated her room then, painted her half a soft yellow with floral decals along the borders of the walls. "This isn't right," she'd said when she was done. Iris's half stayed the same dingy off-white with posters of the Monkees taped to the wall.

Daisy started to eat sitting at the kitchen table. She would move away the *Reader's Digests* and unopened bills that covered it, set a place for herself with a plate and napkin and a glass of water, and eat. "This," she would say, "is how a normal person eats."

Donna read cards for a living. Never at home, always for groups of six or more. She did parties mostly and was booked for months in advance. She used a regular deck of playing cards and gave the same advice she gave to her daughters. "There's a dark haired man. Am I right? What are you doing with him? One woman's garbage, honey, is another's dessert." She told Mrs. Porter that she was a counselor. "The problems I see," she told her, shaking her head. "What kind of counselor are you exactly?" Cal had asked, pronouncing each word, each syllable, with disbelief. "Psychic counselor, honey," Donna said.

That first year that Daisy dated Alexander, she came home a few weeks before Christmas, mad again, screaming.

"Can't we even have a Christmas tree? Like normal people? A little tree, that's all."

As children, Iris and Daisy had done any holiday decorating for the house, using things they'd made in school. Red paper hearts pasted to doilies stayed up all year, hung beside turkeys traced from their hands and rough silhouettes of George Washington and Abraham Lincoln. Construction paper chains, meant to hang on Christmas trees, draped instead over the kitchen cupboards until the links tore and sent them to the floor. One year they made pine cone trees, stuck with plaster of paris into empty tunafish cans painted white and green. Those sat among the papers on the table until the pine cones dried up and the paint flaked off and no one could remember why they were even there.

"I've had it up to here with the Porters," Donna had said. "What with their roast beef and their Cape Cod vacations."

But she bought a tree.

It was silver. The branches stuck out from a center post and came to a pom-pom-tipped end. It had no decorations. Instead, a multicolored light rotated in front of it, changing the tree to shiny blue, then red, then green, and finally yellow. The tree stayed up until March, gathering dust, the pom-poms drooping until they looked like silver streams of tinfoil.

That same year, just before Christmas, the Porters invited the Blooms to their house for dinner. Daisy panicked. She went through Donna's closets, pulling out clothes. "Don't you have anything understated?" she said. She sat on Donna's bed, surrounded by flowered chiffon blouses with ruffled cuffs and tight black dresses with slit skirts and drop backs and screamed. Daisy's back was pressed against her mother's satin headboard like a cornered cat, the mascara running down her cheeks and her hair long and straight and yellow. She had tiny feet for such a tall girl, and she was wearing small brown suede moccasins with eagles beaded on the fronts. "Can't you just look normal?"

Donna had bent her head, as if in shame.

"I have the midnight blue. With the beaded top."

It was her funeral dress, prim, with a high neck and long sleeves. Daisy forced herself not to blurt out something about that being her mother's funeral dress.

"Wear that," Daisy said. "Wear the blue."

Iris was well into her purple period when they went to the Porters that first time. She had decided that purple was an extension of herself. Of Iris. Her hair went from light brown to lavender, violet, eggplant. She wore metallic purple nail polish and makeup in all shades of purple, almost like a death mask. To the Porters', she wore a bright purple jumpsuit and plum boots.

Years later, after Alexander had left her, Daisy thought of how ridiculous the three of them must have looked. There were the Porters, in corduroys and sweaters, Mackenzie and Cal in plaid wool skirts, each wearing a single strand of pearls. And there were the Blooms. Daisy, in an effort to look sophisticated, looked like a child playing dress-up, her skirt sticking out from under the hem of her coat, her sweater too tight, the jewelry she wore clanking cheaply together. Donna looked overdressed in the midnight blue with the beaded bodice. She chatted away nonstop. "I had the original flower children. Iris and Daisy. Get it?" When Grammie saw Iris she gasped, and grabbed her heart.

But all Iris could do was stand in awe. The house smelled the way a real home should, a mixture of cinnamon, peppermint, and pine. The table was a deep polished wood draped in lace, with a centerpiece of pine boughs and red berries. She pricked her finger on the needles to see if they were real. Then she picked up a knife, heavy and silver with a curved edge. She put it down quickly, seeing that all the silverware was in some mysterious and repeated order at each place.

"She's just trying to find herself, honey," Donna had told Grammie.

A huge tree loomed in the living room—the parlor, the Porters called it. Each branch held a shiny treasure, finely striped balls, longer ones with silver stars pressed in their centers, others with fluffs of white, like clouds, poking through gilt. The fireplace was trimmed in pine branches and holly. The logs snapped. There was mistletoe and poinsettias and silver bells, all the things of a fairy tale Christmas. And the Porters moved among the rooms with perfect ease and grace.

Donna grabbed Daisy's arm and whispered, "These are real Chinese rugs."

Daisy looked down at the carpet where she stood, its bright colors woven into an intricate design of birds and flowers.

"I've seen three so far," Donna said. "And I haven't even been upstairs yet."

They drank egg nog, Mackenzie pouring it from a silver-handled ladle into tiny silver cups.

Every few minutes, Mr. Porter cleared his throat and then poked the logs in the fireplace.

When Mackenzie's red sweater brushed Donna's hand, she'd whispered to Iris, "Cashmere, I bet."

"We have a goose," Cal had said. "I hope you like goose."

Grammie had laughed.

"Who doesn't like goose, Cal? With oyster dressing. A good goose with oyster dressing. I'd like to meet the person who doesn't like that."

Everyone had smiled politely then.

Cal's lips kept sticking to her big horse teeth.

"Not everyone does," she'd said. "Like goose."

Later, back in their own house, the Blooms sat silently amid the litter of dirty dishes and empty bags of food. The wheel sent color across the tree. Already the light had burned through the sliver of yellow, so that every fourth turn left the tree bare and silver.

"As for me," Donna said finally, "I could live without ever eating goose again."

When no one responded, she said, "They're a little hoity-toity for my taste. But to each his own."

Eventually Donna moved to Mexico. She had never

37

paid taxes on the money she made from her readings, and she moved to a village full of other tax evaders. Daisy got letters from her describing the villa she lived in, the ocean view, the white beaches, and the bushes heavy with large red flowers. "Hibiscus, maybe?" she wrote. "I don't know. All I know is their perfume is like a rich woman's."

When Alexander left her, and Daisy thought she'd lose her mind from loneliness, she went to visit her mother. There was no ocean view, no white marble villa. She lived instead in a pink stucco apartment complex with bad plumbing. Whenever her neighbor flushed the toilet, her wall dampened. The sinks held old water, sluggish and rusty. The smell was not of a rich woman's perfume, or of perfume at all. The air was full of chemicals from a nearby factory, which shot dark gray soot into the sky and left ash on rooftops.

They took a hot, dusty bus to the beach. The beach was littered with beer cans and cigarette butts. The water swirled a milky green around their ankles.

"Ma," Daisy said, "are there chemicals in this water?"

Donna lifted her head toward the sun, looked up, and smiled as if the clouds weren't tinged with ash.

"Chemicals?" she said.

When they got back to shore, their blanket was gone. They walked in circles around the beach, looking for the spot where they had left it. But it was gone, stolen by some village children. They'd also taken a big straw basket, woven with red flowers, that Daisy had bought while they waited for the bus.

Mackenzie cleared her throat.

"Sorry," Daisy said. She smiled weakly. "My mind wandered."

She sat on the couch, a sinking feeling in her stomach from remembering. Sometimes, she thought, it's better to pretend you have no past at all. That your life just started yesterday. Like on *Dynasty*, the way people were always getting amnesia and starting new lives for themselves. They married different people, became a part of a new family.

"I guess we should get Sam," she said, without even looking at Mackenzie. "If he'll leave his bed. Sometimes he lies there for hours without even moving."

When she looked up, there was Mackenzie kneeling on the rug. Sam had come into the room, his koala bear knapsack dangling off one shoulder.

"Well look who's come out of hiding," Daisy said. "'Now you two can hit the road."

She thought of her house without Sam's silence. She imagined meeting a man and having him spend the whole night with her. She would go out tonight. To a bar or a party. She would be like Fallon on *The Colbys*. No memories. No past.

CHAPTER FOUR

M emories of Cape Cod kept Cal going through Missouri and Kansas and Nebraska.

The snow was deep, so white against the road that it blinded her. She wished she had sunglasses with her. The road ahead and behind seemed flat and endless and Cal thought of Cape Cod. She remembered warmth, sunshine and beaches, shells in the sand and the smell of Coppertone. Sounds came to her in a cacophony of wind chimes and waves, children and boats and sea gulls. It was like a symphony. At one point, she rolled down the window and the clean midwestern air shocked her, as if she had really expected to smell Cape Cod.

Every August for ten years the Porters had rented a beach house. They moved everyone from the house in Rhode Island to a cottage on the Cape—Jams, Cal, Alexander, Mackenzie, Aunt Hope and her son John-Glenn, and Grammie. It was always the same cottage, a small weatherbeaten shingled house with slate blue shutters and trim. It was owned by an old couple, the Sweetlowes. Photographs and portraits of the Sweetlowes' ancestors hung in dusty silver frames and wooden ovals on the wall, their eyes following the Porters everywhere. One summer, Hope had taken them down and hid them in a drawer. "They give me the creeps," she'd said. The empty walls had white marks then, in squares and circles where the portraits had hung.

In the backyard there was a cement slab that the Sweetlowes called the patio. They had hung Japanese lanterns around it on a clothesline, long accordian-pleated ones in off shades of pink and green and yellow. The first summer, Jams had installed a mosquito repeller back there, an electric box that attracted the insects, then electrocuted them. All through the night they heard the zzzzzzt of mosquitoes against the coils that glowed blue in the dark. At the end of the summer, Jams had left it there for the Sweetlowes, and the next year when they went back to rent, the old man had gazed severely at Jams and Cal. "Mother and I don't kill insects," he'd said. He'd had a throat operation and spoke through a box covered by a bright ascot. The children were afraid of him and his wheezing electronic voice. The Porters bringing the mosquito zapper each summer became another ritual of the house, like Hope hiding the portraits.

The house wasn't really big enough for everyone, so Alexander slept on a sofa bed on the back porch, and Mackenzie had a cot out there. Hope and Grammie slept in a tiny attic room that was hot and stuffy and smelled, faintly, like cedar. Cal used to believe she could feel the house moving from so many people breathing in it. Jams felt it too, the walls expanding as if to accommodate all those lungs, but he said it was actually the ocean breezes moving the house slightly. Cal used to lie there and listen to the waves and the seagulls and the children whispering together and she'd dream of escapes. It seemed that with so many people, she wouldn't be missed for a very long time.

One summer, Cal used to get up early and walk down to the docks to watch the fishermen set their lobster traps. The men never paid attention to her as she sat, huddled against a post in an old black cardigan. She watched them work, mesmerized by their muscles straining and pushing against their T-shirts as they lifted the traps and prepared the boats to go out. The air then, at that time of morning, was so full of salt that it stung her face like a slap. She used to imagine being a stowaway on one of those boats. Although she knew that they didn't really go anywhere, just out into the ocean for the fish, she still pretended they could carry her somewhere far away and exotic, that they could save her somehow.

That summer—it was 1968—was the same year all the kids bought bell-bottoms at a surf shop in town, gaudy purple ones and light blue and white pinstriped ones and some just plain white denim. Everyone wore tight bracelets woven out of rope that got dirtier and dirtier as the summer wore on, and no amount of reason could make them take them off. In autumn, a thin bracelet of white flesh slashed their wrists, separating the tanned hand and arms.

Cal planned elaborate escapes that summer, fanciful ones full of miracles in which she'd go for a swim, start out in the water right near the cottage, and then resurface on a distant shore. Africa, somewhere. Or an island in the Mediterranean. And the air was heavy with spices and hope. Sometimes she'd imagined flying away, rising out of the attic or the chimney of the house and looking down at it, a cloud within arm's reach. She would watch the walls of the cottage pulsate and swell, watch the cottage

43

until it became a speck below her like the whitecaps on the water.

Then she discovered the docks and instead of lying in bed daydreaming, Cal went down there with a thermos of sweet Dunkin' Donuts coffee and watched the men through salt-stung eyes. She came to know the boats, their names captivating her like a magic spell, enchanting her—*Halcyon, Byzantine, Eloise.*

One morning, she remembered it as if it had been this very morning, she had sat and watched them work in a dull gray drizzle. A radio somewhere played a count-down of the best one hundred songs since 1960. She listened to "Big Girls Don't Cry" and tried to remember the group who had sung it.

A man came up to her. He wore a long yellow slicker and a droopy hat, like the picture of the Gorton's fisher-man on frozen fish boxes.

She'd thought of that and laughed right out loud.

"What's funny?" he said. He had the slightest bit of an accent.

"You look like a picture on a box of fish sticks," she said.

"Fish sticks, huh? You look like someone in a movie, the way you sit here every morning."

She thought he might be Italian.

The radio announcer said, "That was number ninety-one. The Four Seasons."

She imagined getting on his boat and sailing to Italy with him. Although she had never been to Italy, her friend Missy had gone during college and told her about the old churches, and the way the Roman wall ran, crumbling, through the city. Missy had gone to Pompeii, and watched them excavate the city. Loaves of bread, whole, covered in ash. And fish. Cal wanted to go with this fisherman and find treasures, too.

The hat partially hid his face, but Cal could see that he was younger than her. Maybe twenty-five or thirty. He had long sideburns, two big pork chops hugging his cheeks, and a full mustache. Blonde.

"Which one is yours?" she asked, gesturing toward the boats.

He stood very close to her and she felt a shiver deep inside. She licked her lips and tasted the ocean, imagined he would taste the same, salty.

"That one." He pointed to a small white boat rocking against the rain. "The *Santa Maria*," he said.

"Ah," Cal said. "So you are Italian."

He laughed. The Herman's Hermits sang "Mrs. Brown, You've Got a Lovely Daughter."

"You Americans," he said. "Queen Isabella paid for those boats."

"I know," she said. "Isabella and Ferdinand."

"I'm from Portugal," he said.

"Oh, of course," she said. "I see that now."

"Or maybe I'm from off the cover of a box of fish sticks. Huh?"

She was going to go to bed with him, she knew that then. And he knew too. Perhaps that was why he had come over in the first place.

"If I don't go out there," he said, "I'll lose two, maybe three hundred dollars."

She didn't answer.

"My partner didn't show up today. He thinks maybe he'll melt in the rain. Huh?"

"Will you melt too?" Cal said. "If you go out there?"

He'd taken her hand and pulled her away from the post she'd been leaning on.

"Into you," she thought he said.

His accent seemed thicker now, and the sound of it made her light-headed.

Inside, the boat was small and cramped, and smelled so much like fish that it almost didn't smell at all. The rain sounded like people marching on the roof. They drank sweet wine his mother had made. He was twenty-four, and full of curly blonde hair, under the hat and all over his chest and stomach and legs. She had forgotten what young men were like.

When she left him, it was late morning and all the other boats were gone. The rain fell sure and steady. She stopped for breakfast by the water, at the Crab Claw, a place she sometimes took the children for clam rolls. It smelled like mildew inside. Cal sat at the big window and gazed at the dark water. She ached all over. She could smell him on her, a smell not of the earth, but of the ocean. Sand and seaweed and shellfish.

She sat and ate a full stack of pancakes, drenched in syrup she squirted out of a plastic Mrs. Butterworth, and thought of the other men she had known. Her best friend, Vivvie, years before, had made a list of 108 men she had been with. Cal had read the list, delighted at Vivvie's adventures.

"Fourteen Vincents," Vivvie had said. "Seven Pauls."

On some lines, instead of names, there were descriptions. The red-haired guy from Boston College. Gina Ward's cousin.

Cal hadn't needed a list. There were two before Jams, a Harvard divinity student named Matthew and a poet, Isaac. She and Vivvie would go into Boston and she'd meet up with one or the other of them. They would go to foreign movies or coffeehouses to hear poetry read. Isaac had a cold-water flat in the North End. He would read the poems she'd written and criticize them, the meter, the rhyme. They ate tabouli and wheat crackers in bed. Matthew lived in a boarding house on Mt. Auburn Street. He ate raw refrigerator cookie dough and sketched faces in torture, wide eyes and twisted mouths.

She finished her pancakes and went to call Vivvie. The phone booth had graffiti carved into the wood. FUCK. PEACE. FUCK PEACE. Vivvie had lived in Vermont then, teaching literature at Middlebury.

"I slept with a Portuguese fisherman," Cal said as soon as Vivvie answered.

"What? Is this a joke or something?"

Cal tried to picture her friend on the other end. She had gained weight over the years. She wore blood-red and violet scarves with fine gold threads running through them that she'd bought when she'd studied Persian poetry in Iran. Her earrings hung, heavy and gold.

"I did," Cal said. "Just now." She started to laugh. "My God," she said, "he's twenty-four years old."

"Where's Jams?" Vivvie said. "You left him?"

Vivvie had never liked Jams. Dull, dull, dull, she'd said. She'd refused to go to the wedding. "I'd jump up when they asked if anyone had a good reason why these two shouldn't be united. I'd scream, my friend needs excitement. She needs—more. Let's just call it a boycott of conscience."

Cal watched the clock over the bar. It stuck out of the mouth of a stuffed marlin.

"He's at the cottage," Cal said. The face of the clock had a bright green liquid sloshing up and down. Waves.

"Wait. You're at the Cape, right?" Vivvie said.

Cal heard her strike a match, then inhale.

"He's entertaining the kids right now. Probably playing Monopoly."

"You left him?"

"No," Cal said. "Not really."

When she got back to the cottage, everyone except Alexander was crowded into the living room. The rug, a

black and white knobby tweed, had damp footprints on it.
Jams and the children played Monopoly. Grammie was
reading a short story from the *New Yorker* out loud,
though not loud enough for anyone to really hear the
words clearly. Hope was giving herself a manicure. All
the files and polishes lay out on top of the television.

"Auntie Cal," John-Glenn said as soon as she walked
in, "Alexander never came home until just now." He
pressed a Monopoly token, the top hat, between his fingers. "He's in big trouble, right?"

Cal felt as if she filled the small room with the smell
of fish.

Mackenzie looked up.

"I own Boardwalk *and* Park Place," she said. She
held up the two deeds, the blue stripes across the top of
each.

"So what? So what?" John-Glenn said. A fine spray of
spit streamed through the gap in his front teeth. The teeth
didn't grow in until years later, when he was already in
junior high. "I have all the light light blues. All of them."

Grammie stopped reading.

"They're not worth peanuts," she said.

She and Mackenzie giggled together.

Jams cleared his throat.

Cal looked around her. She felt as if she had walked
into someone else's life. She sucked in her bottom lip,
tasting still the sweet wine.

Grammie sniffed loudly. "You smell," she said.

Jams led Cal by the elbow to the porch where Alexander was sprawled on the glider, wrapped in one of Mrs.
Sweetlowe's afghans. As Mrs. Sweetlowe lost her eye-
sight, the gaps in the crochet and the edges had grown
more and more erratic.

Jams cleared his throat again.

Alexander opened his eyes.

"Tell your mother."

"I'm too embarrassed."

"That's all right," Cal said. "As long as you're okay."

"Emma Matlock's parents don't think it's all right," Jams said.

Cal pictured the girl. She was a year younger than Alexander, her parents August people too. She was small and skinny, frail-looking, with round wire-rimmed glasses and pale hair. She went to Hunter High School in Manhattan and always told Cal the things she had done in school the year before. Just last week she had seen Emma on the beach. "I did a paper on the old Jack Benny radio show," she'd said. "For my communications class. I went to the Museum of Broadcasting and just sat there for hours listening to them."

"I'm in love," Alexander said.

Emma's voice was so soft that people tended to tilt their heads toward her, even when she wasn't speaking, in case she started. She wore an old black one-piece bathing suit and a smear of zinc oxide across her nose.

"They spent the night up at Truro," Jams said. "Slept there. In the dunes."

"She's like an angel," Alexander said. "And to think I ignored her all these years." He sat up. "I mean, last year she started to tell me about African tribal masks and I walked away."

"Well," Cal said. "That's fine."

She went into the bathroom and stood under a hot shower until the water turned icy.

She never went back to the docks.

Once, before they left that summer, she saw the fisherman at a crafts fair in Hyannis. He held delicate silver earrings in the palm of his hand. There was mother-of-pearl inlaid at the bottom of the tear shape, and it glistened in the sunlight. Mackenzie tried on rings, interlocked silver hearts. Cal had looked right into his eyes across the table of silver, shocked by their color, a velvety violet. It was a cool day and he wore a white cable knit sweater. She saw that his front tooth was chipped, and wondered if it had always been that way. He held the earrings like an offering.

Cal turned away abruptly.

She thought he said, "I waited for you."

Her impulse when she'd left Rhode Island last Labor Day had been to run away from home, like a child. She used to threaten this sometimes when her own children were young. Jams would be at one of the liquor stores he owned, Grammie would be demanding dinner or a card game or her attention, Hope would be crying because her husband, Ricardo Havana, had left her, and John-Glenn would be in trouble somehow—popping all the fuses in the fuse box or trying to shave the cat with an electric razor— and Cal would state calmly, "I'm going to run away." She would get in the car and drive around and around the block until she was ready to go back in the house.

Grammie used to have a large map of the United States hanging in her bedroom. She would stick pushpins into the cities she'd visited. New England was a mass of red and yellow pins. A solitary green one jutted out from Atlantic City. One blue one pointed into Lancaster, Pennsylvania. That memory of her mother's map had led Cal to keeping the one in the car. She marked off city after city as she drove, cluttering it with X's.

Last September, Cal had stood in her kitchen and watched, unmoving, as a pan of water boiled over on the stove. Jams had come in moments before, looking sheepish. Cal had known immediately what he had done.

"What did you take?" she had demanded.

Jams didn't answer. He kept his eyes focused on the big green and yellow squares of the floor.

She had hit his pockets lightly with her hands, like a policeman frisking a criminal. His jeans hung too low off his hips, the belt the only thing holding them up at all. Cal's fingers found something in the pocket of his blue cardigan, the alligator on its chest grinning at her.

"Why are you doing this?" she'd said, her hands frozen on the outside of the pocket. He had earned the nickname Jams as a child because he was always getting into trouble. No one ever called him Jared, even though as an adult he had become quieter and less likely to make waves. Yet, in the past three months he'd stolen corkscrews, packs of gum, even tubes of lipstick.

Slowly Jams shook his head. The blondeness there was turning, rapidly, to silver.

Cal reached into the pocket and pulled out a small tangerine.

"We have a refrigerator full of food," she shouted. She wanted to hit him.

Mackenzie, her skin so tanned she looked foreign, stood in the doorway.

"We have to stop this," Mackenzie said.

"A refrigerator full!"

Jams remained silent. He took the tangerine from her, held the tiny orange fruit to his nose, and inhaled.

"Dad," Mackenzie said.

From downstairs, Cal could hear John-Glenn's high-pitched laughter.

Jams pressed his thumb into the fruit and began to peel it, dropping the torn skin into his pocket. Cal walked over to the refrigerator and yanked the door open. She pulled food off the shelves and threw it, hard, at him. Strawberries. A small block of cheddar cheese. An egg that hit his leg and then rolled onto the floor without breaking. Then another egg, this one cracking open immediately, its yolk bleeding on the green and yellow squares. Mackenzie was yelling "Stop" over and over but Cal kept throwing food. The milk carton oozed milk as it flew out. A jar of mustard cracked into two perfect halves. Jams stood there, peeling the tangerine until all the skin was off. Then he pulled a canoe-shaped section off and ate it.

The water on the stove began to boil, tiny bubbles erupting into bigger ones. Cal had stopped to watch it boil over, the water hissing as it splashed onto the flame below the pan. Mackenzie, crying, had turned the stove off and then started to clean up the food on the floor. The egg slid off the paper towel like a tear.

Jams didn't move at all. He just kept eating the stolen fruit, piece by piece.

"I'm going to run away," Cal had said quietly, watching the bubbles die in the pan. "I can't stay here anymore."

Then she'd really left. She had gotten in Alexander's car and had driven away. She wanted to contact them somehow but could only bring herself to send postcards without any messages written on them. She had no message for anyone yet. But this way they'd know she was all right.

The sign ahead of her now said: WELCOME TO COLORADO, THE ROCKY MOUNTAIN STATE.

Cal sighed.

In front of her, a car with a full ski rack on top had broken down. Teenagers in brightly colored ski outfits stood beside it. They blazed color against the white snow—turquoise, orange, fuchsia. One girl held a handwritten sign, HELP!!!

Cal drove past.

The girl, she thought, had looked a little like Emma Matlock. That same hair, so pale it really had no color. Even the same glasses, and they'd been long out of style now. Maybe it was just that she'd been remembering Emma.

52

Alexander and Emma had gone out through most of college. She came home with him every Christmas and brought chestnuts and tiny pine trees decorated with miniature ornaments, doves and balls with angel's hair. Her father was in advertising and not long after she and Alexander started dating, her father grew a mustache like a walrus and long hair. He wore paisley shirts and left her mother for a model named Coco who had starred in one of his soft drink ads. Emma always had stories to tell them, about ski trips he took with Coco, rock concerts they went to, and the gifts he gave her.

Emma majored in French at Smith. When she went to study in Paris her junior year she met a man there, Armand, and never came home. He was a diplomat now, and they lived all over the world. Postcards still came to Alexander written in her backward left-handed slant, from Hong Kong, Venezuela, New Zealand. The day Alexander got the letter from Emma telling him about Armand, he'd collected all the things she'd ever given him, and burned them. He had stood over the flames crying. "Armand," he'd said. "What kind of stupid name is that?"

For a long time, Cal had a fantasy in which Emma left Armand and came back to Alexander. She imagined them in a high-ceilinged room together, with bookshelves and Oriental vases and a piano playing Chopin. His life, in contrast, since Daisy had been noisy and out of sync. Their apartments had been a series of rooms filled with unpacked boxes and makeshift shelves. After Sam was born, the smell of spilled milk lingered beneath Daisy's perfume. It had seemed to Cal that Alexander spent his life with Daisy running from something.

Cal laughed. Who was she to talk about running away? It's what she was doing now, what she had imagined doing for a very long time.

She had even tried it once, a half-hearted effort their

last year at the Cape. Alexander drove down on weekends with Daisy, who greased herself in cocoa butter and lay in the sun until someone went to get her to come inside. John-Glenn got hepatitis halfway through August and Hope and Grammie took him home to recuperate. Jams's niece, Jodi, was visiting from Pennsylvania, overweight and sullen. She tried a different fad diet every week, gorging herself on grapefruits until she broke out in hives, then eating only leafy green vegetables. Finally, she settled on something called BARF. A day of bananas, a day of apples, a day of raisins, a day of frankfurters. Then repeat. The hot dog days made Cal ill; the smell of boiling frankfurters clung to the sticky air.

That year the temperature stayed above ninety-five degrees for almost two weeks, and the fans did nothing more than blow hot air back at them. Mackenzie had met a boy in Falmouth, and worried that her boyfriend, Felix, from back home would show up. She kept saying to Cal, "What should I say? What should I do?" and retelling how she felt and what her options were until Cal had said to her, "You are not the only person here, you know. Everyone has problems this year." And she had screamed at Jodi, "Can't you grill those hot dogs? Or fry them? Do they have to boil like that?"

Cal found a trunk in the attic full of Mrs. Sweetlowe's old clothes and letters. She started going up there that summer and sorting through them. There was something oddly comforting about the feel of the worn lace, the faint smell of floral sachet, and the world the letters spoke of. Cal sat in front of a small fan and pretended this life was hers—parties on the veranda where the girls snuck away for a cigarette, boyfriends away at war, and one exciting Saturday spent watching an airplane fly by.

She could not imagine that the Patsy Sweetlowe whose things were in this old steamer trunk was Mrs. Sweetlowe, who she'd seen in the car, blind, with thinly curled bluish hair. The one whose letters Cal read was funny and smart and independent. She turned down three marriage proposals, then ran away with an inventor who took her across the country, trying to peddle his inventions. When Cal went up to the attic, she entered a different world.

Then one day, their last week there, Mr. Sweetlowe called and told them his wife had died. Cal thought not of the eighty-six-year-old woman, but of the young girl in the letters. That day, Cal had found a hard peppermint candy in one of the dress pockets in the attic, and it was as if the young Patsy were still alive.

"She was old," Jams told Cal when she'd cried. "We didn't even know her."

But the loss seemed real and near to her. She felt that it was a sign of sorts, a message that she had to do something before it was too late, before she lost the young girl in herself. Cal had thought of going to Vivvie's, but it seemed too far. And she wasn't really sure what she would say when she got there. She needed to sort things out. So she drove up to Provincetown and checked into a small inn on a curving road that overlooked the beach.

The room was too expensive, but the heat wave broke that night and a cool breeze came in right from the sea. Cal lay under the sheet and listened to two men in the room next to hers making love all night. One said, "Aaaaargh" over and over, in a guttural voice, like a wild animal. In the morning, they ate breakfast beside her at the inn's outdoor patio. She had tried to guess which one had made that sound, but they were each polite and soft-spoken and she wondered if it *had* been a wild animal. Or just her imagination. When she stood to leave, one of the men smiled at her and said, "Good day," like a country gentleman.

She'd had no money, certainly not enough to spend another night there. After she'd walked around the town, through galleries and shops, she'd headed back to the cottage and her family. The house was noisy and cool when she got there, and the smell of barbecue sauce drifted in from the grill on the patio. Daisy and Alexander were there, and had brought Grammie with them. Felix had driven down to see Mackenzie, and everyone talked about Nixon, and what would happen to him, whether he'd be impeached or not, whether he'd resign.

Cal waited for Jams to ask her where she'd been. But he didn't.

That night in bed, with the fan off and the window opened to bring in cool air, she'd said, "I went to Provincetown yesterday."

He was quiet.

"I almost didn't come back," she said finally.

In the distance she heard a foghorn.

"Well," Jams said, "I guess it's a good place to go and think."

A good place to go and think.

Cal said the words silently, then out loud. Around her now the Rocky Mountains rose like outstretched arms. Colorado blended into Utah. She'd reach her destination soon. San Francisco. She could start a new life there. Be a poet, just like she started out to be long ago. The hills and fog and gingerbread houses would be a constant inspiration. Already, she'd submitted the poems she'd written on this trip to a journal there, using, of all people, Iris Bloom's address on the return envelope. It was the only address Cal knew out there and it made her feel good to think of San Francisco as her new home. The roads were winding and icy. She watched a jeep in front of her fishtail. Once.

Twice. Cal held her breath. The jeep regained control, vanished around the bend.

Sometimes, when she turned a corner, the view was so spectacular she gasped. She wished they had had Alexander cremated and had thrown his ashes here, over these mountains. It seemed more right than putting him in the ground off a highway in Warwick, Rhode Island. But it had all happened so quickly—hadn't she spoken to him that very afternoon?—that things came to her too late. She would think of songs they should have had played at the service, poems that the family could have read.

One night shortly after the funeral she had woken up trying to remember a particular Beatles song he had liked. She'd known that the words, if she could only remember them, were beautiful and appropriate.

Mackenzie was asleep down the hall, in her old bedroom, and Cal had run to her. The room was lit by a plastic nightlight, the type that sat flush into an outlet. Cinderella or Sleeping Beauty.

Cal shook her awake.

"There's a song," she'd said when Mackenzie opened her eyes.

Cal tried to hum it.

"What song?" Mackenzie said.

"Something about places I remember," she said. She hummed again softly. "But of all these friends and lovers, something . . ."

"I don't know it," Mackenzie said.

Cal turned on the overhead light.

The furniture was the color of eggshells, with tiny yellow and pink flowers stenciled on it. The sheets on the bed were a soft yellow, like melted butter, and Mackenzie's hair, bleached from the sun, seemed white against them.

"You have the record," Cal said. "I know you have it. You used to play it all the time."

She opened the closet and rummaged deep inside, to the back. She pulled out an old album case, orange with black kaleidoscope swirls.

"Sing it again," Mackenzie said. "Maybe I can think of it."

"There's something in it about places I remember that have changed," Cal said, pulling albums out of the case and sliding them across the floor as she discarded them. "And how you never forget people and things that came before."

Meet the Beatles. Jan and Dean's Deadman's Curve. The Herman's Hermits.

Mackenzie smoothed each cover down as her mother tossed it aside.

Until finally Cal said, "This is it. 'My Life.' "

Mackenzie nodded.

"Now I know it," she said.

"We should have played it at the funeral," Cal said.

There were other things she thought of later. But here, in the mountains of Utah, she saw that all those things were wrong too. Cal pulled over at a lookout. She stood, staring down at clouds and mountaintops. She could make out the *S* shapes of ski trails. She had read once that if a person was cremated, he or she didn't just dissolve into fine ash. Rather, there were chunks of bone like rock candy and ash thick with crystals, and more ash grainy like sand. Cal imagined having that now, Alexander's body crushed in her hands like seashells, and she opened her hand over the railing, stretched it into the cold blue air, as if she really were scattering his ashes here.

CHAPTER FIVE

Even though Mackenzie knew people had rented the house, when she drove up she expected to find it abandoned. Instead, Christmas lights blazed and laughter came from inside. Cars lined the sidewalk in front and she had to double park the rented Buick.

"Well," she said. "Home."

She looked at Sam. He sat beside her, his seat belt fastened across his chest.

Blinking multicolored lights bordered the windows and all the lines of the house.

"Grandma Cal would never have stood for this," she said. "We used to have make-believe candles in the windows with little white lights for flames. That's all."

Sam craned his neck. The lights blinked on and his eyes reflected their flash of color. He leaned back again.

"Do you remember those make-believe candles?" Mackenzie asked him. She felt the desperation in her voice. "And on the lawn over there was a plastic snow-man with a white light in his belly. I mean, you couldn't see that the light was there. It spread a glow all through the snowman so he looked bright and jolly."

The front door swung open. A woman's voice floated out. "I don't think you drunks should drive." Mackenzie wondered if she was the woman renting the house. Two men staggered out, arms thrown sloppily around each other's shoulders. One sang the drumming part of "The Little Drummer Boy." He wore a stocking cap with rein-deer and evergreens on it. The other man had on a baseball cap with red antlers sticking out on each side. He was doing a drunken imitation of Bing Crosby.

"I'm dreaming," he crooned, "of a white Christmas..."

They stumbled down the front steps and onto the sidewalk.

Sam sat straight up and watched the men.

"You can unfasten your seat belt," Mackenzie told him. She watched the men too.

"Where the treetops glisten, and children whistle—"

The man in the stocking cap stopped rat-a-tat-tatting.

"Those aren't the words," he said.

"What?"

"Children don't whistle. They listen."

"Where treetops glisten, and children whistle—"

"That doesn't even rhyme."

The door flew open again and a woman in a black fur coat came out laughing. She held a big square box wrapped in red foil. Mackenzie wanted to scream at all these people to leave, to get away from her house.

"Sing 'White Christmas,' " the man with the antlers said to the woman.

"I'm not sure I know that one," she said. "I mean, I know the movie, with Bing Crosby and Rosemary Clooney and all that. And I know there's a song. A theme, or whatever, to the movie. But I don't know the words."

Mackenzie rolled down the car window.

"Where treetops glisten, and children listen," she shouted.

The people on the sidewalk stopped talking and looked at her.

"See," the man in the stocking cap said. "I told you."

Mackenzie rolled up the car window and leaned forward. Her head rested on the steering wheel. She wished she were a magician, that she could wave a wand and make herself vanish, make everything vanish and reappear the way it used to be.

"God," she said.

Sam sat back in his seat. She heard his seat belt click into place. And from the outside she heard the woman laugh and the two men sing the last bars of "White Christmas."

For as long as Mackenzie could remember, Aunt Hope and John-Glenn had lived in the basement apartment in the old house. But when the house was rented, they had to move too. Their new apartment was in a Spanish-style complex, with papery stucco walls and imitation wood beams. Aunt Hope had taken a lot of furniture from the old house and crowded it into her new apartment.

The heavy mahogany mantel at home had always held photographs of people Mackenzie didn't know. As a child, she thought it must be a great honor to get your picture up there. When she grew older, she realized all the people in the pictures, great-uncles and grandparents, were dead.

And now, above Hope's small white gas fireplace, pictures of Alexander stared back at her. To see him there, tanned and alive, made Mackenzie weak. "You see all those people?" he used to whisper to her when they were children. "They were dying to get up there." And now there he was.

All the pictures seemed out of place here. They belonged, Mackenzie thought, over the fireplace in her childhood home. She wondered briefly what was there now. It too was probably lined with blinking Christmas lights. Or a vase with artificial flowers. Or a pair of brass baby shoes. She winced.

"Ah," Aunt Hope said, "it's a shame. All of them gone. And your father. Locked away like that."

Mackenzie clutched the edge of the mantel. It tipped slightly. For an instant she expected all the pictures to smash to the floor. But she steadied the shelf in time.

"And now here you are," Aunt Hope said. "With the boy, no less."

Sam stood, fascinated by the butterflies on the wall. There were hundreds of them, their wings pinned to white boards, the boards covered by glass, the glass framed and then hung on the walls. The colors gave the room its only source of life.

"You like the butterflies?" Aunt Hope asked.

Sam frowned.

"They are lovely," she said. "So majestic. We must have three or four hundred. John-Glenn knows exactly. He catches them and catalogues them. He has an entire file cabinet full of information about his butterflies."

Mackenzie pictured John-Glenn as a boy, overweight and sloppily dressed, chasing butterflies, pushing his tongue through the gap where his front teeth should be.

"He's a little slow," Cal always explained. "It's probably something in the Havana blood," Grammie would say as she watched him. "No," Aunt Hope told her. "Since Ricardo left, we both just suffer from broken hearts."

"We went to the old house," Mackenzie said.

"Ah."

"You should see the Christmas decorations they have up. Garish lights flashing. Like it's a truck stop or something with neon lights."

"A pity," Aunt Hope said.

"Remember the snowman we used to have? We used to put it on the lawn. His shovel said 'Happy Holidays' on it."

Aunt Hope shook her head. "No," she said. "I don't remember any snowman."

"Sure you do. A plastic one with a light in its belly. Alexander used to say it must have eaten a flashlight."

"Well," Aunt Hope said. "Alexander. Maybe he had that in Georgetown."

Mackenzie swallowed hard. Sometimes, like now, she felt as if she had made all these people up. No one remembered them the way she did. She watched Sam. He reached up and tapped on one of the panes over a butterfly. With his pinky he traced the shape of a small yellow and black one.

"Oh, now, Sam," Aunt Hope said, "don't do that. Don't bang on the glass like that."

Once, Mackenzie had mentioned to Daisy that when Sam got mad, he looked just like Alexander. His eyebrows tightened and his eyes darkened, from a clear blue to the color of a muddy lake. I just don't see the resemblance, Daisy had said. "Sam looks like my sister Iris. Eyes and all. Mad or happy." But Mackenzie had insisted. Didn't anyone, she had wondered, remember Alexander's eyes?

"Now, honey, Sam, don't bang like that." Aunt Hope led him away from the butterflies and sat him down on the couch, the crushed blue velvet one that used to be in the Porters' parlor. When they sat, a lace doily slipped from the arm.

"There," she said. "John-Glenn is so particular about his butterflies." She fluffed her hair, a habit carried over from long ago when she wore a blonde poodle cut. Now her hair had grown flat and thin on top.

"Do you see," Mackenzie said, "that he has Alexander's eyes?"

Sam swung his tiny sneakered feet back and forth.

"Mackenzie," Aunt Hope said gently, "I really don't."

"Everything is upside down," Mackenzie said.

She thought she was going to cry. She focused on an orange spotted butterfly on the wall across from her. Don't, she told herself. Don't cry. Her mother had a trick. When you're going to cry, she used to say, stare hard at something pleasant. Mackenzie stared hard at that butterfly, stared away the tears and blocked out an image—a constant one—of her mother on the beach at Cape Cod, staring at the ocean.

"We lived in that little apartment for so long," Aunt Hope was saying. "John-Glenn just can't get used to this place. Even with some of the old furniture here. I thought that would help him adjust."

Mackenzie nodded. The butterfly's spots danced in front of her eyes.

Aunt Hope hesitated. "I got another postcard."

Mackenzie watched her aunt walk out of the room to get it. She was a pear-shaped woman, a shape John-Glenn had inherited. Since her husband had left, she always wore sleeveless cotton housedresses and backless slippers. Mules, she called them. Tonight, her dress was blue and white checked with violets on the big square front pockets. Her slippers were pink. One had a safety pin hanging from the toe.

"Where's it from?" Mackenzie called to her aunt.

Aunt Hope came back, dusting the postcard with the hem of her dress.

"Where's it from?" Mackenzie asked again.

"That's a good question," Aunt Hope said. "She's trying to confuse us."

She held the postcard tightly, as if it were a valuable prize, not even allowing Mackenzie to glimpse it.

"Now this one here," Aunt Hope said, "has a picture of a desert."

She reached into one of the big square pockets on her dress and pulled out a pair of oversized glasses. A wadded old Kleenex was tangled in the glasses and Mackenzie fought back an impulse to grab the postcard out of her aunt's hand. It was, after all, her mother off in that desert.

"Is she in a desert?" Mackenzie asked. Her mind ran through all the deserts she knew of—Mojave, Gobi, Sahara. "Which desert is it?"

"Well, that's the funny thing."

Aunt Hope bent to pick up a bobby pin that had fallen from her pocket. Then she put her glasses on and read from the back of the postcard.

" 'Giant cactus in Arizona.' That's what's printed on the card. And sure enough, that's what the picture is on the front."

Aunt Hope held up the postcard for Mackenzie to see. A huge cactus was in the foreground with a few smaller ones behind it. Sam came over and looked at the picture. Gingerly, he touched the big cactus, then pulled his hand away quickly, as if he'd been pricked.

"Is there a message this time?" Mackenzie asked impatiently. She was tired. And tired of her aunt's slowness.

Aunt Hope shook her head.

"Just her initials on the bottom, like always. CP. Now the funny thing is this is a desert in Arizona somewhere and this postmark says Seattle. I said to John-Glenn, now I may not be a geography whiz but am I right when I say

Seattle is not in Arizona? Is nowhere near Arizona? And of course John-Glenn has to show me in the atlas. He points out Arizona and then Washington. Washington state. Not DC. And they're this far apart.'' Aunt Hope holds her hands out to demonstrate. The postcard dangled from the Seattle hand. "Nowhere near each other.''

Mackenzie snatched the postcard from her aunt's hand. She studied it for some clue about her mother. Years ago, her parents had gone to Montreal for a few days. They had sent Mackenzie and Alexander a postcard of their hotel. A window high in the hotel had been circled in black magic marker. OUR ROOM, their mother had written in the sky above an arrow pointing to the circle. But this postcard had no such intimacies. Just the initials CP.

"Nothing," Mackenzie said.

"The last one was postmarked Denver," Aunt Hope said. "It had a picture of the Jefferson Memorial. At night.''

"You told me.''

"And the initials CP on the bottom. What would it take for her to sign her name at least. Just sign her full name instead of the initials.''

Mackenzie sighed and laid the postcard on the coffee table. Sam picked it up and traced each of the cacti.

"It's from Grandma," Mackenzie said.

Sam nodded.

Mackenzie touched the top of Sam's head, ran a few strands of his fine blonde hair through her fingers. She thought of her brother. Alexander's hair had been just this fine and this blonde when he was a child. Later, it had darkened to the color of straw.

The door burst open then and John-Glenn stood there, surrounded by cold air and snow flurries, his bulky body framed by the dark night. He was wearing a bright red down coat. Lime green mittens hung from a hook on each sleeve. On top of his head sat a pointed brown and yellow striped hat with golden arches embossed on the front.

"Oh, no," he said. "Company."

"This is not company," Aunt Hope said. "It's Mackenzie. And Sam. Look at Alexander's boy."

John-Glenn stamped the snow off his feet.

"Company is company," he said.

"Close that door now," Aunt Hope said. "You're letting all the cold in. And snow. Look at the carpet."

He walked in and slammed the door behind him.

"Aren't you going to kiss your cousin Mackenzie?"

"No."

"Let me get you a cherry Coke," Aunt Hope said. "You sit down here and talk."

John-Glenn took off his coat and dropped it on the floor.

"Why are you here?" he said to Mackenzie.

"What kind of a question is that?" Aunt Hope called from the kitchen.

"We're visiting," Mackenzie said. "I wanted Sam to see the old house."

"Is his crazy mother around here somewhere?"

"No. She's back in Maryland."

"Daisy," he muttered. "And her crazy sister with the purple hair. The *dyed* purple hair."

"Most purple hair is dyed," Mackenzie said.

"I'm mad at you," John-Glenn said. "I'm mad at your whole family. Making us leave our home like that. It isn't fair."

"You stop talking like that," Aunt Hope yelled.

Despite the cold air he'd brought into the room, John-Glenn was sweating. He stood in front of Mackenzie with his red coat at his feet, dressed in his brown striped McDonald's uniform, jumping up and down slightly.

"One time," he said, pointing his finger at her, "Alexander said to me, 'Does your face hurt?' and I said, 'No. No, why?' and he said 'Because it's killing me.' And then he fell on the floor laughing. But Alexander's the one killed, right? He's the dead one. Not me."

Sam's mouth opened and closed quickly. He clutched the postcard to his chest.

"That was our real home," John-Glenn said. "Alexander went and died and ruined everything."

Aunt Hope came into the room carrying a silver tray with a liter of cherry Coke, four glasses full of ice, and a Waterford crystal bowl of corn curls in it.

"I don't like this kind of talk," she said. "You're getting everyone upset. Just sit down now and have your snack. And you should apologize to your cousin."

John-Glenn looked at Mackenzie.

"I don't care what anyone says," he told her. "Aliens killed Alexander. And they shut Sam up too. For good."

"That's always been his theory," Aunt Hope said. "Aliens. I showed him the article in the *Globe*. He just can't believe it was the telephone that killed Alexander."

"People talk on the telephone every day," John-Glenn said. "Every day. Nobody dies from it. These aliens took Sam's voice and now everybody on their planet talks like a little boy. They reproduced it up there—"

"Please," Mackenzie said. "Stop."

Sam folded the postcard into tiny accordian pleats.

Mackenzie leaned her head back. She closed her eyes. Aliens, she thought.

CHAPTER SIX

Mackenzie could remember when Aunt Hope was young and single. She used to drive a white convertible and wear big dark sunglasses and brightly colored kerchiefs to protect her hair from the wind. Looking down at her now, asleep in the bed that had been Hope's her entire life, Mackenzie had trouble reconciling that twenty-one-year-old Aunt Hope with the middle-aged woman she saw now. This Aunt Hope's face was covered with a thick, lumpy masque—honey and almond, she had explained as Mackenzie watched her slather it on her face— and her hair was wound around pink rubber curlers with bobby pins stuck through them. On the bureau was her wedding picture in a gilt frame, Aunt Hope, her hair like a Barbie-doll's, being carried away in the arms of her husband, Ricardo. He wore a canary yellow suit. His hair was jet black and so heavily lacquered that it shone like chrome. It rose high and stiff above his head, the front a mass of perfect curls. He had a mustache, a thin black slash between his nose and lips. A short cigar stuck out of his mouth. Mackenzie knew that if she looked very close at the photograph she would be able to make out a thin stream of gray smoke floating above them. Aunt Hope clutched a bouquet of spring flowers, tulips and irises and daffodils. Those flowers were pressed, and used to be in the dictionary in the living room, under the letter *L*, dried and cracked, their colors faded to the faintest shade, a blotted red, a grayish purple, a yellow that had turned almost white. Once Mackenzie picked up one of them, a shriveled, pale tulip, and it disintegrated in her fingers like a trapped ghost. She wondered if they were still in that book, the light blue bouquet streamer hanging out like an old banner.

Ricardo had been the lead singer in a group called Ricardo Havana and his Havana Hoochie-Coo's. The group played at an old ballroom, left over from the forties Swing Era, where Aunt Hope and her friends went dancing on Friday nights. The group played Caribbean music under imitation palm trees and a blue paper moon. Sometimes, as an encore song, Ricardo sang " Say, it's only a paper moon, sailing over a cardboard sea. But it wouldn't be make-believe if you believed in me." Sometimes Mackenzie would watch as Aunt Hope and her friends practiced their dancing. They taught her to cha-cha. "One, two, cha-cha-cha," she would repeat with them, and their full pastel skirts would lift and balloon around them like parachutes. Aunt Hope would lean in the doorway and imitate Ricardo Havana singing "Paper Moon," her voice sultry and heavily accented.

Aunt Hope and Ricardo eloped on a Sunday night in the spring of 1960. The family was watching Ed Sullivan when the phone rang. Grammie was sitting in her rocking chair, and Alexander and Mackenzie were squeezed into the big overstuffed chair, the color of butterscotch candy. Their mother and father sat together on the pale red sofa. Grammie answered the telephone.

"Hello," she said, her voice, as always, demanding. She listened, her grip on the receiver tightening every second. Her face grew pale. She picked up her paper fan with the ornate Japanese scene of bridges and blossoms and birds painted on it and began to move it jerkily up and down, a signal for everyone to jump up and go over to her.

"What, Mom? What?" Mackenzie's mother, Cal, shouted, as if to wake her from a daze.

Behind them, on the screen of the old Zenith, Czecho-slovakian gymnasts formed a fuzzy pyramid of bodies. Alexander crouched in front of the set and counted them quickly, his finger pushing against the screen, touching each person for an instant, climbing up the pyramid until it reached the top. Then he said in awe, "Twenty-one. Holy cow."

"Mom," Cal said again. "What?"

Grammie closed her eyes and shoved the receiver into Cal's hand.

"Hello, hello, hello," Cal said. "Who is this?"

Mackenzie heard tinny laughter from the caller. She inched closer, trying to make out words.

"Are you drunk?" Cal demanded.

"For God's sake," Jams said. "What is going on here?"

Cal pressed the heavy black receiver into her shoulder.

"Hope married Ricardo Havana. They're in Seekonk now."

"Tell her," Grammie whispered from under her fan, "to get home now."

"Jams," Cal said to her husband, "tell her."

71

Mackenzie watched as her father took the receiver from her mother.

"Why didn't we get invited?" she asked. "Mom?"

"Not now," Cal said.

"Does she have a bride gown?" Mackenzie said.

"Hope," Jams said into the phone, "we think you should come home and talk this over."

"Or else," Grammie said.

"Tell her or else," Cal said.

"Well, now," Jams said. He put a finger in his free ear to block out the voices in the living room. "That sounds reasonable to me. We'll see you Wednesday then."

"Wednesday!" Grammie shrieked. "It will be too late by then."

The Czechoslovakians leaped backwards out of the pyramid.

"Yikes!" Alexander said.

"They want a little honeymoon," Jams said. He never raised his voice or spoke quickly. It was always the same even pace. Grammie said that was because he was a Pennsylvania Quaker. "They're in Seekonk and they thought they'd just keep on going. To Boston, maybe. Or New Hampshire. Ricardo has to sing Wednesday night so they'll be back sometime before that."

"Ricardo Havana," Cal said.

"That man," Grammie moaned. "I don't trust anybody with a skinny mustache. And that fake accent."

"He talks like Ricky Ricardo," Mackenzie said.

"Yeah," Alexander said. "Babaloo-oo-oo."

Jams laughed along with his children.

"Don't encourage them," Cal said.

Later, up in Alexander's room, Mackenzie asked him where Seekonk was. "Right over the state line," he told her. "Aunt Hope had to go there to get married because the legal age in Massachusetts is younger than in Rhode

Island. To get married here, Grammie would have had to sign a permission slip and she would never do that. Not in a million years." "Why not?" Mackenzie asked him. "He seems like a nice man. He brings me those little bananas." Alexander held up his hand and counted the reasons. "Ricardo Havana is foreign, number one. Number two, he doesn't have a real job. And number three, he drinks too much."

Mackenzie went into the kitchen. The clock above the sink said three o'clock. When she looked out the window, the sky was daytime bright, illuminated by the lights at the mall across the highway. They stayed lit all night, to keep people out. A patrol car with silent red flashing lights drove by slowly. Mackenzie picked up the telephone and dialed, pushing at the tiny squares quickly, listening to the familiar tune the numbers played.

"Hi," a mechanical taped voice said, "this is Jason Fine. I can't come to the phone right now . . ."

She wanted to hang up. But instead she waited for the beep at the end of the message, then said, "Jason, it's me."

"Whoa," the real Jason cut in. "Wait a minute."

His voice was thick with sleep. She heard the machine whir, then click off.

"Mackenzie?" he said.

"Hi."

She could picture him in his railroad flat in the East Village, each room gaping open into the next, the red bathtub in the middle of the kitchen like a strange centerpiece. Mackenzie imagined him sitting on his bed, two doors topped with a thin piece of foam. Above it he had hung two old posters from the Avalon Ballroom period. They had psychedelic swirls and fat elongated letters advertising concerts by Big Brother and the Holding Company and Creem. Jason had tacked them up over a water spot shaped like the state of Florida. She saw him there, his thick brown hair curling in every direction, flat where it had lain on the pillow, wildly poking out everyplace else.

"Are you naked?" she asked, seeing him so.

"Yes," he said. "I was sleeping."

"I'm sorry," she said. "I'm in Rhode Island," she said. "I made it."

Mackenzie sat on one of the stools at the kitchen counter. The overly bright mall lights washed the rooms in a fluorescent glow and she could see, clearly, Sam asleep on the couch. The ghosts on the mantel stood watch over him from across the living room. A blanket was twisted around his legs, the sheet, covered with a design of violets, was tangled around him like a snake. A violent sleeper, Mackenzie thought. She heard Jason's voice, a question.

"I'm sorry," she said. "What?"

"How is Sam?"

Mackenzie put her fingers through the curly loops of the telephone cord.

"This is so hard," she said.

"I know," Jason said softly.

"Somehow, I knew that if I didn't show Sam, or tell him, that all those things would disappear."

"I know," Jason said again.

"Now I woke up with this crazy idea that maybe I can find my mother and bring her back. I mean, even though Alexander died, we can still be a family, can't we? Aren't we stronger than that?"

"What can I do?" Jason said.

Mackenzie reached out in the air, the way she did sometimes at night when they were together and she needed to touch him, his shoulder or leg.

"Feed the cats for me," she said.

"Of course. Anything else?"

She tried to think. "Those pictures are done. They're in the bathroom, hanging on the clothesline. You can drop them off at the magazine."

"Okay. What else?"

"I can't think."

"Call me when you can. Okay?"

"Yes," she said.

"Mackenzie?"

"Me too," she said, knowing what he was going to say. "I love you too."

She hung up and went over to the couch where Sam slept. John-Glenn had bunk beds in his room, but he was afraid to sleep on the top bed and Mackenzie was afraid to put Sam up there. So he had been put down, half-asleep, here.

Mackenzie thought of Jason, probably already back to sleep. He could wake up and answer ringing phones or doorbells and then fall immediately asleep again.

Sam's legs moved in his sleep, kicked against the blanket. Mackenzie tried to straighten the bedding, to untwist it. She pulled the blanket away, and shook it out gently. Then she began to disentangle the sheet. She had to lift him up slightly to free him from its grip. Sam's mouth moved, noiselessly. Across the wall, the patrol car's red beam flashed, bathing the room and Mackenzie and Sam in its light, then passed by.

CHAPTER SEVEN

After Mackenzie left, Daisy poured herself a big glass of white wine and paced the living room floor. Goddam that Mackenzie, she said out loud. Goddam the entire Porter family. They hadn't liked her from the first day she walked in that house, a gangly seventeen-year-old with blonde hair full of brassy highlights from too much Sun-In and a hot pink miniskirt that allowed flashes of white silk panties when she sat down. She remembered how she had chewed gum nervously, popping it loudly and wrapping it around her tongue as Alexander's family surveyed her.

Even back then Mackenzie had been bold and arrogant, all full of herself and the books she was reading, dropping names of poets and painters like she knew them personally. She was only a few years younger than Daisy, but that first night, as she talked on and on about some incredible book and this amazing artist she'd just found out about, Daisy had felt like a child beside her. And then Mackenzie had run out to take some photographs while the light was just right, and Daisy had watched her, a camera hanging down her chest and a tripod in her hand, and she had known that forever this girl would be her enemy, like all girls like that were to all the girls like Daisy.

Mrs. Porter and Grammie had shot disappointed looks at Alexander as they served iced tea with fresh mint leaves crushed into it and butterscotch brownies they called blondies. The tea, she thought now, had been too strong and bitter and she recalled the look of horror on their faces as she kept adding more and more sugar to her glass. "They're just not used to you yet," Alexander had told her when they left. But in the ten years that she was involved with the Porter family, right up until Alexander died, she had never felt a part of it.

Daisy stopped pacing and dug her bare toes into the carpet. Every time she thought about the Porters she got angry. All the years she had struggled to understand their conversations, to get in on their litttle family jokes, had made her dislike them even more. Once, during an argument Alexander had with his mother while Daisy sat in the car, she had heard Mrs. Porter say, "She dresses like a streetwalker, Alexander. What will she wear to faculty parties with you?"

She looked at the little Christmas tree she had put up for Sam. It was sitting on top of the coffee table, covered in tinsel and blinking red and green lights. She thought, for an instant, of the tree the Porters always had, a tall, perfectly shaped one that Alexander and his father cut down. It used to be full of ornaments that had been in the family for years—red porcelain apples with Cal's and Hope's names painted on in white scroll, construction-paper angels that Alexander had made in school, glass and silver and angel's hair shaped into bulbs. Daisy used to sit near that tree and wish she had grown up in a family like that. "Don't worry," Alexander had told her, "our kids will have traditions just like these." She looked back at the little dime store tree on the table, its skinny plastic branches almost blue. She fought back an impulse to take the tree apart and throw it out.

Here I go again, Daisy said to herself. All I've got to do is think of the Porters and I start doubting myself. She had gotten farther since Alexander left her than she did in all the years they were together, shuffling from school to school so he could get all his degrees, and then shuffling even more so he could teach. When he moved to Boston without her, his whole family acted like she was the one who deserted him. She could imagine them shouting "I told you so" in unison.

She refilled her wineglass and walked into the kitchen. Sam's See-and-Say toy was on the table. Daisy picked it up and turned it on. A picture of an apple lit up on the screen and a robotlike voice said, "Apple."

"Jesus," Daisy said.

Sam's speech therapist had given the toy to him, hoping that alone with it he would talk, follow the mechanical voice and recite words after it. He never did, although he listened over and over as the different objects were identified. Cat. Dog. Car.

"Ball," the toy said now.

"Fuck you," Daisy said, and turned it off.

She needed to talk to someone. She brought the bottle of wine into the kitchen and sat at the table with it in front of her.

"Iris," she said. Then she flipped through her address book until she found her sister's number in San Francisco.

Iris was a good person to talk to when she felt this awful. She was always going through a crisis herself and into some new way to relieve her pain—EST, TM, Pyramid Power.

Daisy and Iris looked as different as sisters could look. Daisy had always been too tall and too skinny. She still wore her hair in the same shag she'd had since junior high, and she still dyed it an off-yellow. The last time Daisy saw her sister, Iris had platinum blonde hair and dark black eyebrows. "My therapist says my purple phase and purple hair were just a reaction to being named Iris," she'd explained. "I act out my fears and desires through my personal appearance rather than passive or aggressive acts."

Daisy counted the times the telephone rang. On the tenth one she started to hang up when she heard Iris answer.

"Hello," she said. "Iris Bloom here."

"Daisy Bloom here."

"Porter."

"I switched back," Daisy said.

"What's wrong?"

"Who said anything was wrong?"

"'You never call when things are right," Iris said. "When Alexander left you, you called a thousand times a day."

"He didn't leave me."

"Oh. My mistake. I thought moving to Boston without you indicated leaving you."

Daisy didn't respond.

"How's business?" Iris asked.

"Great. I told you I earned a car, right? A pink Cimarron." Daisy's voice sounded flat, even though earning that car had been one of her biggest triumphs. Every Saturday she and Sam took it to the drive-through car wash. She paid the extra two dollars to have it waxed as well. Then the two of them cleaned the interior, vacuumed and buffed every inch. "It's a gorgeous car," she added.

"So what then?"

"Mackenzie took Sam to Rhode Island for the holidays."

Daisy felt like she was going to cry. I should not feel guilty, she told herself. She bit down on her bottom lip, hard, until she felt a little pain there. Alexander used to say it was better to cry than bite your lip off. Thinking of that, she bit down harder. She tasted the faint rusty taste of blood.

"Listen," Iris said, "did you know that Iris was like a goddess? A goddess of rainbows? My therapist told me. I feel so liberated now. I mean, that is really a beautiful thing. Goddess of rainbows. You should see what I've done with my hair."

"What?" Daisy pictured Iris with a multicolored afro, the top arcing like a rainbow, the colors in the exact order of the spectrum.

"It's *brown*," Iris said. "How about that? Number 22, Clairol brown."

"Oh, God," Daisy said. Her tongue ran over her bottom lip. She could feel a tiny ridge where she'd bitten down.

"There probably aren't any name therapists in Maryland, but you should check it out. You'd feel so much better if you explored your identity through your name."

Daisy thought of the time Alexander had given her books with characters named Daisy in them for her birthday. *The Great Gatsby. Daisy Miller.* "For my own heroine, Daisy" he'd written.

"Maybe," Daisy said, "I should have gone to Boston with Alexander."

"What? Listen here, you blossomed after he left. You've made something of yourself. When you were with him all you did was live in his shadow. Period. Now you earned that car. And you bought that condominium. Do you hear me?''

Daisy nodded.

''You and Alexander were wrong for each other. All wrong. You were always saying that.''

''I don't know,'' Daisy said.

''Well I'm reminding you.''

''One time,'' Daisy said, pouring more wine in her glass, ''he brought me one hundred daisies. He did. He covered me completely with daisies.''

''He could have taken a job in Washington,'' Iris said. ''In the Washington area, anyway. You moved plenty of times for him. Plenty.''

''I fell in love with him the minute I saw him.''

''You did not, Daisy. You say that now because he's dead. People always speak fondly of the dead, no matter how they really feel. Alexander was so stodgy. So stiff.''

''He wasn't. You hardly knew him. When I met him, my heart fell,'' Daisy said. ''It did.''

''Fine,'' Iris said.

Daisy closed her eyes and remembered that day. It was summer and she was working at the candy counter in Jordan Marsh, kneeling behind it and sneaking Godiva chocolates into her mouth.

''I saw that,'' Alexander had said.

She could remember looking up at him. He was so tall, much taller than her. His hair was somewhere between blonde and brown, and fell over his forehead. There was a slight cowlick in the back, and short sideburns. Daisy remembered thinking it was funny to see such short ones. Later, she convinced him to grow long, thick ones. He would itch and pull at them like they had no business on his face. The first time she saw him, he had on madras shorts, the magenta and green bleeding together in such a way that it made her blink to look at them, as if blinking would clear the blurry plaid.

"Nice shorts," she'd said, standing up, pushing the candy in her mouth to the side, against her teeth, so she could talk better.

He'd looked down, confused. It was as if he really didn't know that no one wore shorts like that or big tortoiseshell glasses.

Daisy had laughed. He was holding a bag from Waldenbooks, tightly, as if it were precious cargo.

"What's in the bag?" she'd asked. "Gold?"

He'd opened it and let her peer inside. Her eyes scanned the titles. She had never heard of any of them. That night, when he took her to the Barnsider for a drink, he'd read passages to her from them. In the soft light of the bar she could see the blonde shadows on his face. They looked almost silver. Beneath her feet, the floor was littered with peanut shells that cracked as she leaned closer to him, to catch every word he read. She could smell him, a rich, spicy smell that made her think of tropical islands, of fruit and ocean spray and exotic herbs. Sometimes still, Daisy would open a drawer or a closet and get a whiff of Alexander, and it made her ache deep inside.

"There are things," Daisy said quietly into the telephone, "that no one knows but me." She remembered sitting in his car, a blue Mustang convertible that he still had when he died, and kissing him. Someone's watching, Alexander had whispered. She'd followed his pointing finger to the sky, where a white full moon hung, its cratered face gazing back at them.

"I've got to go," Daisy said. She could still hear Iris talking as she hung up the phone.

Daisy slipped on her shoes and refilled her wineglass. She went outside, past Sam's rusty swingset to her friend

Allison's condo across the courtyard. All of the units were the same—long and rectangular windows against wooden exteriors painted in flat blue or green or yellow. Daisy's high heels clicked against the cobblestones, slipping occasionally into a crack and sticking there for an instant.

She could see Allison through the open window, smoking a joint. Motown blasted out and she swayed to the music, her eyes shut. From here she looked like a teenager, all freckles and long shiny hair. Close up, though, Daisy knew there were lines around Allison's mouth and eyes. They went out a lot together, to different bars, country and western mostly. They drank and danced and usually took men back with them for the night.

The door wasn't closed all the way and Daisy walked right inside.

"Hey," she said.

Marvin Gaye was singing "I Heard It Through the Grapevine."

Daisy lowered the volume on the stereo and Allison opened her eyes slowly. Alexander would have said that she was a bad influence on Daisy. He always said that she was too easily influenced and that's how she got into trouble.

"Hey," Daisy said again.

Allison smiled up at her.

"I need to go out," Daisy said. "Maybe to the Country Western Playhouse. What do you say?"

"Sure," Allison said, but she didn't move.

Daisy took the joint from her and puffed on it hard, begging it to soothe her.

"Should I change or something?" Allison said. She ran her hands down her boyish body, over her Michael Jackson Victory Tour T-shirt and tight Levis.

"You look fine," Daisy said. Then, "I need to get out."

Allison opened the elaborately carved teak box that sat on the coffee table. My dope box, she called it. She took out two thick joints.

"For the road," she said.

Daisy looked in the mirror over the couch. She reached into her purse and pulled out some makeup—mascara, blush, lipstick, all in little pink cosmetic cases.

"You have enough of that stuff on already," Allison said as she tugged on a pair of red cowboy boots. Thick swirls were etched into the sides and toes.

Daisy brushed on more mascara, licking the tip of the wand first.

"It's December, you know," she said. "You'd better grab a jacket or something."

Allison stared into the closet until Daisy grabbed a suede jacket off a hanger and pushed it into her hands.

"Let's go," she said.

They always took Daisy's car when they went out. It was Allison's opinion that a pink Cadillac attracted more attention than her white Hyundai. Daisy's license plate said I SELL.

On the way to the bar, as they drove along the curvy country roads, Bruce Springsteen pounding from the back speakers, the two women shared a joint. Allison's foot moved in time to the music. Softly, she joined in the chorus of "Rosalita."

Daisy looked over at her. She wanted to tell Allison about Sam, but Allison's ex-husband had custody of their daughter, and Daisy was afraid to open up the subject. She didn't want to listen to Allison's complaints about visiting privileges and lawyers. She just wanted someone to tell her it was all right not to spend Christmas with her son. That is was okay to want him out of her life for just a little while.

At the bar, Daisy ordered them each a shot of tequila.

"Bad day, huh?" the bartender said as he poured the drinks.

She avoided his eyes. Once, very drunk, Daisy had spent the night with him, in his pickup truck under a scratchy gray blanket with USN stamped in black on the front. She had lost her shoes somewhere between the bar and the parking lot and had hitchhiked home, barefoot, at dawn, her back sore from leaning against the spare tire in the back of the truck.

Allison's eyes darted nervously around the room. Although it had never happened, she always feared that her ex-husband would follow her some night and try to get evidence to keep her from seeing their eight-year-old daughter, Brandy. Finally she relaxed, sure that he wasn't there.

"Some day," she said, emptying her drink, "I'm going to turn around and Carl will be standing there with a Polaroid. I just know it."

Daisy shook her head.

"From them," the bartender said. He refilled the women's glasses and cocked his head toward the end of the bar.

Daisy looked at the two men and raised her glass in thanks. A few minutes later the guys came over.

"You old enough to drink?" one of them asked Allison.

"This one sure is," the other man said. He ran his finger up the length of Daisy's arm.

He was shorter than Daisy and she could see a bald spot the size of a half dollar on the top of his head.

"What's your name?" she asked him.

"Jim," he said.

"Jim," she laughed softly. "Hey, Jimbo." She felt the tequila burn the back of her throat when she swallowed. The tension had started to ooze out of her, like there was a little hole in a dam and the water could seep out. Right then, with Jim's finger dancing across her throat, pausing on the spot where her pulse beat, then moving down to her collarbone, Daisy didn't think about Mackenzie or Sam. She didn't wonder if she should have gone to Boston or not. She just felt free. She reached for her glass and slipped. Jim grabbed her arm.

"Steady," he said.

"How many have you had?" the guy talking to Allison said.

Jim led Daisy to the dance floor. Willie Nelson croaked "Let It Be Me" through the crackly speakers. Daisy formed herself against him. He smelled like Old Spice. His head rested against her shoulder. His hands cupped her buttocks, kneading. She pressed against him. Nothing mattered.

Back at the bar, he whispered to her, his fingers tracing her neckline, scooting across her skin like a spider.

"Daisy, Daisy, give me your answer do."

She looked past Jim for Allison. She didn't see her anywhere.

"Come on, Jimmy," Daisy whispered. "Let's go and be nice to each other."

They went back to her place. As he moved on top of her, Daisy's hands clutching his back, she felt the dam break, the tension pouring out of her, gushing, until she was the freest she could be. She heard herself scream, grunt.

It was always this way. Later, in the early morning, with the sky through her window a rosy pink, as she pretended to be asleep, her mouth thick from smoke and liquor, she watched him dress and leave the room without looking back at her. It was then, when she was alone, naked, that Daisy felt like she was just the kind of person Mrs. Porter always said she was.

CHAPTER EIGHT

Mackenzie still half expected to see Grammie in the doorway when she drove up to the house. Up until Grammie had died ten years ago, every time Mackenzie had turned the corner onto their street she had been met by the sight of her grandmother, framed in the picture window of the front room of the house, like a portrait of a New England home. Grammie always used to dress formally, as if she were expecting very important company. She wore a catch of lace at her throat, held there by a large imposing cameo. The laces were scented like flowers—lilies, violets, and roses—and they scratched any face that tried to hug her. She was not a woman given to affection. Even though Mackenzie had grown up in the same house as her grandmother, she'd never once seen her barefoot, or without powdered cheeks.

The woman Mackenzie saw now in that window had her hair tied up in a bright orange kerchief. Her gray sweatshirt had Greek letters on it, in faded maroon. For months now, Mackenzie had tried to come to terms with the fact that other people—strangers—were living in their house. When her father had called and told her he had rented it, she had screamed "No!" and had hung up without hearing more. The next time they had spoken, Jams had told her, "They're good people. They have two little girls," as if that somehow made it all right for these people to be there. She thought again of those garish Christmas lights. They hung now like misshapen fruit from the bushes, dull and hard.

She tried to imagine what was inside the house as she walked up the path toward the front door. The path wasn't shoveled. Instead, the snow had been beaten down by people walking on it, leaving small mounds in the way like miniature igloos. Her parents used to hire a neighborhood boy to shovel the path in winter and trim the hedges and lawn in summer. He lived in that small fieldstone house down the street. She struggled to recall his name. Suddenly it seemed important to remember it. She imagined his face, round with tiny spaced teeth and rubbery looking ears. Walker? she thought. Jeff Walker? Her toe nudged one of the mounds of snow. Mackenzie looked down. Someone had stuck a pink flamingo swizzle stick into it.

"Great," she said, and climbed the steps to the front door.

It was hard for Mackenzie to ring the doorbell, like a visitor. She wanted to grab the clear glass knob and push the door open, to yell "It's me!" and have her mother call to her from the kitchen. On her way through the front room, she'd say hello to Grammie, who wouldn't look up, but would just wave her hand like she was shooing a fly. That hand had a ring on it, clustered with the birthstones of her children, and her grandchildren. A pearl and two rubies, a diamond, and an emerald. The stones formed no specific pattern, just nestled against each other in a careless group.

From inside, she heard a baby cry.

Mackenzie rang the doorbell. She saw the doorknob was cracked.

She rang the bell three more times before the woman, Patty, finally opened the door.

"Sorry," Patty said, "I had to choose. Baby or door." She looked beyond Mackenzie. "Look at that," she said, laughing.

She walked out, past Mackenzie and down the stairs. She kneeled beside the snow mound with the pink flamingo stuck in it.

"You know," Mackenzie said, "there's a neighborhood boy who will come and shovel. For very little money really. He lives in that fieldstone house. Jeff Walker, I think."

Patty didn't look up.

"It would look so much neater if it was shoveled," Mackenzie said.

"This looks like those pictures of the moon," Patty said. She twanged the swizzle stick. "You know, with the American flag stuck in a crater somewhere."

Mackenzie peered into the house. Except for a Christmas tree, the front room was empty. All of the old furniture was crammed into Aunt Hope's tiny apartment and these people hadn't even bothered to move in any of their own. Pushed into one corner sat a playpen, empty except for a blue ball.

"We had a party last night," the woman said.

Mackenzie thought of those lights, the men singing "White Christmas."

"Yes," she said.

"I think I'll leave that swizzle stick there," Patty said. "I sort of like it."

She stood and looked at Mackenzie. "Did you say you were looking for the Walkers?"

"I'm Mackenzie Porter. I—"

"Oh, God." Patty's face wrinkled. "I'm sorry."

Mackenzie shrugged, thought, Sorry? For what? For living in my house? For putting up these stupid lights like a circus? Sorry that you and your husband are alive and well with your two little girls while my family has fallen apart?

Out loud she said, "I left some things here. I thought maybe I could retrieve them."

"Come on in," Patty said. "I just figured you were from UNICEF or Christmas seals or something."

Mackenzie followed the woman inside. The house smelled of cigarette smoke and strangers.

"I was just straightening out from the party," the woman said, and touched the orange kerchief, tugged at its corner. "I don't always walk around like this, in my husband's fraternity shirt from a million years ago. Anyway, I'm Patty. We're renting for a year." She laughed. "But I guess you know that."

"My grandmother used to sit right there, every afternoon, and read." Mackenzie pointed to the spot where the Christmas tree stood. "She'd fill the silver teapot and drink the whole thing herself. With lots of sugar. She used cubes. Lumps, she called them. Like that old joke, one lump or two."

Patty was frowning now, shifting her weight from foot to foot.

Mackenzie laughed nervously. "Listen to me ramble," she said. "You have to excuse me. I haven't been myself lately."

Patty nodded, smiled. "Of course. Your father says that too. That he's not quite himself yet."

That's for sure, Mackenzie thought. She imagined his pockets, full of stolen dime store items. A plastic whistle. Bubble gum. Erasers shaped like animals, Hershey Kisses and Mr. Goodbars.

"You're a photographer, right?" Patty said. "Your father says you go all over the world taking pictures. I did a lot of traveling too. I was a stewardess." She blushed proudly. "I guess you know that too."

Mackenzie motioned toward the stairs.

"Don't mind me," she said. "I just want to check and see if I can find—"

"I could just go on talking forever. Go on up. You didn't come here to socialize."

"Actually," Mackenzie said, "I left this box full of pictures in my room. In the closet. Maybe you moved them."

"Well, which room was yours? There's a couple rooms we haven't even looked in yet. You can look through every closet in the house as long as you don't wake the kids."

"Great," Mackenzie said.

She walked up the stairs. The center was still carpeted with the same oriental pattern. Midnight blue background with red and green flowers on a vine, climbing upward. She stopped three steps from the top. When she was eleven, she had sat on this step and smoked a cigarette with Alexander. She had coughed so hard the cigarette had fallen and burned a hole in the carpet. There it was still. Mackenzie bent forward and poked her pinky into it. When it had happened, her forefinger had been the size of that hole. It had gaped at them, enormous.

At the top of the stairs, she sat on the chintz-covered window seat. Patty had pinned three swatches of fabric to the seat. Was she recovering it? Mackenzie groaned. One had a pattern, eagles and cannons.

"Not eagles," she said out loud.

She looked away, out the window. One autumn she had sat on this seat every Friday night, waiting for Alexander's blue Mustang to come around the corner. She was fifteen that fall, and Alexander had gone off to college in Massachusetts. Every Friday he came home with his roommate, Mackenzie's first secret love, Mark Hayden. They would take her to a movie where she'd sit between them, unable to concentrate, listening to Mark breathe. Sometimes he'd look over at her and smile and she would have to clutch the armrest of her seat, afraid she might fall to the floor. By winter, he'd started going out with a girl named Kate. She had a long red braid that hung down her back like a horse's tail. It swooshed when she walked. Mark stopped coming on Fridays but for a while Mackenzie still sat there, on the window seat, looking out.

My first broken heart, Mackenzie thought. She could almost see that blue Mustang now, coming around the corner, could almost hear the old eight-track tapes playing. "Surfin' USA," "Good Lovin'," "Do You Believe in Magic?" For an instant, her heart skipped a beat, the way it used to back then, when she thought that Alexander and Mark were coming just for her—college men!—and the songs were playing just for her.

Years later, at Alexander and Daisy's wedding, she had danced with Mark. He had grown soft around the middle and wore too much cologne. Kate's hair was cut like Farrah Fawcett's, all wispy waves. They'd made a fortune by buying a Datsun dealership. As they had danced, Mackenzie realized for the first time how short Mark was. Inches shorter than her. But despite it all, during that one dance, while the band played a bad rendition of the Carpenters' "Close to You," Mackenzie had once again felt dizzy with that feeling of first love. When she'd told Alexander, he'd laughed. "Mark had an enormous crush on you too. I told him if he laid one finger on you I'd kill him." "Thanks a lot," she'd said. "If it wasn't for you I'd be driving around in a brand new Datsun now."

Mackenzie walked down the hall, afraid to open any doors, afraid of what was behind them. Or of what was gone. When she opened her own bedroom door, she was surprised that everything was as she'd left it. She wished she could walk inside, close the door, and go back in time to the days when she'd lie in this bed and practiced kissing on her pillow, pretending it was Mark Hayden.

It looked as if Aunt Hope had made a halfhearted effort to pack some things up. There were a few cardboard boxes, closed shut with masking tape, and neatly labeled in Magic Marker. COIN COLLECTION, the top one said. The boxes were old ones from the liquor store, Seagram's and J&B.

She opened the closet, was surprised to see clothing hanging inside in plastic dry-cleaning bags. She peeked into the first few and saw old sweaters of hers and her mother's. On the floor, behind an orange and black psychedelic case full of Herman's Hermits and Jan & Dean albums, was a large white box, just where she'd left it a few months ago.

From downstairs, she heard a little girl's voice. "WHY? WHY? WHY?"

Mackenzie held the box in her arms. As if she could see through its lid, she pictured the prints inside, each carefully matted in white, and negatives beneath them wrapped in tissue paper. Although for years she had worked as a travel photographer, had shot the Great Pyramids, the Wailing Wall, the Bridge of Sighs, Alexander had loved the fact that she'd always had her own projects too. "My sister," Alexander had told her, "keeping art alive." She'd had small shows in galleries around the country. A study of trees, from gnarled oaks to delicate cherry blossoms to massive redwoods. Then, a study of hotel lobbies, a grand, gilt-trimmed one in Bangkok, the check-in station at the LA-Z-DAZE motel on Route 1A. In this box was the project she'd been working on when Alexander had died. A black and white study of brothers and sisters. The developed prints were of strangers—a young sister and brother in Beijing, dressed in identical Mao jackets and standing as straight as soldiers, twins in a stroller in Rock Creek Park, an old man being wheeled down a city street by his ninety-year-old younger sister.

The negatives were of Mackenzie and Alexander. She'd taken them only last Christmas. A year ago, she thought. How can so much change in just one year? She didn't open the box. She remembered holding the negatives up to the light when Alexander had first died, as if these images could recreate him, bring him back to life. In one, their heads were such that her hair bled into his. They looked like they were one person, connected.

"Recorded for posterity," she had told him the day she'd taken the shots.

"Like the Beatles," he'd said. " 'Strawberry Fields Forever.' "

As children, they'd worshipped the Beatles. Mackenzie had a red wallet with a picture of all four in collarless suits on the front, and a charm bracelet full of gold records and guitars. She still remembered all their birthdays.

"Gee," Alexander had laughed, "do you think they'll ever get back together?"

Mackenzie remembered she'd hit his arm playfully. "Not funny," she'd said.

For one picture they'd worn moppy black wigs and crooned like their childhood heroes. YEAH, YEAH, YEAH.

She couldn't do it. She could not open this box.

Back in New York she'd started a new project. Doorways. It had seemed, when she'd started it, like a way to stay calm, open. Jason had told her she had to let go. Close one door, he'd said, and open another. She still refused to say Alexander's name out loud most of the time. It was too painful. She could not look at these pictures. The ones that haunted Aunt Hope's mantel were older, distant. A boy in a Little League uniform, her grandmother frozen in 1962. But the photographs in this box were real. This was who Alexander had been when he died.

Back downstairs, Patty was in the kitchen, mixing mayonnaise into a bowl of tunafish.

"Find it?" she asked.

Mackenzie shook her head. She knew with certainty that she would never find what she had really come for.

The radio played an easy listening version of "Lady Madonna."

"Did you look in the attic?"

"It's gone," Mackenzie said.

"Do you want to stay for lunch?"

Mackenzie thought of all the meals she'd had in this house. She thought of her grandmother's veal stew, with round pearl onions and a touch of curry.

"I've had so many—" Mackenzie started. Then, "No. Thank you."

She zipped her jacket. Behind her, as she closed the door, she heard a little girl. "I hate tunafish." "You do not," Patty said. "You love tunafish."

Mackenzie sat again in the car and stared at the house, the way she had the night before with Sam. Then she pressed her eyes shut, tight. When I open my eyes the present will vanish, she thought. Grammie will be in the window sipping tea. Alexander's car will be in the driveway. She didn't open her eyes for a very long time. Not until Patty called to her from the doorway.

"Car trouble?"

Then Mackenzie waved and smiled and shrugged, all at once, and drove off. She kept her mind focused on Sam, whose eyes were just like Alexander's and nothing like Iris Bloom's. Sam, who was sitting and waiting for her to come to him.

The first thing Mackenzie noticed when she and Sam got to her father's that night was his shoes. They were white, the kind old men in Miami wore. Pat Boone shoes, Alexander would have called them. For as long as she could remember, Jams wore either oil-stained Topsiders or, for dress-up, black wingtips. In her childhood there was a Friday night ritual in which Mackenzie polished her father's shoes and he paid her fifty cents. Jams would spread out part of the newspapers from the Sunday before on the kitchen floor. With a big glass of Pepsi beside her, Mackenzie would open the shoeshine kit and spread its contents on the papers—the smudged chamois cloth, the metal tin of wax, and the bottle of black shoe polish with the tip of squishy foam. Once, while Mackenzie was carefully unlacing the wingtips, Alexander took the bottle of polish and painted Groucho Marx eyebrows on Babar, the family dog. Mackenzie had felt like a holy ritual had been ruined. She felt the same way now, looking at the unfamiliar shoes, white with long tassels.

"Where are your shoes?" Mackenzie said.

"On my feet," Jams said, laughing.

They were sitting in his room at Oakdale. It was sunny and small, like a motel room. On the walls were paintings of clown faces that looked as if they were done with a paint-by-number kit. The rug was a scratchy shag. The television was on a swiveling pedestal. Mackenzie and her father sat on white wicker chairs, sipping iced tea. Jams had crushed fresh mint in it like they always did at home. In a small bowl on the table were assorted nuts—cashews, almonds, filberts.

Jams had moved to Oakdale just a few weeks after Cal left Rhode Island. There was therapy for his shoplifting habit, for dealing with Alexander's death. "The people here aren't crazy," a nurse had assured Mackenzie when Jams first went there, "they're just troubled. Or lonely. Think of this as a social club, not a hospital." On the bulletin board in the lobby, Mackenzie had seen sign-up sheets for bus trips to Plymouth Rock, Mystic Seaport, Sturbridge Village. A bookshelf in her father's apartment was cluttered with cheap souvenirs, plastic domes with fluorescent colored scenes inside—a neon green Plymouth Rock, a shiny pink lobster. When the domes were shaken, glittery snow fell.

"I have a whole drawer full of your letters," Jams said. "And the clippings you send me of your work."

Mackenzie hesitated, then asked, "Any word from Mom?" She tried to make her voice sound casual.

Jams shook his head.

Sam picked up one of the domes and shook it, watched the silver snow fall.

"Auntie Hope gets these postcards," Mackenzie said. She kept her eyes fixed on her father's white shoes. A glimpse of pale yellow showed above them.

"So I hear," Jams said. "Blank postcards." He shook his head again.

"Those shoes are awful," Mackenzie said.

Sam gasped slightly. He was peering into one of the domes, nodding. Mackenzie went over to him and looked inside too.

"Boston," she said, reading the name that sat below a pot of fluorescent yellow beans and a bright blue Prudential Center.

"He remembers," Jams said quietly. "He remembers visiting Alexander there. Don't you, Sammy?"

Mackenzie took the souvenir from Sam, shook it, and watched the sparkling flakes fall onto the Boston baked beans.

"Alexander had him there for Memorial Day weekend right before—"

"I know," she said quickly.

"Your mother and I met them at Durgin's Park for lunch. Last time I saw Alexander, sitting at one of those long tables there eating strawberry shortcake."

"Why did you go and buy those shoes?" Mackenzie said angrily. She felt like she was standing on ground that was shaking loose from an earthquake, more and more of it crumbling into a chasm.

"It's better to talk about it," Jams said. "Everybody's just running away from it."

Sam took the souvenir from Mackenzie.

The room was silent.

"These shoes," Jams said finally, "reminded me of some I use to have a long time ago, back when I first met your mother. I swapped them for three Izod shirts at a swap meet we had here."

Sam moved to the next shelf, this one lined with row after row of miniature liquor bottles like they sold on airplanes. Sam unscrewed the cap of a Grand Marnier, smelled it, and wrinkled his nose.

"Spitting image," Jams said.

Mackenzie nodded.

"Just the other day," he continued, "I read about a boy in New Jersey who died talking on the telephone. Did you read that?"

"No."

"It happens sometimes. It really does."

Mackenzie thought of all the Saturdays she had spent

with her father in the liquor stores he owned. There were two of them, as large as supermarkets. He would put her in a shopping cart and wheel her up and down the aisles, explaining the processes it took to make champagne and wine, what grains and fruits went into each liquor. She loved the bottles that had fruit in them best, black cherries or pears, and the liquor from Portugal that had a branch laden with sugary crystals inside. She was allowed to run free in the big cooler room full of beer in the back of the store. Mackenzie used to pretend she was traveling on an ocean liner, each case of beer a country. "I'm in Australia," she'd say, sitting on a case of Foster's.

She watched as Sam rearranged all the bottles by their height, and wondered how many of those her father had stolen. The first thing he took, right after Alexander had died, was a miniature of Tanqueray from one of the stores he used to own, its tiny red seal and ribbon in place.

Sam examined a bottle of gin.

"Sloe berries," Mackenzie said.

Her father smiled at her. "Do you remember all of them?"

"A lot of them, anyway."

"I remember when you were doing photography for the Smithsonian, you brought me liquors I'd never even heard of one Christmas. Made from plants I'd never heard of."

She remembered too. The last Christmas they were all together.

"Last year," she said.

"That boy in New Jersey," Jams said, "was talking to his girlfriend on the phone. She heard a loud crackle, like static, and then silence. No screams or anything. No pain. I was glad to learn that."

"I was thinking we'd go to the Barnsider for dinner," Mackenzie said.

"Key West."

"What?"

"It's not the Barnsider anymore. It's a Mexican place now. Key West."

Alexander had taken her to the Barnsider on her eighteenth birthday and bought her her first legal drink. It was a Cape Cod, cranberry juice and vodka, and it came in an oversized tumbler. There were baskets of peanuts on the table and everyone threw the shells on the floor. Her brother had looked at her, and clinked his glass to hers. "Eighteen more," he'd said. "And we'll come right back here in eighteen years to drink to eighteen more," Mackenzie had made him promise.

"No more peanuts on the tables?" she asked her father.

"Chips. Like Doritos. And salsa for dipping."

"I won't go there, then," Mackenzie said.

"The food's not bad," her father said.

Mackenzie began to cry. She wanted her father to put on his real shoes. She wanted to be in their house, to have Alexander drive up in his Mustang and take her to the Barnsider.

"Hey," Jams said.

He got up and went over to her. She pushed her face against her father's stomach, a small white button on his shirt pressing into her cheek.

"I want Sam to know what it was like," she said.

"What?"

"What it used to be like," Mackenzie said.

CHAPTER NINE

The next day Mackenzie and Sam ate chowder and clam-cakes on the breakwall that stretched from the beach into the sea. Between the rocks, the water swirled a dark green. They huddled together, an old plaid blanket from Aunt Hope's around them. A large ship sat on the water, as if frozen to the horizon.

"I wish I had my camera," Mackenzie said.

Sam slurped his chowder.

"Your daddy and I used to come and sit out here," she said. "Grandma and Grandpa would wave to us from the shore. Every time we'd turn around, they'd be there waving. We used to try to see if we could catch them not looking. But we never did."

Sam turned toward the shore, as if expecting them to be there.

"Do you know what a cocoon is, Sam?"

He lifted his face to hers and nodded.

"I feel like I lived in a cocoon. All of us did. And when Alexander died, it was as if we were all forced out. Grandma said that was the final straw. But to me, it was the first and most awful thing. Everything else was like an adventure. It didn't seem so bad." She thought of Aunt Hope and Ricardo Havana in his big convertible. They used to let her sit on the top of the back seat and wave to passing cars like she was a beauty queen in a parade.

Sam looked out at the ship.

"Come on," Mackenzie said, helping Sam to his feet. "Let's walk on the beach."

They made their way off the breakwall. Mackenzie kept her eyes on Sam's sandy Nikes. He clutched the blanket around him like an Indian chief. Once off the wall, they followed the shoreline. The waves were small and gray. The sea foam soaked into the sand, eating their footprints as they walked.

Sam stopped and bent down to pick a stone out of the sand at the water's edge. It was shaped like an egg. He brushed the sand from it. Veins of pink ran through the off-white. Sam held it up and licked the salt from it. Head bent, he ran ahead of Mackenzie and picked up more stones. Some, after he studied them, he threw back into the ocean. Watching him, Mackenzie remembered Alexander doing the same thing, on this very beach. He used to skim stones across the water's surface. He could make them dance, touching down three or four times before they sank.

She thought of Jason, back in New York. She had promised to bring him here someday, when her mother came back and things were normal again. She had told him about the famous Porter turkey dinners that they had on special occasions. Mackenzie made sweet potatoes with Kahlúa and marshmallows. Jams had a secret recipe for stuffing with apricots, Grand Marnier, and raisins. "That's what we'll make when you come," she'd told Jason, "our special Porter turkey dinner." "I'll bring string beans," he'd said, "made in a casserole with Lipton mushroom soup and fried onion rings. That's my specialty." "That's all right," Mackenzie had said, laughing. "You don't have to bring anything."

Sometimes, when Mackenzie thought about her family, she wondered if the warmth she had felt between them had been real. Or was it something she imagined now to sustain her? If it had been as wonderful as she remembered, how could it all fall apart so quickly? Mackenzie shook her head. Her breath came out in streams of whitish gray air. It had been real, she told herself. She looked around her at all the familiar things on this beach. The saltwater taffy shop. The seafood restaurant. The distant lighthouse. She had come here often to be healed, not only after Alexander had died, but earlier, for broken hearts, decisions, and lost friendships.

Sam ran back to her, his red scarf coming loose from his neck, one end dangling longer than the other. Smiling, he dropped a dozen stones into her hands.

"For me?" she said.

He nodded.

They were all worn smooth from the waves beating against them. Mackenzie ran her fingers over a black triangular-shaped one.

"Stones," she said, "are a wonderful gift because they last forever."

Mackenzie filled her coat pockets with the stones, and pulled Sam close to her. His cheeks were red and cold.

They turned away from the ocean and began to walk back to the car. A seagull squawked overhead. Sam raised his head and watched as it cut into the gray winter sea air in a perfect arc.

*   *   *

Mackenzie's grandfather had died long before she was born. He appeared in his World War I uniform, sepia toned and starched, on the mantel, and in an oval wedding picture, standing straight beside Grammie, whose hair fell to her shoulders in soft ripples. Great-uncle Bill, Grandpa's brother, spent his life winning and losing fortunes. There was a story that he had been in love once, but the woman had left him for another man. He lived a wild life, trying to forget her. The way Uncle Bill did that was by drinking too much and going to Las Vegas to gamble and pick up showgirls. Alexander had discovered this by finding a five-by-seven picture of Uncle Bill with a leggy blonde in a red sequined leotard and gold feathers in her hair. The woman's name was Gigi and she sent Uncle Bill postcards. One of them had a donkey on the front and said "I lost my ass in Las Vegas." That was Alexander's favorite. Mackenzie liked the one that had a hot pink kiss imprint on the front. When he wasn't in Las Vegas, Uncle Bill hung around with Ricardo Havana. "This behavior," Grammie told him, "has to stop." "We're only going bowling," he used to say.

In the end, it had been Uncle Bill who told Aunt Hope that Ricardo Havana had another wife and three daughters in Miami. By then, the Havana Hoochie-Coo's had split up and John-Glenn was born. Aunt Hope took the baby and moved into the basement of the Porter house. For a while, Ricardo stood on the front lawn and serenaded her, trying to get her back. But she never spoke to him again.

Uncle Bill drove Ricardo back to Miami to meet up with his other family. Steamer trunks full of the Hoochie-Coo's costumes—blue velvet tuxedos and ruffled shirts—and various musical instruments crowded the back seat. Despite the cold January morning, both Bill and Ricardo wore brightly colored Hawaiian shirts, decorated with parrots and hula girls.

"They're bombed already," Alexander had said.

He stood with Mackenzie and watched from an upstairs window as Bill and Ricardo packed the car.

"We can all forget the name Ricardo Havana," he added.

From downstairs, Grammie yelled, "Ricardo Havana, don't you ever show your face here again."

A month later, everyone was in the living room watching a new group called the Beatles on the Ed Sullivan show. The cameras showed close-ups of each one as they sang, and flashed their names on the screen. Alexander read each name out loud as it appeared. Mackenzie screamed along with the girls in the audience.

"Paul," Alexander read.

The girls screamed.

"What is happening here?" Grammie said. "Look at the hair on these singers. They look like a bunch of women."

"This," Jams said, "is Beatlemania."

"John," Alexander read.

The girls screamed.

"Sorry girls," he read, "he's married."

"I like Paul anyway," Cal said.

The front door opened then and Uncle Bill called into the living room.

"Anybody home?"

Grammie grabbed her fan and started to wave it. "Go and look," she said, "and see if he's brought back that two-timing Ricardo Havana."

Aunt Hope jumped up from the ottoman she was sitting on and started to cry.

"George," Alexander read.

"I'll go and see what's happened," Jams said.

But he didn't have to go very far. In the doorway stood Uncle Bill, dressed in a white suit and pink shirt, open at the collar. On his head sat a Panama hat. Beside him, clutching his arm, was a beautiful woman in a flaming red dress that fell in a million soft ruffles around her hips and thighs. Her hair was long and curly, the color of coal. Her own eyebrows had been tweezed off and replaced with thin penciled-in V's.

"Ringo," Alexander read.

No one listened. Everyone faced the doorway.

"What is this?" Grammie demanded.

"Everybody," Uncle Bill said, "this is Carmen Havana."

There was shouting and confusion. Had Uncle Bill really brought home Ricardo Havana's wife?

"How could you?" Aunt Hope wailed.

"Get that woman out of here," Grammie said.

"My new wife," Uncle Bill said.

All noise stopped, except for Ed Sullivan. He said, "Ladies and gentlemen, the Beatles." And the audience screamed.

"Your what?" Cal said.

"She's Ricardo's cousin," Bill said. "I met her in Miami."

"I wanted him to marry Gigi," Mackenzie whispered to Alexander. "Then we could all have moved to the desert and eaten cactus."

Carmen extended her arms. "Now where are Mackenzie and Alexander?" Her voice was husky.

No one moved.

"This woman," Cal said, "will not touch my children."

Mackenzie thought that Carmen must be very bad. At family gatherings she always sat slightly apart from everyone. She brought earthenware bowls full of paella, steaming with shrimp and chicken and sausage. Aunt Hope never tasted it. Because of Carmen's connection to Ricardo Havana, Aunt Hope completely ignored everything Carmen said or did.

After a few years, Carmen left Uncle Bill and moved back to Miami. She said she couldn't get used to the cold up north, even though in winter she wore two coats and brightly patterned mittens and fur-lined boots. She sent Mackenzie postcards of beautiful palm-tree-lined beaches, which she used to sketch in big drawing pads she took to carrying everywhere with her. The first Christmas after Carmen left, she sent the children three pet alligators. The animals lived for a few days in the red sink in the Porters' basement. John-Glenn was afraid of the alligators. He thought they would grow large and eat him. When they were found drowned one morning, everyone suspected homicide. Alexander even started an investigation, but Cal stopped him, suggesting that it was most likely an accident and that it was probably better that they were gone anyway. For years, Alexander and Mackenzie speculated about who had drowned the alligators. He was sure it had been John-Glenn. But Mackenzie thought Aunt Hope was the murderer and had killed them out of some misplaced revenge against Ricardo Havana.

The late afternoon winter light was gray and white. The clouds hung low and heavy with the cold. Mackenzie and Sam shivered when they stepped from the heated car into the December air. Sam's eyes widened at the sight of the rows and rows of stone monuments marking the graves. Mackenzie had wanted to come here before she left Rhode Island. She had told Sam as they drove away from the beach that she was coming here. "I'll drop you off at Aunt Hope's," she'd said. But he had shook his head violently, back and forth. "You want to come?" she'd asked, her mind racing, wondering if it was all right to take him to Alexander's grave.

He seemed calm now as they stood on an icy path between two rows of tombstones. The daylight was fading quickly. Mackenzie tried to orient herself. She had only been here once, the day of the funeral. Nothing had seemed right about that day. It was hot and sunny, the kind of day that Alexander would have called a definite beach day. They would have driven to the ocean with the top down and a Beach Boys or Four Seasons tape playing full blast. No one at the funeral wore black. Instead, they stood around the coffin in thin summer clothes, pastel colors, cotton and sleeveless. Someone, an old friend of Alexander's from high school, had worn a bright orange T-shirt: MOONDOGGIE'S SURF SHOP, it said in sunshine yellow. Mackenzie could remember watching as Daisy swayed in her high-heeled white sandals, like a willow tree in a breeze. And no one had cried. They had all stood in stunned silence instead.

"I don't know exactly," Mackenzie said as she led Sam by the hand.

She felt his fingers tremble inside his mitten.

"It all looks so different in this light," Mackenzie said. "In the winter."

She remembered Daisy saying, "His tombstone should reach into the sky. Like Alexander himself. Reaching upward." She wondered if her parents had agreed to that, if his monument was tall.

Mackenzie saw, a few rows away, where she thought the spot might be, a headstone, taller than the rest, pointing upward.

"Over there, I think," she said.

Sam paused at a child's grave, his mouth open. JENNI-FER, DARLING BABY OF . . .

"Come on," Mackenzie said, pulling him away.

She shouldn't have brought him, she thought.

"I'm going to walk you back to the car, Sam," Mackenzie said.

She heard his breathing, hard and fast. He walked faster, ahead of her now. Mackenzie felt the stones he had given her at the beach in her pocket, heavy against her hips.

"Sam," she said, but he didn't stop.

He walked right to the taller headstone.

Mackenzie stopped just behind him.

ALEXANDER PORTER.

She heard a moan, then realized it had come from her.

The name, carved into the stone like that, seemed to belong to someone else, someone she had never known.

Mackenzie looked at her own brother's name on his grave. She remembered that when they had visited their ancestors' graves in Pennsylvania, Alexander had stood beside her touching the name PORTER. "Gross," he'd said, sticking his finger into the carved-out P.

A white poinsettia stood next to the grave, its pot wrapped in shiny foil, a red bow draped around the base. Beside it was a blue basket of large pine cones, their tips dipped in white paint as if they had been frosted with snow or cake icing. Under his name, etched into the stone, it said: "The ball I threw in the schoolyard had not yet reached the ground."

Mackenzie frowned. Her mother had picked that, had shown her the quote in a book of poetry. Dylan Thomas.

Mackenzie looked down at Sam. He was stuffed into his bright blue ski jacket. The down inside it made creases and squares on the coat. He dropped to his knees. Mackenzie knelt beside him. The ice cracked beneath her. She put her arms around him, the jacket squishing in her hands. His body felt rigid.

"Sam," Mackenzie said.

She waited, half expecting him to answer, to suddenly talk. She felt, somehow, that, if he did, she would understand everything, that he held some key to it all. But he simply leaned against her and they stayed like that for a very long time.

Sometimes Sam considered talking. Thought about it until he almost actually did it. Like when his aunt brought him to the cemetery.

He hadn't known what exactly to expect there. He remembered his father's funeral, the quietness of it, the way the air felt thick and still. His mother had told him that his father was in that big box covered with flowers. The box was the color of his crayon called Burnt Sienna. His mother read the words on the ribbons that hung off the bouquets to him. Beloved Son. Brother. Nephew. He hadn't understood. "Who?" he'd kept thinking. The night before the funeral, everyone went out. His mother had wanted to take him along. "He should be able to say good-bye to his father," she had said. "It's the kind of thing," Jams had told her, "that sticks with a child. It's not good." In the end he had stayed behind with Aunt Hope. "It's all right," she had told him, "I didn't look at my own mother." What was that supposed to mean? he'd wondered, and he imagined Aunt Hope as a child, blindfolded.

This time it was cold at the cemetery, and Aunt Mackenzie kept saying that maybe he should go back to the car. But he wouldn't. He had to see whatever there was to see at his father's grave. He had hoped there would be something of his father there. Maybe the Red Sox hat he always wore. But the only thing that was left was his father's name.

Sam had thought then about calling out. "Daddy," he would shout, "I'm here." But couldn't his father see that he was there? If his father was indeed under this stone, in the ground, then he would see Sam and come out. Sam had knelt and banged on the icy dirt with his hands, as if to wake him. But he didn't come out. And Sam didn't speak. He was sure he had been right all along—his father had stopped talking and disappeared.

After the funeral, everyone asked him the same questions, over and over. What was your daddy saying? Did he scream? The questions, to Sam, seemed silly. It wasn't what his father had said, it was that he had stopped talking that was important.

Sam had been asking him about Boston, which was where his father lived. There were streets made out of brick, a building that looked like an icicle, and once, there had been a war there. A war against England. "Was Princess Diana in the war?" Sam had asked. Sam loved Princess Diana. His father cut pictures of her out of magazines and kept them for him. "This war," his father had told him, "happened a long long time ago. Before the Beatles or Princess Diana. Even before Jams."

His father knew about everything. He taught Sam songs and words all the time. That day, he taught Sam the word "itinerary." "Here's our itinerary," he had said, "for when you get here." They were going to eat lobsters, and even his father would wear a bib while he ate. One day, they would drive to Cape Cod, which was a beautiful place near the ocean. "By the sea," his father had said, and Sam had sung, "By the sea, by the sea, by the beautiful sea." "You and me," his father sang, "you and me, oh how happy we'll be."

Boston had an aquarium with seals and whales and sharks. It had museums too. One with glass flowers, and one with scientific things, and one just for children. "Boston," Sam had said, "sounds wonderful."

And then there had been the slightest crackle, the way the television sometimes sounded when the neighbor used his ham radio. Like a short buzz. It had been nothing like everyone asked him about. Not a jolt or a bang or a loud zzzzzt.

Sam had waited for his father to tell him more.

"What else?" he'd said.

He had waited a very long time.

Sometimes, when Sam talked on the telephone, he got tired or thirsty. He'd put the phone down for a little while and get a drink of water or watch television. But his father had told him if he did that he must say, "Hold on, please." Maybe, Sam thought that day, his father had gotten thirsty and forgot to say, "Hold on, please."

It had been a long while before Sam got really frightened and started to scream. It was, he'd thought, as if his father had just disappeared. That thought frightened him because things that disappeared never came back. They stayed gone forever.

It was like the lost continent of Atlantis.

His father had told him the story about Atlantis. It had been a beautiful, beautiful place to live. A utopia, was the word he'd used, which meant perfect, like heaven. Until one day there was a bad earthquake and Atlantis sunk into the sea. "Where did it go?" Sam had asked. "It just disappeared," his father told him. And no one ever found it again.

Sam had stopped talking and so far he hadn't disappeared. But that was what he wanted. To vanish, just like his father had. When he finally did disappear, he expected to find his father and maybe even the lost continent of Atlantis. Every morning he would look in the mirror, expecting to find nothing. But instead, he always saw his own reflection staring back.

His speech therapist, Miss Knight, was old and fat. Sam thought her neck looked like a turkey's gullet, loose and saggy. She wore half-glasses that hung around her neck on a gold chain or sat on the very tip of her nose. Her hair was white, but sometimes, in a certain light, it looked vaguely blue, and Sam could see the pink of her scalp through her tight curls. Miss Knight kept a dish of animal crackers in front of him during the entire session, but wouldn't let him have one until right before he left. He always chose the elephant, and ate it slowly—first the trunk, then the tail, and finally the head and body.

Miss Knight usually sat in front of him on a velvet bench and made noises with her long, pointed tongue.

"Th. Th. Th."

Or she said words that rhymed.

"Spoon. June. Moon."

Then she waited, looking at him down her nose and through her small glasses.

One day she said, "Sam, I'm going to tell you a story about a woman named Helen Keller. Helen Keller was born with the ability to see and speak and hear, but she got terribly ill and lost all of those senses."

Miss Knight stared at him for so long then that he had to look away. He focused instead on a lion animal cracker on the white plate.

"But she picked herself up by the bootstraps, Sam, and learned to talk all over again. Despite every obstacle."

Miss Knight was pretty nice, but there were times when she got mad at him, like the day she told him about Helen Keller. And sometimes, after sitting in front of him making sounds and waiting, she'd take off her glasses and let them fall around her large bosom and Sam would know she was mad at him.

She'd shake her head and say, "Do you know what I think, Sam Porter? I think you can talk just fine. You're just a very stubborn, very selfish little boy."

What Miss Knight didn't know—what no one knew—

was that if he talked, he wouldn't disappear. He'd just keep right on the way he had been, living with his mother, going to school, except he'd never see his father again.

CHAPTER TEN

The woman sitting beside Jams was named Ursula. She always sat next to him at dinner, and looked at him shyly with her marmalade-colored eyes. She had hair the color of carrots and very white skin that was covered with freckles. She had come here to escape a husband who beat her. A bruise still lingered on her cheek, yellow like an old autumn leaf.

"He hit me all the time," she said. "If *Taxi* was a rerun or the electric company man misread our meter. Anything."

Jams nodded. He sometimes felt saturated by other people's problems. Sometimes he wished he could propel himself backward into time. There would be a puff of smoke and then his chair at this table would be empty. Ursula would gasp when she realized he had disappeared. Her orange eyes would grow wide. Maybe she'd even faint, while all the time he would be back in Pennsylvania, in his boyhood room, like Peggy Sue in the movie *Peggy Sue Got Married*.

To Jams, his life had been a pleasant blur sandwiched between two periods of glaring reality. He remembered more details about his childhood and about the past few months since Alexander had died than he did about all the time in between. He could clearly recall the taste and feel of that tangerine he'd stolen right before Cal had left, yet he could not remember his own wife's scent, or the way her skin felt. And he could startle himself with recollections of his childhood in Pennsylvania, with things that seemed too trivial to remember.

"The final straw, though," Ursula was saying, "was when he strangled a litter of kittens. Our cat had three kittens, little black ones, and he killed every one of them."

And then Jams surprised himself by telling Ursula a story of something he had seen long ago, using details he had no idea he recalled.

"I had a friend when I was a boy," he said, "named Jay Hogue. His family had a farm nearby and I'd ride my bike out there. We lived in the center of town, right off the main street in a big white house surrounded by porches so that any time of day you could sit in the sunlight. My grandfather designed it that way." As he spoke, Jay Hogue's face—crooked nose, hair the color and texture of hay— loomed in front of him with great clarity. Jams saw his old bike, a red and white one with red, white, and blue streamers on the handlebars.

"Yes?" Ursula said. She was trying to get the connection, pulling her face tight as if that might help.

"Well," Jams said, "one day I rode out there. My God! This is incredible. It had rained earlier that morning and I had to ride through a lot of mud and puddles. And even once I got to the farm I had to sort of traipse through even more mud. My jeans got filthy. And my sneakers too. We went to the barn. We used to like to hang out in there. Jump around on the hay, things like that. My father owned a hardware store in town. Sometimes we'd help him out, sometimes we'd help Jay's father on the farm. Make a little pocket money. Anyway, on this particular day, we walked in the barn with a stack of comic books to read and found their dog—a big golden retriever name of Tops—gobbling up a litter of kittens. Five of them. Little bitty things, too.''

Ursula frowned, disappointed with the story. She bent her head and avoided his eyes while she finished her meal. He watched her eat the green Jell-O with white grapes, her bites small and precise. She had, he expected, wanted a story of abuse. Jay's father beating up on the boys or the dog, maybe. But despite her disappointment, Jams felt exhilarated. The story had unfolded in his brain like a home movie. The dog, Tops, licking his lips and growling softly, the way the barn smelled, a horse's tail swishing against its stall, and then the sound of more rain, falling hard and smelling like springtime.

There were times when he could completely recall his childhood room, right down to the bed with the scratchy white sheets that smelled of bleach and the sheer curtains against a window that had one cracked pane forever.

But from the day he arrived in South Station in Boston to help his Uncle Andrew with his liquor stores until the day that Alexander died seemed like a pleasant, fuzzy dream. Images and events blurred together and he could not distinguish one from the other. Certainly he had felt love for his wife, and joy when his children were born, and pride as his business grew, but all the emotions seemed jumbled to him.

He could recall easily the phone call and what followed became marked and clear, like his boyhood memories. One Christmas, Daisy had given them a cribbage board that was like a maze, the holes a twirling spiral, and that was what they were doing when the call came. He and Cal were playing cribbage with that board. They had eaten pork roast stuffed with apricots and prunes for dinner. Or perhaps it was roast beef. A roast, anyway.

"Let's have a big barbecue here on the Fourth of July," Cal had said. "Sam will be up and Mackenzie will be back from New Zealand."

Maybe he had suggested the barbecue. Jams wasn't really sure. He remembered someone suggesting it, looking at his cards, and the phone ringing. All of that as if it were one movement instead of three separate ones. A man's voice, high and thick with a Boston accent, told him then that Alexander was dead. "Do you," the man had said, "know one Alexander Porter." The r's had come out like sighs. Ah.

In that instant, Jams's senses woke up, as if from a long sleep. They jumped to life and assaulted every part of him. The taste of the sweet fruit he had eaten turned sour in his throat. The pendulum on the grandfather clock swung in slow motion, its large black hands pointing to eight-twenty. Cal leaned toward him.

"What?" she said. "What?"

"I'm sorry, Mr. Porter," the policeman said. Behind the voice, Jams heard a typewriter clacking.

And then Jams thought of all the things he hadn't told his son. How, when he was a boy in Pennsylvania and he worked in his father's hardware store, his hands would turn black from counting and sorting nails. They turned black and smelled like metal. And that once his family had been snowed in for a week. Just when they managed to get out, an ice storm came and turned the entire town into a crystal palace.

When Alexander was in junior high, he entered a statewide social studies fair. He had chosen Italy for his project. For weeks he'd researched it, bringing every new piece of information to Jams like it was a wonderful discovery. The largest cities. Its imports and exports and natural resources. ITALY, he had stenciled on the poster board, RICH IN ART AND HISTORY. Jams had helped him make the map, using colored rice to make it 3-D. Italy was a pale yellow boot, the Alps rose red and high in the north, and the Mediterranean stretched out in grains of food colored blue.

"I have to know everything about it," Alexander told him every night, "for the oral presentation."

And Jams quizzed him, over and over. Capital city, largest city, bordering nations.

In the end, Alexander won first place along with a girl whose map of Hawaii included a bubbling volcano.

For years, like a ritual, Jams would ask Alexander when he called, "Capital city?"

"Rome. Roma."

"Language?"

"Italian."

"Founders?"

"Romulus and Remus."

But never, Jams thought, had he told him the things that mattered.

He considered saying this to Ursula, telling her about the unimportance of Italy, the importance of snow and metal. But she had slipped away, unnoticed. A smear of green Jell-O lay on the table.

Jams hated going back to the house. But once a month he had to go there to pick up the rent check from Patty. He feared that he would walk in and horrible memories would come to him in vivid detail. Tonight he drove over after dinner.

Patty insisted he stay for a drink. "To warm you up,"

she said. She had thick curly hair that extended outward and formed a triangle in the back. She had hung studio portraits of her wedding and the children at various stages of their lives so far, all over the family room walls. As Cal would have said, Patty was not a woman of taste. Jams hated to sit there, surrounded by those pictures of strangers. In one picture Patty stood in front of a silver jet in her stewardess uniform. It was bright blue with tiny airplanes on it. Her hair was cut like some ice skater's he had seen once. "That was right before my first flight," Patty said. "Don't I look terrified?" He nodded. "And this is Jolie when she was two . . ." She took him through a tour of each picture, wedding and children's bath time, vacations and picnics. All the time Jams smiled and nodded, waiting for the perfect moment to get out of there, away from Patty and her smiling family.

It wasn't until he got back to his building that he realized he'd forgotten the check. He stood in the parking lot, paralyzed. He did not want to go back to that house. He inhaled, smelled snow. Across the lot he watched two figures approaching and sighed with relief when he saw it was Mackenzie and Sam. Good, he thought, happy for the reason to skip the trip back to Patty's.

"I smell snow," he said to them.

Mackenzie looked beautiful, he thought, in the cold air and lamplight.

He held a hand under Sam's chin. "We'd get snow up to here when I was a boy. In Pennsylvania."

"He needs stimulation," Mackenzie said.

"Like a good snowfall?"

She frowned at him. "To talk. He needs stimulation to talk. Daisy leaves him alone, by himself. That's not going to get him talking. He needs to be shown things. Reminded of things."

Jams shrugged. Sometimes, he thought, it's not such a good thing to be reminded of the past.

"I believe with the right stimulation, Jams . . ."

"Do you think," Jams said, "that nuclear explosions could affect the snowfall?"

"When I take him back I'm going to talk to his speech therapist. I know what he needs."

Sam started sliding on the ice, his arms held out into the air.

"All he needs," Mackenzie continued quietly, "is to be stimulated the right way. When he saw Alexander's grave—"

"You didn't take him there, did you?"

"He wanted to go. We can't keep pretending that Sam doesn't have feelings about his father. About Alexander."

"When my grandfather died," Jams said, "they showed the body right in our living room. My brother and I were told to stay in our rooms. But of course we crept downstairs in the middle of the night, after all the people had gone home. He was there in a coffin lined in powder-blue silk and he looked like a statue in a wax museum we had gone to in Philadelphia. That museum had wax statues of Benjamin Franklin and all the presidents. 'He looks like John Quincy Adams,' my brother whispered. Then we ran back upstairs and put all the lights on because we were so afraid."

"Well, Sam wasn't afraid. He was emotional."

Sam had slid away from them, and now he made figure eights back to them.

"I know," Jams said to Mackenzie, "how hard it's been on you."

Sam reached them and bowed elaborately.

"Wonderful," Jams said, applauding.

Mackenzie looked at him, impatient. As a child she used to ask him every morning, "Is it tomorrow now?"

"I've got something I want to show you," he said. "Upstairs."

"So what do we do?" Mackenzie said.

"You'll tell Daisy when you see her. About stimulation. About Alexander."

"A lot of good that'll do," she said.

Mackenzie hung back for a moment. Jams turned to her.

"I hope it's so," he said. "I hope he's getting ready to talk. I want to know what happened that day. Just like you do."

The ride in the elevator was silent. Sam closed his eyes and felt the numbers in braille.

"This came in the mail today," Jams said once they were inside his apartment.

Mackenzie and Sam stood in the little hallway. Jams could smell the sea on them.

"You were at the beach," he said.

Sam stood on tiptoes to see the postcard he had handed Mackenzie.

She turned to the back immediately.

"Nothing," she said, holding up the blank message space. "Only her initials again."

Sam took it from her and studied the front. There was a picture of the arch in St. Louis. Sunlight sparkled off it. In red letters it said, GATEWAY TO THE WEST. A fat red cardinal perched on the word WEST, a baseball bat poised for a hit in his wings. In the distance, the Mississippi River curved.

"Oh, no," Jams said. "There's a message there."

Sam looked at him, surprised. The boy turned the card over.

"Take your coats off," Jams said. "I'll make some hot

chocolate if you don't mind the instant kind. Your mother would never stand for it. But . . ." He held his hands up.

Mackenzie and Sam dropped their coats on the couch and sat next to each other. Sam held the postcard.

"St. Louis," Mackenzie said, then noticed the post-mark also said St. Louis.

Jams put three cups of hot chocolate on the table. A big marshmallow floated on top. The cups all said I LOVE BOSTON, with a red heart.

"She's going west," Jams said.

"She's been out west," Mackenzie said. "She's sent Aunt Hope postcards. Mount Rushmore. Hollywood. All of it."

"Your mother," he said, blowing on his cocoa, "is a poet. She likes to speak in symbols. Metaphors. It used to drive me crazy, trying to figure out what she meant. When she found out she was pregnant the first time, she told me by serving pickles and vanilla ice cream for dessert."

"So?"

"So have I heard from her in months?"

Mackenzie shook her head.

"Now I get this postcard. Gateway to the West. It's not a coincidence that it says that. It's her way of telling me she's going west."

"But she's already been there."

Sam fished the marshmallow out of his cup and sucked on it. A thin stream of chocolate ran down his hand.

"I think," Jams said slowly, "that she plans on staying there."

He heard panic in Mackenzie's voice. "Where? St. Louis?"

Jams shrugged. "Maybe. Probably further west. I don't know exactly."

"But she'll come back," Mackenzie said.

"Mackenzie," Jams said, "when she left I told you I didn't think she'd be back."

"You're wrong," she said. She slumped back against the couch.

Sam held his sticky hand into the air, waving it. Jams wrapped a paper napkin around it.

He looked at his daughter, her hair tangled from the wind, her eyes blazing turquoise, and wished that she would never again be hurt. He wanted to keep her safe in that blurry world he'd created for them long ago. People used to say that she led a charmed life. "Everything she touches," a college friend had said, "turns not to gold, but to platinum." And suddenly everything was turning rusty.

"Jams," she said, "wouldn't she call?"

"She will, sweetie," he said. "But I want you to be prepared."

Mackenzie smiled, a small, sad smile.

"You'll see," she said. "She'll come home."

In the air, Sam drew a big, invisible arch.

CHAPTER ELEVEN

Daisy had developed a lot of marketing techniques to increase her sales of makeup. For one thing, she thought everything should be color coordinated to match the soft pink cosmetic cases and brochures. She always wore either a pink knit dress or fuchsia spandex pants with a satin blouse. She even served Entenmann's raspberry coffee cake to carry through with the color motif. Another thing she did was to dab the company's own perfume on all the light bulbs, which sent the aroma throughout the room. On a tour once of the mansions in Newport, Daisy had heard that Mrs. Vanderbilt always rubbed her perfume into the lights before a party. To Daisy, her makeup demonstrations were an event.

Daisy smiled at the four women sitting at her dining room table. They all lived in her condominium unit.

"For daytime," Daisy said, "we can offer you an

entire array of soft colors." She opened a sample case of Rose Whisper blush.

"Now this," she continued, leaning toward one of the women, "is perfect for you." Recently, Daisy's voice had picked up the slightest hint of a twang, as if she really came from Maryland or Virginia.

"I don't know," the woman said. "I usually only wear lip gloss during the day." Her hair was cut like Dorothy Hamill's.

Daisy smiled. She knew the woman would end up buying the entire daytime line. She had a knack for sizing her customers up and zeroing in on exactly what they would buy.

"I know you aren't used to wearing a lot of makeup during the day," Daisy said, "but just let me put a dab of this on you and I guarantee you will change your mind forever." Daisy had on a gold headband across her head with tiny gold leaves dangling from it. The leaves chimed softly as she brushed the blush on the woman's cheekbones. "Why shouldn't you look beautiful all day long?" Daisy asked her.

The other women craned to watch.

Daisy opened more cases.

"Now," she said, "a touch of this."

The woman blinked rapidly as the brushes stroked her lids and lashes.

"I can see a difference already," Daisy said.

One of the women stood close behind Daisy. She was pregnant, her face slightly blotchy. The skin care line, Daisy had thought when the woman arrived. Now she stood, spilling coffee cake crumbs onto the floor.

"Meg," she said, "you look amazing."

"Really?" Meg reached for the mirror.

Daisy grabbed her wrist.

"Not yet," she said. "Not until I'm finished." She

could feel their excitement. When she finished with Meg, they would be like schoolchildren—"Do me next. Me next." Daisy smiled at the women. "We want to really wow Meg," she said.

The tall one with long straight hair and tinted aviator glasses nodded.

"Right," she said.

Daisy loved to work on women who wore glasses. She liked to use the disco line on them—glittery blush and copper eye shadows. Already she could envision how this one would look.

"Not too much lipstick," Meg said.

Daisy wet a brush. "Lip gloss is for little girls," she said. "Women need color. If you wear nothing else, promise me you will wear lipstick. Promise me you will never leave the house without putting on the lips."

The women laughed.

"I mean it," Daisy said. "You never know who you'll run into, even at the supermarket. Why, I know someone who saw Richard Gere in a Safeway once and had to run the other way because she forgot her lips."

The telephone rang, startling all of them.

Damn, Daisy thought. The mood was broken. She heard it break, in a series of sighs, chairs creaking as the women settled back down.

She looked right at Susan, the one wearing glasses.

"You have got to promise me that you won't let Meg look."

"Please," Meg said, "let me."

The phone rang a third time.

"I need a promise here," Daisy said, clutching the round silver hand-mirror to her chest.

"All right," Susan said.

Daisy picked up the phone mid-ring.

She knew, even before Mackenzie spoke, that it was her, checking in, being considerate.

Daisy tried to picture Mackenzie, her blonde hair falling around her shoulders. She thought of a weekend she and Alexander had spent with Mackenzie when she lived in Washington, before they'd moved there. A short, pale peach kimono hung on a hook behind the bathroom door in Mackenzie's apartment. Its sash hung down, as if pointing to the pair of frayed ballet slippers on the floor below it. The slippers were scuffed and worn, not from dancing but from shuffling around the apartment. The robe and slippers had seemed perfectly placed there, like Mackenzie herself. Daisy had seen them and put them on while Alexander and his sister ate nachos and drank piña coladas in the living room. The slippers had been too small for Daisy and she had been able to just press her toes into them. She had wrapped the robe around her. In its pocket, she found the silver back of an earring and an empty matchbook from a restaurant. F. Scott's, it said in silver against a shiny black background. She tried to imagine herself at such a place. It conjured images of blue smoke and Sinatra music and beautiful people. Finally, Alexander had shouted to her, "Hey, did you fall in or something?" and she had scrambled out of the robe, dropping its sash to the floor.

Mackenzie appeared to her now in that pastel kimono and worn slippers, even though those things had been very old when Daisy last saw them.

"There's snow everywhere and in town they've hung those awful Christmas decorations across Linden Street," Mackenzie was saying. "You know the ones I mean? They're made of that squishy green stuff and there's bells hanging in the middle."

Daisy didn't answer.

From the other room she heard Meg say, "Will Brian think it's too much?"

And another voice, "He's going to love it."

"Daisy?" Mackenzie said.

"I'm here."

"Listen," Mackenzie said, "I'll bring Sam back Christmas Eve. Something's come up."

"But you were going to keep him through the holidays." Daisy struggled for an image of Sam. She could not even remember what his voice had sounded like. He had been a pilgrim in his first grade play. He had put a tiny black shoe topped with a construction-paper buckle on top of a papier-mâché rock and he had said something. But in her memory of that day, Sam only moves his mouth silently.

"No!" someone shouted in the other room. "You can't look."

"Look," Daisy said, "I'm in the middle of something. You'll have to call back."

"Can't we just make arrangements now?"

"No. I have to think about it." Daisy hung up the telephone and frowned. Had Mackenzie said she was going to go looking for her mother? How do you look for someone who doesn't want to be found? she wondered.

Daisy curled up on the brown corduroy bean bag. She had come to this Christmas party with Allison. It was in one of the newer condominiums in their complex, off of the U-shaped stretch of wooden apartments. The ones down here were all brick, as if the builder had suddenly run out of wood.

The couple giving the party passed around pictures of a teenaged guru on a laminated card. The guru sat cross-legged, suspended a few feet above a small maroon rug.

"He's flying," the woman, Aubrey, said as she handed Daisy a card.

Daisy stared at it. It reminded her of the prayer cards that people handed out at funerals.

"Flying?" she said.

"Yes. Jonah flies too," Aubrey said, and pointed to her husband across the room. He was very tall and skinny with a long red beard.

"Really?" Daisy said. She watched Aubrey shuffle the cards nervously. Her fingers were lumpy with calluses. She was a quilter, and the apartment was full of her quilts. They were draped over the couches and chairs and some hung from the walls.

"Of course," Aubrey said, "Jonah can't fly as high or as far as the guru."

"How high can he fly?" Daisy's nose twitched at the smell of sandalwood incense. She felt like she had been blasted backward in time.

"About five and a half inches," Aubrey said.

Across the room, Daisy spotted Susan. She still had on the makeup from the afternoon demonstration. She had removed her glasses and squinted beneath the dramatic copper eyeliner Daisy had used on her.

"That's really incredible," Daisy said. "Flying like that."

"Nothing," Aubrey said, "is incredible."

Daisy watched her walk away, stopping to hand out more cards. She settled back into the bean bag chair. Hadn't Iris had a chair like this? she thought. Hers had been purple, of course, and vinyl. After a while small pieces of Styrofoam started to come out. She would find them here and there, like mouse droppings.

Allison kneeled down beside her. "Having fun?"

"Let me just double check something with you," Daisy said. "What year is it?"

Allison laughed. "They're all artists."

Earlier, a man wearing a shirt covered with tiny mirrors had pressed his nose against hers and said, "Your eyes are yellow."

"Artists, huh?" Daisy said. She stretched her legs out and watched the candlelight reflect in colored swirls across the shiny blue spandex. "A guy told me my eyes were yellow."

"He says that to everyone," Allison said. "There's another guy walking around here reading auras."

"Give me a break," Daisy said. She took a sip of her egg nog. It was thin with a thick layer of froth on top.

A man with long gray hair stopped in front of them. "You hate me because I fought in Vietnam, don't you? Admit it." His hands were tattooed with snakes, curling from his wrists up each finger.

"Here I am," Daisy said, "I can do anything I want for five days without worrying about Sam, and I'm at a party full of weirdos."

"They're just in the wrong decade," Allison said.

Daisy thought briefly of Alexander's old dorm room. His roommate had hung a black light poster of Jim Morrison on the wall and an Indian bedspread on the ceiling. He would sit in the corner and carve hash pipes and incense burners out of sandstone.

"Let's go to a bar or something," Daisy said.

"It's still too early for that. Let's just wait a little while longer."

"Let's not stay here all night," Daisy said. "All right?"

"Fine. Now I'm going to get my aura read."

In front of Daisy, a barefoot woman lifted one foot to her face and pulled at her toes, her knee bent at a perfect angle. The gray-haired man held up his thumb and forefinger into an imaginary gun and shot it at the barefoot woman, over and over.

On one of Daisy and Alexander's first dates they had gone into Cambridge to see a play in the basement of an old church. The actors had pantomimed different situations—war, sex, death. "Experimental theater," Alexander had whispered to her. At the end, all of the actors took off their clothes and marched in a circle playing toy instruments. Some of the audience undressed and joined them. Daisy had wanted to take off her clothes too, and march with them, playing a tinny kazoo or a plastic harmonica. But as she began to unzip her jeans, Alexander had grabbed her wrist. "Come on," she'd said. "I hope you're joking," he'd said. She still remembered how cloudy his eyes looked right then. Daisy thought, at that instant, that there was something very different about the two of them, something that couldn't be resolved. And that image of his hand over hers, frozen above her zipper, haunted her. She had sat and watched the sweating bodies parade around her, hip bones, swaying breasts, soft penises, and wondered why she wasn't getting up there with them. Later, in a traffic jam on the Southeast Expressway, she had unzipped Alexander's pants and taken him into her mouth. His hand gripped her head, tight and steady.

A penny fell onto her lap from above. Daisy looked up from the bean bag chair. A man stood beside her. He had silver hair and a thick salt and pepper beard. His eyes were a clear, light blue.

"For your thoughts," he said.

"Actually, I was wondering if everyone was going to take their clothes off and parade around the room playing kazoos."

"Kazoos?" he laughed. "Are they?"

"It's too early to tell."

The man extended his hand. "I'm Willie Forrester,"

he said, "and I've been watching you for a long time now. I had to meet you."

"Daisy Bloom," she said. She didn't take his hand.

"Your drink has been drunk," he said.

She put her glass in his still-extended hand.

"Willie," she said, "if you're going to fill it up, put some real liquor in it. That egg nog is disgusting."

"I hear you," he said.

She watched him walk away. He was short and solid. His painter's pants had speckles of black paint all over them.

"Daisy? I didn't know you were here." Susan stood in front of her, blocking her view of Willie. "I can't see a thing without my glasses."

Daisy smiled into the elephants that danced, trunks linked, around the border of Susan's skirt.

"You have changed my life," Susan said. "I'm getting contact lenses and my hair hennaed. I feel like a new person."

"Great." From around Susan's skirt, Daisy watched Willie come toward her, holding two glasses.

"How do you know Jonah and Aubrey?" Susan asked her. "From the complex?"

"No. I'm here with a friend who knows them."

"Jack," Willie said, and handed Daisy a glass.

She took a long drink of the Jack Daniel's. "Much better," she said.

"Why did you bring her that," Susan asked, "when there's homemade egg nog?"

"Daisy and I prefer the egg nog straight from a carton."

"Do you notice anything different about me, Willie?" Susan tilted her head upward for him to see better.

Daisy thought about standing up so she didn't have to keep craning her neck to see everyone above her. But she didn't. She scanned the room for Allison.

"Daisy did it," Susan said. "The makeup, I mean. I decided not to wear my glasses. She's an artist too, don't you think?"

Willie looked down at her.

"I'm a saleswoman," Daisy said.

"I think you're an artist. Only, instead of canvases, you use skin."

Daisy yawned.

"Remember on *Laugh-In* they used to body paint Judy Carne and Goldie Hawn?" Susan said.

"Goldie Hawn wasn't on *Laugh-In*," Willie said.

"Of course she was. Wasn't she, Daisy?"

Daisy struggled out of the bean bag chair. Willie bent to help her up and she steadied herself on his arm. Standing, and with her high heels, she was a good six inches taller than him.

"You sort of look like Goldie Hawn," Susan said to Daisy.

"I think my friend and I are going to listen to some music," she said. "I'd better try to find her."

"Wait a minute," Willie said. "You can't leave yet."

"Why not?"

"Because we haven't settled the question of whether or not Goldie Hawn was ever on *Laugh-In*."

Daisy thought of the Porters. They always played games like that—Facts in Five, Trivial Pursuit, arguing over which river was the world's longest or which director won the most Oscars. Silly, useless stuff.

"Who cares?" Daisy said.

"I do," Willie said. "I won't be able to sleep tonight unless I know."

"The point is," Susan said, "she was the sock-it-to-me girl. And they always threw water on her. I think even Richard Nixon threw water on her once."

"Tell her," Willie said, holding Daisy's elbow so she

couldn't leave." Tell her Judy Carne was the sock-it-to-me girl."

"If I tell her that," Daisy said, "will you let me go?"

"Yes."

"Judy Carne was the sock-it-to-me girl." Daisy pulled her elbow free and walked away.

"The point is," she heard Susan saying, "Goldie Hawn was on that show."

Daisy felt Willie's eyes on her back.

She worked her way through the crowd. She recognized a lot of the people from the complex. Most of them looked more ordinary than the earlier guests. Daisy looked out on the patio. A group of people in business suits watched a man in a small sandbox build a sand castle. He emptied dixie cups full of water onto the sand, then shaped the wet earth into turrets.

Sam would love this, Daisy thought. She remembered a trip she and Alexander and Sam had taken to Cape Cod once. Sam had buried Alexander in the sand, up to his neck. Then, like Frankenstein rising from the laboratory table, Alexander had pushed out of the sand and chased Sam into the water. She felt a pain in her chest at the image. Daisy wondered how she could feel both mad at Alexander and so in love with him. That had always been the problem, she supposed. She had let him stifle her, try to shape her more into what he wanted because she had loved him so much.

Maybe she had been wrong to let Mackenzie keep Sam. She thought of his bed at home, made up in Garfield sheets. "I never met a lasagna I didn't like," Garfield smirked across the pillow. Sam should be home, in his own bed. Daisy remembered how excited she had been when she had read *Jonathan Livingston Seagull*, with its wisdom about freedom. Alexander had laughed that she'd read it. "Oh, Daisy," he'd said, "the things you do."

She caught sight of Allison talking to a good-looking blonde man in the corner of the patio. She had on a big navy-blue ski jacket, the tips of her fingers just poking out of the sleeves.

"Hey," Daisy said.

"Hi," Allison said. "Listen, Brad and I are going to get something to eat." She looked at the man she was with. He had very pale blonde hair and a tan. "Mexican, right?"

"Sure," he said.

"Great," Daisy said.

Allison turned from him slightly and whispered to Daisy. "Could you check the parking lot? Make sure no one's following me?"

"All right."

"Thanks," Allison said. She turned back to Brad. "Olé."

On her way to the bedroom closet where she had hung her coat, Daisy stopped and refilled her glass. She saw Susan in the kitchen and waved to her, but Susan was squinting intently at someone else. "There was Ruth Buzzi," Susan said, "and Judy Carne . . ."

"Do you want to dance?" a man in a gray flannel suit asked Daisy outside the bedroom.

Great, she thought. First the party was full of old hippies, now IBM has infiltrated.

"A little horizontal boogaloo?" the man said.

"Get lost," Daisy said. She pushed past him into the bedroom.

Jonah and Aubrey were in there. They didn't look up when she walked in.

"It was nothing," Aubrey was saying.

Daisy opened the cluttered closet. It was so large she could walk right inside it, which she did, squeezing between the mounds of coats. She felt for hers amid the layers of Army jackets and Burberrys. Her hand settled on what she thought might be it.

The closet door opened.

"It wasn't like it was a breast or anything," Aubrey said.

Willie pushed into the closet and closed the door on Jonah's voice.

"I followed you," Willie said.

Daisy spilled some of her drink onto the stack of coats.

"This is a closet," she said.

"I know."

"My friend doesn't want to go." She tried to sip her drink but her arm was wedged between Willie and the coats.

"I know," he said. He pressed his glass to her lips. Vodka.

Outside glass broke.

"What are they doing?" Daisy whispered.

He smelled, a little, like turpentine. In the darkness she caught a flash of silver and turquoise in one of his ears. She put her glass down on something—a suitcase or typewriter case.

"I think you could be dangerous," Daisy said.

"Yes."

He put his glass on top of the coats.

"Come here," he said. But he didn't wait for her to move. Instead, he pushed toward her. She felt his drink spill, felt the liquor trickle down her leg.

Outside, Aubrey said loudly, "Jonah. Don't."

"I want you," Willie said.

"Here?"

Her mind flashed back to the basement in Cambridge, the naked bodies all around and Alexander's hand keeping hers back.

"You tell me," Willie whispered, his hand inside the waistband of her pants.

"Yes," Daisy said. "Here."

CHAPTER TWELVE

Willie lifted the garage door open.

"This is it," he said, and turned on the light.

The floor was covered with a large canvas splattered with gray and black paint.

Daisy shivered in the cold air. She felt goose bumps on her skin.

"Well," she said.

Willie held up a spray paint gun.

"I use this," he said.

Daisy stared at the canvas. She felt him watching her, waiting for a reaction. Once, Mackenzie had shown her a portfolio of her photographs, blurred colorful images matted in white. Daisy had had to stare hard to discern that the purple smudge was a sailboat, the glaring red circle the sun. As Mackenzie explained how she played with the color processing to get that purple, Daisy had wondered why she hadn't just taken a picture of a sailboat and kept its real colors instead of making this vague, blurry print. She had known that these pictures were considered good and that some had even won awards or had been published, and staring down at the swaying purple strobe-like image that Mackenzie said was a palm tree, Daisy began to feel inferior to the pictures.

Willie cleared his throat.

She looked up quickly, pulled her coat tighter around her.

"Cold, isn't it?" he said softly, and turned on a quartz heater that sat in a corner. It slowly glowed on, orange.

"It's very interesting," Daisy said, looking back at the canvas.

They had been together since the party the night before. She kept expecting him to avoid her gaze, put on his worn brown bomber's jacket, and leave her. Instead, he kept staying. They had made love all night. His beard had scratched her, and left tiny red blotches on her shoulders and neck. At noon, he woke her up with a cup of coffee and an omelette filled with sharp cheese and mushrooms and hairy sprouts.

"You don't have any food here," he'd told her.

"In the kitchen closet," she'd said, wondering why he was still here.

"A Spaghetti-o omelette?" he'd laughed. "Forget it."

He'd gone to the store and had picked up a few things. The cinnamon raisin toast was warm, and smelled like a home Daisy had never known.

Afterward, they'd driven here, to the garage where he worked.

Willie did everything with the excitement of a child. Lovemaking, cooking, painting. "You've got to see what I'm working on," he'd told her. Daisy had talked the whole way over. She was a bad driver, stopping and starting in jerky motions, the pink Caddy hogging too much of the road. Willie had laughed. "Where did you get your driver's license?" he'd said. "The Sears catalogue?" Alexander had kidded her with the same old joke. She had hunched over the steering wheel, trying to concentrate, but instead had talked even more, telling him about her work. Her work was her confidence, the one thing she did really well. She didn't tell him about Alexander. Or Sam.

Willie blew on his hands, held them in front of the heater. Around the corner, three other canvases leaned against the wall. They were as big as the one on the floor, and were draped in fabric.

Daisy lifted the material from one. The painting beneath it looked much like the first, black and gray paint splattered on it, thick in spots, thinner trickles running down it. In the center was a blob of pale pink, its spidery veins running into, disappearing into, the black around it.

Daisy frowned.

"It's okay if you don't like it," Willie said.

"I don't get it," she said.

"I call that one 'Heartbeat.' "

She nodded.

The pink blotch, she supposed, could be a heart.

"I'm ignorant," she said.

Willie was crouched beside the heater. His silver hair reflected the orange from it, like a halo.

"No," he said. "Don't say that. Don't ever say that."

"Listen," she said. "You don't know me. You have no idea. I had never heard of Ernest Hemingway until I was eighteen years old."

"Ernest who?"

"In school I used to cut classes and drive to the beach and drink Tango, this bottled orange juice and vodka. I'd drink that and smoke cigarettes and pick up seashells from the shore. My room used to be full of them."

"Why is it better," Willie said, "to have read Hemingway than to have studied the sea and collected shells?"

She looked back at the painting.

"Why not just paint a picture of a heart?" she said. Her voice sounded harsh. She wondered if she was trying to make him go away.

Willie dropped the fabric from another painting.

" 'Winter,' " he said.

Amid the black and gray paint, along the bottom of the canvas, ice blue paint stood in fat strokes. Down the center ran a single red line.

"Once," Daisy said, keeping her gaze focused on the painting, "a man at a party asked me how I liked Updike. I thought Updike was a dry cleaner back in Rhode Island."

"Maybe he is."

Daisy faced him.

"Oh," she said, "he is."

"So you were right."

He kneeled in front of the heater, rubbed his hands together. They glowed orange, like an eerie nuclear light.

"This 'Winter' one," Daisy said, "seems kind of sexual."

"Yes," he said.

"Really?"

"That's what I had in mind. That's why I didn't paint snow-covered pine trees and children skating. It's a different kind of winter."

After Alexander had discovered she hadn't read any Hemingway, he'd bought her a set of his novels, paperbacks in pastel covers. She'd only read one, the one whose title she'd liked the best, *The Sun Also Rises*. "All these people," she'd told him, "seem silly." "You missed the point,'' Alexander had said. But for weeks Daisy had pretended to be Brett and that every man was in love with her.

"I should take a class,'' she said, her voice soft and doubting.

"What kind of class?''

"I don't know,'' Daisy said, and lifted her hands to her hair, touching it lightly.

When she and Alexander had lived in New York, she had taken a literature class at NYU. She was pregnant then, self-consciously pregnant. The name of the class was "American Classics.'' Daisy had bought all the books that were required and lined them up on the shelf that used to hold her seashells, an old wooden shelf that she had painted lilac. She put the shells in a box in the closet, then arranged the books, first by size—the tallest all at one end—then, dissatisfied with that arrangement, alphabetically by author, then by size again. At night, in bed, the books tormented her, their unfamiliar names taunting her. In the morning, she rearranged them again, this time by color, in the order of a rainbow, the purple covers followed by the blue. She used an old shoe, a sparkling red pump, as a bookend.

She had gone to only one class, where she sat in the back cradling her belly, slouching low in her seat. A girl named Nadine had stood up. She had on a T-shirt that said A WOMAN'S PLACE IS IN THE HOUSE . . . AND THE SENATE. "I resent the lack of women authors on this reading list,'' Nadine had said. "What about *House of Mirth?* Or *A Good Man is Hard to Find?''* Daisy never went back. Later, after Alexander moved to Boston without her, she had found the box of seashells, crushed like a bunch of old bones and dust. The biggest shard, a wavy white and purple piece, she had kept and used as an ashtray.

"Then again," Daisy said to Willie, "I never do well in classes."

"You don't need a class," he said. "I'll teach you. We'll go to the National Gallery right now."

Daisy's heart pounded. She wondered again when he would leave her, and hoped that it wouldn't be in the museum.

They sat in a crowded bar called Bullfeathers on Capitol Hill. Even sitting at the table people pushed against them. Outside, a freezing winter rain fell hard against the windows and pavement. The bar smelled of wet wool and beer.

Daisy's feet throbbed in their high-heeled silver pumps. Willie had walked her through room after room of the museum. He spoke quickly, excitedly, as he explained styles, themes, color.

Suddenly, here at the bar, Willie and Daisy seemed shy together, like a couple on a first date. She ordered a margarita on the rocks with extra salt and nachos. He ordered a Budweiser. They didn't speak.

Finally Willie said, "I'm surprised you don't have a husband or boyfriend somewhere."

Daisy shrugged.

"Or do you?" he said.

She watched the people at the bar in their rain-soaked suits and dresses, matted hair and faces shiny from the cold. Her own toes started to tingle as they warmed. Willie picked up a nacho and smelled it before he popped it into his mouth. She thought of Alexander, the way he liked to sniff new books.

"Do you?" she said.

"What? Have a husband?"

Daisy frowned.

"I'm divorced," Willie said.

She nodded.

"You too?"

"Oh," she said. "No."

Willie leaned across the table and moved her face toward him. His calloused thumb and forefinger held her chin.

"I like you," he said. "That's why I'm asking. You are so vibrant. And alive. Not like all those people at that party last night."

She twisted her head free and leaned back, away from him.

"Don't look at me like that," she said.

"Like what?"

"Like I'm one of those deformed women by that painter."

"Who?"

"You know," she said.

"Tell me."

She took a deep breath.

"deKooning," Daisy said.

Willie smiled.

"Let's go," he said.

"Where?"

"Your place."

Daisy stood, and let herself think, for just an instant, that maybe he would stay after all.

CHAPTER THIRTEEN

"Sam," John-Glenn said, "that's your basic monarch. I have a million of those. At least."

His voice, high and tense, woke Mackenzie from a muddled dream. Snowflakes clung to Aunt Hope's bedroom window like rock candy. The room smelled of Aunt Hope's sweet perfume. Mackenzie sniffed. Shalimar, she thought, and smiled at how easily she remembered the scent. Every Christmas she and Alexander gave Aunt Hope Shalimar perfume and talc. She snuggled under the covers. Everything in the room was in pastel colors, the soft greens and pinks and yellows of Melt-away mints repeated over and over in the curtains and bedspread, the throw rugs and bureau scarves.

"Those are cabbages," John-Glenn said. "You can get them easy in the spring. They fly around in flocks of two or three dozen and you just scoop them up."

Mackenzie stretched, John-Glenn's voice oddly comforting.

"I think," he said, "that the American painted lady is the most beautiful of all butterflies. What do you mean? Look at it, then I dare you to tell me no."

The digital clock beside the bed clicked and a number dropped. Ten-twenty-one.

"The mourning cloak has nothing on the American painted lady, Sammy boy."

Mackenzie pulled on her jeans and a sweatshirt and walked across the hall. John-Glenn and Sam sat on the floor of John-Glenn's bedroom, surrounded by butterflies pinned to poster board. Sam looked up when she came in, and waved.

"Oh, it's you," John-Glenn said. "Just when we were having fun."

"You can still have fun," Mackenzie said.

Pens and pencils stuck out from the pocket of John-Glenn's red flannel shirt. The top of one was shaped like a rocket. The eraser of another was a Lady Smurf.

"Where's your mother?" Mackenzie said.

"Which is the most beautiful butterfly?" John-Glenn said. "The most magnificent?"

Sam held up a large one for her to inspect. Its wings were trimmed in yellow and purple. There was chocolate smeared across his cheek.

Mackenzie glanced at the powdery butterflies, frozen as if in flight.

"They all give me the creeps," she said.

"Come on. Come on. Pick."

She pointed to one, a swirl of bright orange and yellow.

"Aha!" John-Glenn shouted. "A red barred sulphur. Very showy. A big show-off. Like you."

"Be quiet," Mackenzie said. She winked at Sam and left the room.

In the kitchen, she searched the cupboards for coffee. All she found was flavored instant. Irish Creme. Dutch Mocha. Chocolate Orange.

"Yuck," Mackenzie said.

She opened the lids and sniffed each one.

In New York, she bought small brown bags of coffee beans and kept them in her freezer. Every morning she ground enough for a pot. If Jason was with her, he scalded milk and ladled it into the coffee with carmelized sugar and a dusting of cinnamon. Right now, she thought, he's probably in his bathtub, reading the *Times*. The tub sat in the kitchen, painted a bright China red.

Jason wrote mostly at night. As if acting out the part of a tortured writer, he paced the apartment, unshaven, drinking black coffee and muttering to himself. He told her that all day, no matter what he did, he felt guilty for not writing. "My typewriter," he said, "screams at me. 'Get out of that tub, you bum.' 'Put that newspaper down!' "

Mackenzie had sat through readings of his plays in church basements and lofts in Tribeca and dusty spaces overlooking the Hudson. He always sat in the back, his head bent as he scribbled notes onto a yellow legal pad. Yellow pages of ideas and changes littered his apartment, covered the countertops and tables and floor.

"That," John-Glenn said, "is my father. He was a famous Latin American musician whose plane disappeared over the Atlantic while his band was on tour."

Mackenzie took her cup of Dutch Mocha coffee and went back into John-Glenn's room.

He had pulled out a large box, the kind a department store might put a new coat in. The box was overflowing with stuff. John-Glenn held up a gold-framed black and white picture of Ricardo Havana and the Havana Hoochie-Coo's.

Sam looked impressed.

John-Glenn tossed the picture back in the box and pulled out a trophy.

"This was your father's," he said to Sam. "Little League."

Sam took the trophy from him. A gold baseball player swinging a bat sat on top of an imitation marble pedestal. The plaque beneath it said: 1961 LEAGUE CHAMPIONS.

"You haven't seen this stuff?" John-Glenn said to Sam.

Sam shook his head. He clutched the trophy with both hands.

John-Glenn began to pull things from the box.

"We've got merit badges from the Scouts. A yearbook. And look at this picture. That's your daddy dressed like a girl for Halloween."

Mackenzie didn't have to look at the photograph to know exactly what it was. Alexander in a long blonde wig and cashmere sweater, puffing on a black and rhinestone cigarette holder borrowed from Carmen Havana. That same year, Mackenzie had been a pumpkin, stuffed so fat with newspapers that she hadn't been able to sit all night.

"Where did you get that?" she said.

"What? This picture?"

He held it up. It was just as she had remembered it, except that the image in her mind blazed in full color. The platinum blonde wig. The rhinestones against ebony. The soft pink cashmere. And in her mind, Mackenzie could see what the picture didn't show. Alexander also wore a pink and black poodle skirt and flaming red pumps. To his right, just out of the camera's eye, stood an orange human pumpkin.

"All of it," Mackenzie said. "Where did you get all

of this?" Her throat felt dry and she sipped at the sweet coffee to moisten it.

Sam's mouth opened in silent laughter as he looked at the photograph. His eyes scrunched shut and he threw his head back in a noiseless guffaw.

"We've got some ticket stubs here," John-Glenn said, burrowing through the box's contents. "Young Rascals. Herman's Hermits. All from the Rhode Island Auditorium." He picked up a handful of creased and torn tickets. "Big deal," he said.

Mackenzie felt like Alexander was somehow being violated.

She slammed her cup down on the night table, beside a plastic Mickey Mouse cradling a bright yellow telephone. The coffee made a watery brown puddle.

"Stop it," she said.

"There's a couple report cards. Seventh grade. Tenth grade."

She grabbed his wrist hard, gripped it until the yellow report card dropped from his hand. Mackenzie saw her mother's neat, private school signature on the back, three times.

"Where did you get this?" she demanded.

John-Glenn twisted his wrist free from her hold.

She began to pile things back into the box. Papers, photographs. Alexander's writing and his face flew past her like an animated slide show.

"How would you like it," Mackenzie shouted, clutching the big box to her chest, "if I threw all your goddam stupid butterflies into the street and laughed while people pawed at them? How would you like that?"

The three of them watched as a piece of paper slipped out of the box and floated to the floor.

"Don't you dare touch it," Mackenzie said.

"Fine."

Mackenzie brought the box into Aunt Hope's room and put it on the bed. In purple script on the sides it said Cherry and Webb, Your Kind of Store. Behind her, in the hallway, she heard John-Glenn's voice.

"Some people," he said.

The box and its contents seemed a pathetic remnant of her brother's life. Every part of her ached and strained to conjure more of him than an old report card or ticket stub. His laugh rang in her ears, distant and faint, fading.

Gently, Mackenzie sat on the bed and peered inside. Poking through the papers, Mackenzie saw a black box covered with colored seashells.

"Oh, no," she said, as she lifted it out.

It was an old cigar box, painted a shiny black that had now dulled. Alexander had taken small oval shells and painted them in bright colors, then glued them to the box in neat, even rows. A few had fallen off in the years since he'd made it, and left hard white spots of dried glue where they had been.

Mackenzie opened the box. In thick red paint on the inside of the lid, Alexander had printed:

TO MY DEER DEER SISTER
HAPPY B-DAY
LOVE 4 EVER & EVER ALEXANDER PORTER
1961

She remembered that birthday, her cake a snowman dressed in coconut and jellybeans. The box had held, at first, her gum machine rings, a sand dollar, and a starfish. Later, she hid her diary there. And lipstick she was forbidden to wear until she turned thirteen. Goodnight Slicker, by Yardley. Its pink striped tube pushed to the back beside a purse size bottle of Tigress perfume, also forbidden. Finally, in high school, she forgot about the cigar box and kept on her bureau a box made of ivory, with a delicately etched scene on its lid, a waterfall and low blossoming trees.

A shell, painted a vivid yellow, fell off the cover and onto the bed. Mackenzie picked it up, tried to imagine Alexander at ten, his hair cut short and bristled on top, painting these tiny shells, writing the message on the lid. 4 EVER & EVER.

She took the stones Sam had given her the day before on the beach and placed them in the cigar box.

Had she once, she thought, years ago, reminded Alexander of this gift he'd made for her, his deer deer sister? Yes. She had teased him, laughed at his sense of colors and the symmetrical design the shells made. "Not to mention," she had laughed, "your terrific spelling." "I had to work with what I had," he'd said. "That glue that came in those jars that you had to get out with a ruler and then plop it down on a piece of math paper. If you ever find that box again, the shells will probably have turned white or fallen off. Or both."

But here it was. The colors bright, almost all of the shells still in place, and smelling still of Tigress and, slightly, of salt.

"She said she was going to throw all of my butterflies into the street," John-Glenn shouted.

The front door slammed shut.

"Let me get my breath," Aunt Hope said.

Mackenzie went into the living room.

Aunt Hope had on a large fur hat and a black coat with a snap-on fox collar. The animal's head sat right under her chin, staring out from glass eyes. She had two shopping bags on each arm, decorated with red and green abstract Christmas trees.

"She said people would touch them and stomp on them," John-Glenn said.

Aunt Hope removed her hat and placed it carefully on the coffee table. It looked like a big, furry muffin.

"Mackenzie is not going to do that," she said.

"I didn't say I was going to throw them into the street. I asked you how you would like it if I did."

"Same difference," he said.

"The mall," Aunt Hope said, "was packed."

She took off her coat, revealing a plaid wool suit that Mackenzie recognized as her mother's.

"What is going on here? Are my family's things just common property?"

"Well," Aunt Hope said, "excuse me. Your so-called 'family' up and left everything. Things in the attic, in the closets. Everywhere."

"She yelled at me because I have a box of junk that belonged to you-know-who," John-Glenn said. "You might think he was a saint or something."

Aunt Hope sighed.

"Mackenzie," she said, "you have got to let go."

Mackenzie closed her eyes. She stood in that room with her aunt's furry hat and John-Glenn panting beside her and Aunt Hope's Shalimar on her mother's Pendleton's suit and she tried, not to let go, but to hold on.

"Here," she heard Aunt Hope say. "This will cheer you up."

Mackenzie wished that when she opened her eyes she'd find herself someplace else. Maybe in her old apartment in Washington, near Dupont Circle, surrounded by damp pictures that she'd taken of the Amazon. The pictures would be coming to life in front of her and the air would be thick with the smell of the developing chemicals. Or perhaps she would open her eyes and find herself back at that long-ago birthday party, her snowman cake uneaten and her brother holding out the seashell-covered cigar box.

Instead, Aunt Hope held out a postcard. The fox stared out at Mackenzie from the arm of the couch, where the coat dangled to the floor.

Mackenzie looked down. It was the same postcard her father had received. The red cardinal perched on the words GATEWAY TO THE WEST.

"The postmark," Aunt Hope said, "is St. Louis."

"St. Louis," John-Glenn said, "is in Missouri."

"Kansas, isn't it?" Aunt Hope said.

"No, no, no," he said. "Missouri."

"And," Aunt Hope said, "there's a message this time."

Mackenzie took the postcard from her aunt and turned it over.

HEADING TO SAN FRANCISCO. C.P.

"San Francisco," Mackenzie said.

"Beats me," Aunt Hope shrugged.

"St. Louis," John-Glenn read from an atlas he held in front of him, "a port city in *Missouri,* on the Mississippi, below the influx of the Missouri, population 750,026."

"Thank you, John-Glenn," Aunt Hope said. "Missouri it is."

"You were getting it mixed up with Kansas City," he said, "which is in both states."

Aunt Hope laughed.

"That boy," she said, "loves geography. Always has."

"You see, you see," he said, bouncing up and down while he read.

Mackenzie watched the Lady Smurf eraser bob in and out of his pocket.

"Kansas City. A city in western Missouri, on the Missouri River, population 475,539."

"All right," Mackenzie said. "Enough."

"*And* a city in Northeast Kansas—"

"Thank you, John-Glenn," Aunt Hope said again.

"I'm going to go to San Francisco," Mackenzie said. "I'll find her and bring her home."

"Population," John-Glenn said, "121,901."

"Well, then," Aunt Hope said, "let's celebrate. I've felt like celebrating all day. Let's go out to dinner."

"What," John-Glenn said, "are we celebrating?"

"Things getting back to the way they used to be."

"I'll go there," Mackenzie said, "and I'll talk to her. We'll work things out."

She expected to feel relief when she said that. Instead she felt dread. A horrible dread. She couldn't even let herself think that she might not find her mother. Or worse, that she might find her but Cal wouldn't come home. Mackenzie laughed a little. That, she thought, is impossible.

She went over to the kitchen counter where Sam sat on a stool drawing. He had drawn an island, pink sand surrounded by sky blue water. On the beach was a purple shell, smiling out.

John-Glenn waved the chopsticks in the air.

"Hold them like so," he said, "and—" He aimed them like giant tweezers at his plate and picked up one perfect grain of rice.

"—viola!" He smiled at them and popped the rice in his mouth.

Mackenzie smiled too. One of John-Glenn's favorite pastimes had always been to turn foreign phrases into English. It was a habit that used to infuriate Alexander. "Stop mutilating language," he would moan. "A fine day," John-Glenn would say. "Next cheese pots?" Then, before he'd leave, he'd say, "As they say in Spain, Add-three-o's."

Sam's chopsticks clicked and crossed each other.

"Now," Aunt Hope said, "isn't this nice?"

The four of them sat in a booth at the Cathay Inn. Between Aunt Hope and Mackenzie on the table was a drink in a large coconut with floating pink and purple paper parasols and foot-long straws. Sam had taken all the cherries and oranges from the drink and had lined them on this plate like soldiers facing off. He clutched his chopsticks as if they were swords, one in each hand, and stabbed two cherries.

"Barbaric," John-Glenn said.

Mackenzie inhaled. In New York, she and Jason had Chinese food delivered once or twice a week. They got steamed dumplings and cold noodles in sesame sauce and fiery Hunan chicken. Sometimes, on Saturday mornings, they walked to Chinatown for dim sum. They sat at a crowded table full of strangers and ate, stacking their saucers high as they finished each dish.

But here, at home, Chinese food meant shrimp, fried rice, beef chow mein, and egg foo yong in brown gravy. Grammie always used to do the ordering, enunciating loudly and slowly into the telephone as if the people on the other end were deaf.

"I'm sorry I won't be able to see you and Sam off tomorrow," Aunt Hope said. "But I've got to get in some Christmas shopping."

"What," John-Glenn said, "are you buying, anyway?" He had the red linen napkin tied around his neck like a bib.

"John-Glenn! It's Christmas. I can't tell you what I'm buying." Aunt Hope sipped her tea.

"And who is there to buy for?" John-Glenn said. His napkin had a large dark spot on it.

"I want to buy the perfect gifts. That's all."

Carefully, Sam picked the shrimp out of his fried rice and placed them on the table.

"Those are shrimp," Aunt Hope said, and smiled.

"He knows that," John-Glenn said. "He isn't stupid, you know. Maybe he just doesn't like shrimp."

Mackenzie leaned forward so the aroma from the steaming silver plates surrounded her. Who would ever think that things like this are the pieces of home we carry with us? she thought.

"I never did like egg foo yong," Mackenzie said.

"It was my mother's favorite," Aunt Hope said. "But I never really cared for it either. I like sweet and sour pork. With pineapples and cherries. You'd like that, Sam."

"I hate egg foo yong," John-Glenn said.

Mackenzie laughed. "Then why did we order it?"

"Because that's what we always get," Aunt Hope said.

"But no one likes it."

"Mackenzie," Aunt Hope said, "sometimes you are so silly."

After dinner, while John-Glenn and Sam waited for the leftover food to be put into cartons, Aunt Hope said to Mackenzie, "I *still* feel like celebrating. What do you say we go dancing?"

"Dancing?"

"Hear some music." Aunt Hope did a fast cha-cha and laughed.

Mackenzie thought again of her aunt dancing, a young woman in love. She smiled. "All right," she said. "Dancing it is."

They drove to a lounge in Attleboro after they dropped Sam and John-Glenn off at home. Aunt Hope had changed into a green chiffon dress. The skirt was accordion pleated and a short, wispy chiffon cape hung over the shoulders. The cape was held closed by a rhinestone clasp at the throat. As they drove, Aunt Hope kept touching the clasp, rubbing it gently.

"I really feel like celebrating," she said.

Mackenzie glanced over at her aunt. The passing cars on I-95 sent moving shadows across her face. She stared straight ahead, the rhinestone clasp first dull in the darkness, then shooting a quick sparkle as a streetlight or headlight found it.

As a child, Mackenzie used to love to sit at Aunt Hope's vanity table, on the long pink cushioned bench, and imitate her as she stroked on rouge and shadows, outlined her eyes and lips with pencils. For a while, Aunt Hope worked downtown, in the Outlet Department Store, at the Revlon counter as a beauty consultant. Cal would take Mackenzie there. As they walked, tall beautiful women would spray perfume on them, and would hand Cal tiny samples of cosmetics and colognes. Mackenzie made it a point to touch each glass counter they passed. Cal would wave her hands as she moved, as if to part the clouds of cologne. But Mackenzie would stand on tiptoe and turn her nose upward to catch every drop of fragrance.

When they finally reached the Revlon counter, they would find Aunt Hope, wearing a baby-blue smock and curly long eyelashes, working on a client. "My appointments," she called them. Cal would wander off to look at scarves and purses until Aunt Hope finished and could join them for lunch. But Mackenzie stood and watched as Aunt Hope turned an ordinary woman into someone special.

"Do you remember," Mackenzie asked her aunt, "when you worked downtown?"

"Which time?"

Mackenzie frowned.

"At the Outlet, of course."

"I had a million jobs in my time," Aunt Hope said, laughing. "I worked in the coat department at Gladyings downtown for a while. I never could fold those boxes up right. I was in shoes there too, I think. Or maybe that was at the Garden City store. Let's see. The Outlet—"

"Revlon," Mackenzie said, irritated.

"Oh, yes. I remember now."

"When did you ever work in the shoe department at Gladylings?" Mackenzie said.

Aunt Hope shrugged. Her shoulders lifting under the green chiffon cape made a slight rustling sound.

"I always loved shoes," she said. "I used to like to get the employee's discount on things. I still have a beautiful pair of gold sandals that I bought when I worked there. Lovely ones. With a T-strap."

Aunt Hope kept all her shoes in their original boxes, her coats in plastic hanging bags, her jewelry in boxes lined with cotton. She could delve into her closets and drawers and produce perfectly kept items from twenty-five years ago—a leopard coat, scarab bracelets, and cashmere sweaters.

"We used to come and watch you do makeovers," Mackenzie said.

"That's what Daisy does, isn't it? Makeup?"

"You used to have appointments."

Aunt Hope laughed. "I never knew anything about makeup. They used to tell us to look dramatic. So I'd put on eyelashes out to here and dark red lips. One time I had a bride come in. She took one look at me and ran out."

Mackenzie pointed ahead to an exit sign.

"Where exactly are we going?" she said.

"Not this one," Aunt Hope said. "The next one."

She gave Mackenzie directions, a series of lefts and rights, counting traffic lights and stop signs until, in the midst of emptiness, she said: "We're here."

"Where?" Mackenzie said.

"Just keep going."

They finally reached a low flat building with a sign

that glowed green, LIZARD LOUNGE, the I faint and dull. In one window a neon lizard moved, eerily, airily, up and then down.

"Isn't this fun?" Aunt Hope said.

"I guess so," Mackenzie said.

At the door, a bald man with no eyebrows asked Mackenzie for an I.D.

"How about me?" Aunt Hope said, smiling up at him.

"You," he said, "I know."

"You know him?" Mackenzie whispered.

Three staples glistened in his left earlobe as he examined Mackenzie's driver's license.

"Hey," he said, "you're older than I am."

The bar was full of people with spiked hairdos dyed in rainbow colors. A lot of the women were dressed like Marilyn Monroe, platinum hair, lips a thick red. Three giggling Marilyns passed them.

"They have a Marilyn look-alike contest on Tuesdays," Aunt Hope said.

Mackenzie nodded.

Behind the bar, in cages, were lizards, horny lime green iguanas, small flat brown ones, fluorescent salmon salamanders, and tiny chameleons clinging to rocks.

"Aunt Hope," Mackenzie shouted over the Talking Heads, "have you been here before?"

Across the room, near the stage, a long-haired man in an Iron Butterfly T-shirt tinkered with equipment.

"Over there," Aunt Hope said. "I like to sit up front."

Aunt Hope pushed her way through the crowd. The smell of leather and beer was strong.

A man wearing round glasses with multicolored psychedelic swirls for lenses stuck his face in front of Mackenzie.

"To the moon, Alice," he said.

Aunt Hope turned to her. "They get a lot of students from Brown," she said.

"He's from Brown?" Mackenzie said, but again her aunt was moving on.

What am I doing here? Mackenzie thought. What is Aunt Hope doing here? She remembered going to a nightclub like this in London once. "Welcome to the future," the doorman had told her. His Mohawk haircut had been metallic blue. A safety pin pierced his cheek. Later, she had sent Alexander a postcard, three punks in front of the Piccadilly Circus tube stop. Welcome to the future, she'd written on the back.

They reached a table where a lava lamp glowed and dripped red.

Across the room, a microphone screeched.

"Two Cuba Libres," Aunt Hope said to the waitress.

"What?"

"Rum and Cokes," Aunt Hope said sadly. "No one knows anything anymore."

"Why are we here?" Mackenzie said. "This is where you like to come dancing?"

The taped music stopped.

Someone blew into the microphone.

"Testing."

"Do you come here a lot?" Mackenzie asked Aunt Hope.

"Of course not. I've only been here twice. This is my third time."

Mackenzie looked toward the stage as a group of musicians paraded on. They wore blue velvet tuxedos and ruffled shirts.

"What is this?" she shouted above the noise. "A wedding or a bar mitzvah?"

Aunt Hope touched her arm.

"What?" Mackenzie said.

The lights dimmed, except for one over the stage that cast a fuzzy green light over the musicians and the people at the front tables.

"Ladies and gentlemen," crooned a low voice, "straight from Havana, via Hoboken, the Hoochie Coos's!"

The crowd cheered wildly.

"Aunt Hope," Mackenzie said.

Aunt Hope shook her head slightly. She kept her gaze fixed on the stage, where Ricardo Havana was stepping up to the microphone. It seemed to Mackenzie that his eyes searched the crowd for Aunt Hope before he began to sing in his thick accent, real or imagined, full of rolling *r*'s and elongated *e*'s.

It was as if no time had elapsed just then. Ricardo Havana's black hair was wavy and stiff, the color of tar, and his face was unwrinkled and tanned. His eyes settled, briefly, on their table and then he sang:

" Say it's only a paper moon . . ."

Mackenzie thought of her aunt imitating that voice, that song, waltzing with her girlfriends in an upstairs bedroom lined with posters of Fabian and Troy Donahue, and she felt, as she watched and remembered, that anything was possible after all.

"I've never really had any friends before," John-Glenn said.

He and Sam sat on the floor of his bedroom. The room was lit by only one light, a tulip-shaped leaded glass lamp that used to sit on the desk Grammie wrote letters at. Sam was wrapped in John-Glenn's plaid bathrobe. Only his fingertips poked out of the sleeves, and the belt looped around and around his waist, ending in a droopy oversized bow at his hip. On his head, he wore John-Glenn's McDonald's hat.

John-Glenn ate the leftover Chinese food from the

stained white take-home cartons. The lids had a dragon emblazoned on them.

"Everyone," he said, "thinks I'm weird."

Sam nodded.

"You too, huh? Sure. I can see that. It's very spooky the way you don't talk."

Sam opened his drawing pad. With a red Crayola he wrote HI, and drew a yellow smiling face below it. His mother had taught him how to do that, to write HI and draw that face, always using the same two colors, always putting the face below the words. She said that could be his trademark, like things that were pink were her trademark—her car and a lot of her clothes, her bedroom with the pink satin sheets and pale pink walls. In the morning, he left her his trademark on the message board by the refrigerator and sometimes she left him pink bubblegum or lollipops.

"Only my mother really listens to me," John-Glenn said. "Well, Grammie used to listen, but only to be polite." He leaned his face closer to Sam. "I have a million theories. People thought Columbus was crazy, saying the world was round, right?"

Sam drew another smiling face. His mother had given him a roll of stickers full of these faces and he had stuck them to the headboard of the bed.

"For example," John-Glenn said, "my martian theory. They are everywhere. I have books that support this, that list sightings, visits, etcetera." He waved toward the bookshelves. "My mother says that science fiction is just that. Fiction. But I say it is real. Fact."

Sam frowned. Martians.

"There are planets we haven't even discovered yet. Whole galaxies. Sometimes I think about us, earthlings, just as a speck in it all. Our entire planet might be just a little dot. Have you ever looked at a drop of water under a microscope?"

Sam shook his head.

"No?"

John-Glenn went to his closet and pulled out a microscope. He set it up on the bureau, beside the tulip-shaped lamp. Sam followed him into the bathroom and watched as he put some water on a glass slide, then followed him back into the bedroom. John-Glenn played with the microscope, turning and focusing, then peering into it.

"Look here," he said. He lifted Sam up and sat him on the bureau.

Sam leaned into the lens, squinting. When his eyes focused, he drew back in horror.

"Viola!" John-Glenn said. "Another world."

Slowly, Sam rested his head against the lens again. He watched as tiny squiggles—bugs?—swam through the tapwater. He would never drink water again. Never.

"Imagine a planet where the people are gigantic. Enormous. A scientist there picks up the earth and puts it under a microscope and watches us move around just like that."

Sam closed his eyes and imagined a gigantic scientist lifting up the planet earth. He had seen pictures of how the earth looked from space in the Air and Space Museum. It was a circle with lots and lots of blue. The blue, his mother had told him, was the oceans. Sam wondered if a martian scientist could see him right now. He looked upward and gave a little wave.

"Anything is possible," John-Glenn said.

Sam wanted to look back at the universe on that slide under the microscope, but he didn't. It seemed the same as opening his mother's door when she had it closed. That was, she had told him, an invasion of privacy.

"Butterflies," John-Glenn said, "are the only beautiful things we have. The most beautiful things anywhere, I bet. On any planet. And to think that they start out as ugly fuzzy caterpillars."

Sam looked around him, at the butterflies on the walls. They seemed, in the dim light, to be floating. It was as if they were alive, suspended in glorious flight.

"You," John-Glenn said softly, "are my friend."

Sam smiled and nodded. He turned his gaze from the eerily beautiful butterflies to John-Glenn's soft, fleshy face. There were scattered pimples on his chin and a light fuzz on his cheeks and upper lip. Sam pointed to him, then covered his own heart with his hand.

"Oh," John-Glenn said. He sniffed loudly, dramatically. "We are friends."

He lifted Sam off of the bureau and sat him down on the bed.

"I wish," he said, "that you weren't leaving tomorrow."

Sam thought of his own room back home. Since he'd left in the car with his aunt, he had not thought much of his house. His mother had hung pennants on one wall of his room. Colts. Orioles. Red Sox. Jets. She hung a Star Trek mobile from the ceiling and models of beautiful sports cars lined one shelf. All the things she thought little boys should have in their rooms. That's what she said whenever she added something new. "Look," she'd tell him, putting a GI Joe or Incredible Hulk on the shelf, "you think I don't know what you like?" But she didn't know.

"Do you want to go back?" John-Glenn asked him.

Sam shrugged. He thought of the way his mother's eyes looked whenever she dropped him off at Miss Knight's for his speech therapy. And the way his mother and Allison sat together whispering and giggling. He thought of the way her voice sounded when the See and Say

asked him to talk. CAT. BAT. RAT. "Come on, Sam,"
she'd plead, "say cat. Say bat." It wasn't that he didn't
like his mother. She was, after all, the prettiest mom he'd
ever seen. And she always smelled good and took him for
fast rides in her big pink car. But sometimes she didn't do
anything at all with him. "Can't you see," she'd say, "that
I'm busy?" Even though she didn't look very busy.

He had wondered if his Aunt Mackenzie would show
him his father. His father had always had something to
say to him. He knew wonderful stories, about poor gov-
ernesses who lived on the moors in England, and or-
phaned children who picked pockets, and a doctor who
could talk to animals. He also knew funny songs, and
riddles, and the names of trees and birds and fish. His
father had never run out of things to say. Not until that
day on the telephone. Sam shuddered. He shook his arms
back and forth.

"What are you doing?" John-Glenn said. "Hey. I am
going to give you a born voyage gift, as they say in
Paree."

He went to the wall, to the most magnificent butterfly, its wings streaked with vivid velvet colors, and handed
it to Sam.

"Here," he said. "From one caterpillar to another."

Sam took the butterfly and imagined it on the wall in
his room. In his mind, the pennants were gone and the
butterfly soared upward, alone, paused on Sam Porter's
bedroom wall.

Sam reached for his drawing pad and tore off a sheet
with his trademark drawn on it. He handed it to John-
Glenn. "I will frame that," John-Glenn said, "and keep it
always."

After the show, Mackenzie and Aunt Hope went to
the State Line Diner. It was an old silver trailer with shiny

countertops and yellow vinyl booths. On every table was a twirling list of songs to play. Aunt Hope selected a few and fed the machine quarters. "Used to be a dime," she said.

They ordered coffee and she ordered cinnamon toast too.

"Chances Are" began to play and she smiled.

"This one's mine," she said.

Mackenzie looked at her, waiting.

"I am alive again," she said.

They had stayed for the entire first set. Although the Hoochie-Coo's had added some new numbers, like "Feelings" and "New York, New York," they sang most of their old numbers. Aunt Hope hummed along, swaying back and forth and clapping her hands in time. When the Hoochie-Coo's took a break, Ricardo sent two more Cuba Libres over to the table and a note on a green Lizard Lounge cocktail napkin. Aunt Hope had read the note and then tucked it into her purse.

"Aunt Hope," Mackenzie said now, "what is going on?"

"He's back," she said.

"But—" Mackenzie said. She remembered the way Aunt Hope had sat, waiting, after Ricardo had gone back to Miami. The way she'd stopped fixing her hair, stopped going dancing.

Aunt Hope held her hand up. "I know," she said. "He's a rotten two-timer."

"A bigamist."

"Do you know," Aunt Hope said, "that if it hadn't been for Grammie, I would have followed him all the way back to Florida. When I first laid eyes on Ricardo Havana I wasn't even twenty years old. And, I admit, I had a history of dating the wrong boys. Grammie used to worry sick about me. Your mother had done just fine for herself. And then I start bringing home these really awful guys.''

"First Name Initial" clicked on.

"This one's mine too," Aunt Hope said.

"What is he doing here though?" Mackenzie said.

Aunt Hope leaned forward. "When I saw Ricardo with that wavy black hair and heard that romantic accent, I felt like I had met a movie star or something. I used to sleep with his picture under my pillow." She ate the crust off a piece of toast. "Those are all the original Hoochie-Coo's. Except for Pepe. He died in a plane crash. I knew all of them. We had a barrel of fun together.''

"Where have they been all these years?" Mackenzie asked.

"Touring." She began to eat the center of the toast. "I'm not kidding myself this time. Ricardo's still got a wife in Miami. And five daughters now. I almost died when he called me up. 'Meet me for breakfast,' he said, 'no questions asked.' Not that he should have any questions. I'm the one with the questions. But I said okay and I've been meeting him every morning this week. Mackenzie, I should have followed him down there when he left. I remember him and Bill driving off and it was like my heart was ripped right out of me.''

Mackenzie thought of Aunt Hope's wedding picture, of the flowers pressed in the dictionary.

'' 'Paper moon,' '' Aunt Hope said. "He sings that one for me.''

The apartment was dark when Mackenzie and Aunt Hope got home, except for the light from the mall.

Aunt Hope opened the refrigerator.

"Damn," she said. "John-Glenn ate everything but the egg foo yong."

Mackenzie groped in the darkness for Sam on the couch.

"Hey," she said as she turned on the lamp, "Sam's not here."

"Maybe he climbed in my bed."

Mackenzie began to panic. She fought back images of John-Glenn frightening him, telling him some scary story about extraterrestrials taking Sam's voice, or killing Alexander. She practically ran into the hallway.

"Sam!"

"It's about time," John-Glenn said from his room. "Where were you two?"

"Where is Sam?" Mackenzie said, pushing past his doorway.

"Hold your horses," he said. "He's asleep." He pointed to the top bunk.

Mackenzie climbed the little ladder that led to the top.

Sam was there, tangled in John-Glenn's robe and blankets. He opened his eyes when she popped her head over the edge.

"Hi," she said to him.

The tips of his fingers waved to her from inside the robe.

"We've got a long day tomorrow," she said. "Places to go. People to see."

But he had already fallen back to sleep.

CHAPTER FOURTEEN

Daisy fumbled with her car keys. The weather had turned bitter cold overnight. An icy wind whipped through her hair and made her eyes tear. She had forgotten to wear gloves, and in the walk from her apartment across the parking lot to her car, her hands had grown numb.

She glanced at her watch. It was already ten A.M. and she had to pick up an order before an eleven o'clock sales meeting. Before she'd met Willie, she had felt organized and in control. At least of her business life. Now, she hated to leave him. She imagined him, warm in bed. He frowned slightly when he slept. Alexander had done that too, although since he'd died, Daisy had found it hard to separate his face in sleep from how he had looked in death. It was strange that the first dead person she'd seen had been Alexander. She had heard people, after wakes, saying things like, "He looked asleep, didn't he?" And so she hadn't been prepared for this false-looking Alexander,

173

powdered cheeks and tightly sewn mouth, set as if he were thinking very hard. His eyebrows had been arched upward, like he was saying, "Oh!" Daisy had studied the face hard, leaning over, looking for a sign that this was indeed Alexander. She had seen a small black thread at the corner of his eyelid and moved to pull it off, like a person would if they saw a thread on a sweater. But she had stopped herself. No one had said Alexander looked wonderful or asleep, and she was happy for that. Yet sometimes, thinking of him asleep but alive, she confused the faces, and saw him instead curled up beside her with that startled expression instead of the wrinkled forehead and tightened brows he'd really had when he slept. She wished she'd never looked in that coffin at all.

Daisy fought back an urge to forget the sales meeting and walk right back home and into bed with Willie. Sometimes he made little noises when he slept, like the chirps of a small bird. While she was away from him, she worried that she'd return and find him gone, completely. If he went out while she was there, she spent half the time getting ready for when he got back—fixing her hair and ironing clothes and rubbing herself with lotions—and the other half of the time worrying that he wouldn't ever come back to her.

The keys dropped from her frozen fingers.

"Shit," Daisy said.

Someone called to her.

"Daisy."

She looked up and saw Allison and her daughter, Brandy, walking toward her.

Whenever Brandy visited, she liked to dress in Allison's clothes. Today, she wore her green wool houndstooth blazer as a coat and her own earmuffs, each ear covered in a round white bunny face.

"Where have you been hiding?" Allison said, leaning against the car.

Daisy shrugged.

"With that guy?" Allison said.

Daisy looked down at her keys laying on the gravel. Sam had given her the key chain for her birthday. A plastic pot of daisies.

"Willie," she said.

"I guess we both scored big at that party," Allison said. "And you wanted to leave."

Daisy looked at her and noticed for the first time that Allison had had her hair cut and curled. She looked like a beauty pageant contestant.

Allison laughed and touched her hair. Her gloves were fuzzy, bright turquoise. When she dropped her hand, tiny turquoise threads lingered in her curls.

"Brad paid," she said. "A perm. A manicure. The works. He wants me to look respectable."

"Brad."

"From the party. Remember?"

Daisy nodded. "The man in the suit," she said.

In her mind, his face was a blank circle.

"Where's Sam?" Brandy asked.

She clutched a present wrapped in red and green plaid paper. She had the face of a very old woman.

Daisy bent down and picked up her keys. The metal was cold in her palm, like an ice cube tray right from the freezer. She thought of Mackenzie's voice on her answering machine. "We're on our way," she'd said. "We'll be there first thing tomorrow." Daisy wished she'd let him stay in Rhode Island through the holidays.

"I have a present for him," Brandy said.

"He has one for you too," Daisy said, trying to figure out when she'd have time to pick something up for Brandy.

"Janet helped me pick it out."

175

"Janet?"

"Her father's girlfriend," Allison said. "A lawyer on the Hill. How do you like that? Brandy shows up last night dressed from head to toe in Esprit. The sweater alone runs fifty bucks. A present from Janet, she says. And her father's sitting out front in a brand new BMW. That's Janet's car, she says. In fact, Janet's about the only thing she's talked about."

Daisy shook her head. Brandy and Allison knew the words to every song from the fifties and sixties and used to sit for hours singing them, until their voices grew hoarse. Sometimes, watching them, Daisy felt sad, as if by having a son she'd been deprived of some things.

"Janet. Janet. Janet," Brandy said. She had on long black cocktail gloves, satin ones that Allison wore on dates sometimes.

"I've got to run," Daisy said.

The key slipped smoothly into the lock. Daisy blew on her hands.

"Wait." Allison touched her arm. Turquoise fuzz clung to Daisy's coat.

"Brad and I are having a little get-together," she said. "Tomorrow night."

"A get-together?" Daisy said. The term seemed foreign coming from Allison.

Allison blushed. Or was it the cold turning her cheeks red?

"Brad wants me to meet his friends. And vice versa." She leaned close to Daisy and whispered, "He says he's never felt so close so fast. He says," she glanced around, as if making sure no one else could hear, "he says we're soul mates."

"Allison," Daisy said.

"He works for IBM."

She said this last like she'd won the lottery.

"You can bring—"

"Willie," Daisy said.

"Are you whispering about me?" Brandy said.

"Willie," Allison said. "And Sam. He'll be back to-morrow, right?"

"Yes," Brandy said in an exaggerated tone. "Do bring Sam."

The clock on the dashboard said ten-thirty. Daisy sighed. She would never be able to pick up the order and get to the meeting on time. But Allison still had hold of her arm.

"Seven o'clock," she said. "All right?"

"All right?" Brandy said.

Daisy twisted free and got into the car.

"Yes, yes," she said, slamming the door. "Yes," she said again, although the windows were closed and she had already started to back up. She turned the heat on full blast.

Allison had started to walk back to her apartment, but Brandy stood, clutching the Christmas present.

Daisy pulled up beside Allison and rolled down the window. In the distance, Brandy was saying, "Seven o'clock. For cocktails."

"Yes," Daisy said, "we'll come. It'll be great."

Sam slept beside Mackenzie, his head bent at an awkward angle to rest on the armrest of his seat. On a screen in front of them, an *Ed Sullivan Show* from 1966 flickered. Paul McCartney sat alone on a stool singing "Yesterday." The tape dragged, Paul's voice ground robotlike to a halt.

"Oh, I believe, in yesterda-a-a—"

On the white-lit screen, Jason's head appeared in shadow.

"What," he said.

A pencil tucked behind his ear stretched like a black rifle in the silhouette.

Mackenzie and Sam had driven directly to the rehearsal of his new play when they'd left Rhode Island. Rehearsals for *Still Looking for Paul McCartney* were in a warehouse on Tenth Avenue, near the meat packing district. Mackenzie smelled, or imagined she smelled, blood everywhere. A draft blew through the cracks in the big wooden sliding doors.

They had left for New York early that morning. Aunt Hope had left even earlier to meet Ricardo Havana at the Pewter Pot for breakfast. Mackenzie had watched as her aunt dabbed perfume on her wrists and neck. "My pulse points," she'd said. She'd put on a pink beaded sweater and skirt. "You know," she'd told Mackenzie, "Jackie Kennedy had an outfit just like this one." The beads formed the petals of flowers, delicate lines leading to a thick and shiny center.

At the car, John-Glenn said to Mackenzie, "You can't open any presents yet. We're waiting for you to come back with your mother."

All through Rhode Island, Sam had opened and closed the electric windows in the car. He wanted to test a weather indicator he'd bought as a souvenir for Brandy. It was a card with a picture of a girl in a lavender felt bonnet. The bonnet changed color with the weather. A code at the bottom of the card explained what each color meant. Every time Sam stuck the bonnet out the window, it came back lavender. Until they reached Connecticut. Then, suddenly, it turned blue.

"Blue," Mackenzie had read, glancing down at the card. "Hazy. Hot. And Humid."

Sam frowned. He rolled the window down again and a blast of freezing air blew in.

"Well," Mackenzie said, "we *are* heading south."

He looked at her, confused.

Mackenzie realized how often she forgot that he was just a little boy.

"It's warmer down south," she'd said. "Like in Florida. And Mexico."

He'd nodded solemnly, his eyebrows scrunched up as if the information were being processed through them.

At a McDonald's in Connecticut, Sam ate Chicken McNuggets with the chopsticks from the Red Dragon and drew palm trees and a blazing sun on the back of his napkin. "That's right," Mackenzie had said. "That's what it's like in the South. Hot and Humid."

Now, in sleep, Sam lay stiff and rigid. Mackenzie wondered if he was dreaming of a sunny beach somewhere.

The lights came on, bright, in the warehouse.

Kyle O'Day sat in front of the screen, her legs wrapped in leg warmers and crossed yoga style. She wore a black Danskin body suit and flowing black skirt. A pink scarf draped around her neck shimmered with silver threads. Jason stood over her, a notebook opened in his hands. Mackenzie watched him as he gestured, drew circles in the air and pointed. Kyle blew a big bubble with her gum.

Mackenzie shifted uncomfortably.

No one working on the play got paid for their time. They all did it in the hopes that a producer or an agent might come and see it. She hated the way Kyle looked up at Jason. For an instant, Mackenzie felt panic. She remembered once accidently finding pictures of Jason with another woman. She had looked in his drawer for a book of stamps and found instead the photographs. In them, he was in the Pacific with a woman, cliffs rising behind them, the clouds above them fat and white, the type of clouds people searched for shapes in. She had studied those pictures and imagined Jason and this woman finding dragons and Nixon's face in the clouds. Mackenzie had tried to figure out who could have taken the pictures. Was there a boat nearby? Or someone on the beach? But the angles and distance seemed all wrong for either of those. For days later she had felt unsettled, remembering the easy way his arms held the woman up, above the waves.

She felt that feeling now, as if the ease in which Jason spoke to Kyle, and the manner in which she looked at him, sweeping upward lazily with her eyes, connoted an intimacy that excluded her.

Kyle studied the tip of her long red braid.

"Jason," Mackenzie said.

Sam sat straight up.

Jason turned toward her.

Somehow, to say his name out loud was all that Mackenzie needed, an affirmation that they were still together, that Kyle was some unimportant person on the far border of their lives.

He shielded his eyes against the light.

Mackenzie smiled and waved, like a beauty queen in a parade.

"Is it fixed?" Jason said. "Are we ready?"

"What?" Mackenzie said, in mid-wave.

Kyle laughed.

A woman's voice behind Mackenzie said, "Ready to roll."

Mackenzie realized how foolish she must look, sitting there, waving like that, when all along Jason had thought it was the projectionist calling to him.

"Jawhol, my commandant," Kyle said, and raised her hand outward. Her voice was high and girlish.

Mackenzie looked around, uncomfortable, unsure if Kyle was imitating her own upraised hand, or responding to the projectionist. She dropped her hand.

Jason winked. Or Mackenzie thought he winked. But

before she could decide, the room went dark and the screen filled with a black and white Paul McCartney.

"Yesterday," he sang, "all my troubles seemed so far away. . . . Now it looks as though they're here to stay . . ."

Sam sighed, a big deep sigh, and rested his head on Mackenzie's arm.

Neat stacks of pink cosmetics cases lined the table in front of Daisy. She stood, pulling papers out of her brief-case. A sticker inside the lid said, THINK PINK! Her sales manager, Brenda, peered over her shoulder into the briefcase.

"I know they're in here somewhere," Daisy said.

"A Meg Griffith called twice today about her order," Brenda said. She had short salt and pepper hair, the bangs pulled back with a giant pink clip, as if a butterfly had landed on her head.

"I can probably remember what she ordered," Daisy said. She thought of Meg's plain round face. "Don't put too much," she had said, over and over.

"Yes," Brenda said, "but what about all the other orders you've lost?"

"Look," Daisy said, "I'm the top salesperson in this district. Almost in the region." She thought of her pink car outside, the smell of its leather. She'd earned that car.

Brenda's face remained the same, expressionless. Daisy saw the penciled outline of her lips, an effort to make them fuller.

"I'm sure it's at home," she said.

She closed the briefcase, the locks snapping shut loudly in the quiet room. Outside the door a woman talked excitedly, nonstop. Daisy imagined Willie, still in her bed. She'd known him one week and was yet to sleep without him. It had been that way with Alexander once they'd started. She'd sneak him into her room at home

181

every night that summer. They could hear the television, her mother and Iris talking, the refrigerator door opening and closing.

Brenda said something that Daisy didn't hear.

". . . you know," Brenda finished.

Since Willie, she'd been unable to think clearly. In the middle of the meeting this morning she'd grown short of breath just thinking about him. She'd looked, confused and inhaling tiny quick breaths, at the graph Brenda pointed to, its points stretching upward like pink fantasy mountains. Yesterday she'd gotten lost driving home from the supermarket. It was only five minutes from home but she'd driven somehow to the Beltway headed toward Washington.

She felt, mostly, afraid. Iris had told her a long time ago that it wasn't right to do so much for a man, to give so much. She used to tell Daisy, "You're losing yourself, trying to be what Alexander wants." And Daisy hadn't listened. Right before they split up, he had told her, almost nonchalantly, that he'd had an affair once, with a student. Daisy had become obsessed with the girl: Who was she? How did she wear her hair? What did you talk about? She had made him tell her every detail, even though he'd insist, "This has got to stop. It was nothing." And then the girl had actually called once, to tell him she'd won some sort of grant. Daisy had listened in on the extension. The girl had a very ordinary voice. She didn't say anything special or brilliant. At the end, she'd said, "I wish you well," like an old aunt might say. And then Daisy had felt awful, because she had tried to be like this girl, like this image she had of this girl, hoping that would make Alexander love her again.

The day he'd left for Boston, she'd watched the Mustang drive away from their apartment in Georgetown, and she'd felt an incredible loneliness mixed with a kind of joy. She'd thought briefly that now she'd be able to sleep late or say whatever she wanted without Alexander's scrutiny. But then, in a flash, she felt abandoned, like a puppy thrown into the woods to fend for itself. And she ran after the car, waving her arms and yelling to him.

"I'll do whatever you want," she'd shouted. "Just come back."

She kept running, even though the car had disappeared from view. By the time she reached Wisconsin Avenue, she was yelling, "Goddam you, you bastard."

A group of girls from the college had stopped walking to stare at her.

"Oh, well," one of them said, "you win some, you lose some."

The other girls had laughed.

"Goddam you all too," Daisy said. She was crying then, and their images blurred before her. "Go and read some books, why don't you? Go to the goddam library."

She'd walked away from them, walked until she could stop crying, then went into Au Pied de Couchon and drank an entire carafe of white wine before she realized that she'd probably left the front door unlocked and she was almost an hour late to pick up Sam at the sitter's. She thought of going home and opening the door and the apartment looking empty, like no one lived there at all, the bookshelves empty and the walls bare, because all of those things had been Alexander's. She'd watched him pack them into liquor store boxes, seal the boxes with sturdy tape.

She ordered another carafe of wine and shared it with a man who said he was famous, a blues singer in town to perform at the Bayou. He was very tall and skinny, like the rubber man in comic books. His mustache was so fair it seemed more a trick of light than real.

"You'll come to my hotel," he'd said. His accent was

a mixture of southern and French, which later she'd realize was Cajun.

She'd nodded. She thought of Sam's sitter, calling the house, looking all over for her. She thought of how Alexander would never come back to her, she had done everything all wrong.

The blues singer brought her to the Four Seasons. On a table in the room sat a huge fruit basket, with pomegranates and kiwi and ripe bananas. He'd left her in bed, where she finished off the bottle of champagne they'd ordered and ate almost all the fruit. She'd wondered if he really was famous. His skinny bones had left tiny bruises on her ribs and hips. She'd known, sitting there, that her life had started to change drastically.

Remembering this, Daisy felt sick, suffocated.

"I'll call in the order," she said.

"You haven't heard a word I've said, have you?" Brenda said. The hair clip wobbled as if it were about to take off.

Daisy walked out of the office quickly. What would she do if Willie had left her? She thought again of the blues singer, his trickle of a mustache, his sharp bones.

In her car, she rolled down all the windows and drove fast, gulping the cold air and trying not to be sick.

"Listen," Jason said. "A traffic jam."

He made a sound like passing cars, honking horns and squealing brakes.

Jason could imitate almost any sound. Gunshots. Birds' wings flapping. Running feet.

Sam and Mackenzie applauded.

"Bravo!" Mackenzie said.

Sam picked the onions off his Tandoori chicken with his chopsticks.

"So," Mackenzie said, "the play."

"Kyle is driving me crazy."

"Oh?" Mackenzie frowned. The girl was bothering her too. Before they'd left the rehearsal, she'd called to Jason and thrown him kisses. She'd kissed her hand and then had blown the imaginary kisses to him.

"She has no frame of reference for this play. She's playing someone ten years older than herself," Jason said. "Everybody's an expert."

Mackenzie tried to quickly calculate how old that made Kyle.

"What is she?" Mackenzie said. "Twenty?"

"When are you coming back?" he said.

"I thought maybe you'd fallen in love with Kyle."

Sam rolled his eyes.

"Everything's like this," she said, and shook her hands back and forth.

"Everything's not," he said.

"Real soon we'll be in Rhode Island having that big Porter dinner."

Sam nodded.

"Mackenzie," Jason said, "San Francisco's a big city."

"I'll find her." She cracked the papadum into pieces.

Jason reached into his bag.

"Your mail," he said.

Mackenzie looked through it quickly.

She wasn't surprised to find the postcard from her mother. A picture of a diner with a rotating sign. The sign was shaped like the earth and pierced by a star. When Mackenzie turned it over, she didn't expect to find a message. "This man," her mother had written, "travels around the country photographing diners. I ate at this one. A double cheeseburger was only 89¢. 89¢ I said to the waitress (whose name, by the way, was Bunny!). And she said, If you don't like it, go somewheres else."

"Your mother?" Jason said. "Does she say where she is?"

Mackenzie shook her head.

"The Galaxy Diner," she said. "Redmond, Colorado. She tells me what she ate for lunch like I saw her last week."

She thought of what Jams had told her about her mother using symbols and hidden meanings. This, however, seemed pretty straightforward. Mackenzie could imagine her mother telling this story, describing the waitress in detail and laughing, hard, at the punchline. For days afterward she would use it in her everyday conversation. If you don't like it, go somewheres else. Until she got bored and found a new story.

"My family," Mackenzie said, "used to be so normal."

"Really?" Jason said. "Mine never was. My sister has anorexia, my brother is screwed up from the war, and my parents moved to Sarasota, Florida, and act like very old people."

"I know what you're trying to do," she said.

"Also, I live here, my sister's in LA and my brother lives in a cabin in Eugene, Oregon. For Christmas this year he sent me a giant pine cone, snow from Mt. Shasta, which of course melted en route, and what he claims is an ear from Vietnam."

"You're making this up."

Jason laughed. "I'm not. My sister wrote me a letter last month and said she calls herself Star now. All her life she's Amy and now she calls herself Star. My mother called me from Florida to ask me if I thought she at least could still call Amy Amy."

"We spent every August in Cape Cod," Mackenzie said. "If it rained, we'd play Monopoly and everyone was always the same piece. Alexander was always the hot rod and John-Glenn was the hat—"

"Baby," Jason said, "nobody's really normal. I mean . . ."

"Please," she said, "don't get philosophical on me. Okay?"

The painting was too large for the living room. It ate up one entire wall. The familiar gray and black blotches of paint hovered behind the twin wicker chairs Daisy had painted white. White with a tint of pink so pale it was almost not there at all. Between the chairs was a small round wicker table in the same shade of white, with a floral skirt around it. And there, behind all that, was one of Willie's paintings.

Daisy stared at it for a long time. Across the canvas, flecks of gold and orange and red shimmered. She tried first to figure out what it was, then why it was there in her living room. Perhaps, since Willie himself wasn't there, he had left it as collateral, proof that he would be back. He'd also left a pot of chili simmering on the stove.

"He's coming back," Daisy said out loud.

Inside, she still felt a terrible sadness, and saw Alexander's Mustang growing smaller and smaller as he left her behind.

The gold in the painting shone like real gold. Daisy leaned closer to it and touched the flecks lightly. She saw then a white ribbon and bow wrapped around one bottom corner. She smiled. It was, she guessed, her Christmas present.

The doorbell rang, startling her.

Allison and Brandy came in before Daisy even reached the door.

"P.U." Brandy said. "I smell Mexican food."

The sky was dark behind them and a lazy snow had started to fall.

"I saw you drive up," Allison said. "I'm desperate for help."

She plopped onto the couch and held up a cookbook.

"What do I make for hors d'oeuvres?" she said. "I mean, ranch dressing and carrots is not going to make it for Brad's friends."

"Why is Sam's room locked?" Brandy shouted from down the hall.

"It's being painted," Daisy lied.

"It is?" Allison said. "What color? I like that blue in there."

"How about buying a party platter at Giant?" Daisy said.

Since she'd met Willie, Daisy had been avoiding Allison, afraid she'd blurt out something about Sam. Or Alexander. She wanted to start fresh with Willie, like he was the first guy she'd ever known. Like all those other men had never happened. She wanted it to be right.

"Janet always has toys laid out for me," Brandy said. She sat next to her mother on the couch. "Coloring books. New crayons. Lady Di paper dolls." She pointed to the painting. "What is that?" she said.

Allison laughed. "See how worried I am? I didn't even notice that huge painting."

"Painting?" Brandy said. "It's a wall, isn't it? Paintings are littler. And they're of something. Janet has paintings in her apartment. One is of a bowl of fruit and one is of . . ." she hesitated, "of flowers. Chris-an-the-mums." She smiled, proud.

"Paintings can be any size," Allison said.

"Willie and I may not be able to come tomorrow," Daisy said. "To the party."

"You have to," Allison said.

Daisy closed her eyes. Why didn't I just tell him all along? she thought.

"Daisy."

"Look, you've got to go," Daisy said. "I've got to figure some stuff out and he'll be back soon."

"Who?" Brandy said. "Sam? Sam's coming back today?"

"Get the party platter from Giant," Daisy said. "It has meats and cheeses. Tiny cream puffs and eclairs."

Allison stood, still holding the cookbook open.

Peasant Caviar, Daisy read across the top of the page.

"Please come," Allison said.

"One time," Brandy said, studying the painting, "Janet took crackers and put a little piece of cheese and an olive on some, and ham and cheese on some other ones."

"Stop it," Allison said. "I'm sick of Janet. Do you hear me?"

Brandy turned around to face her.

"Brad's fingers," she said, "look just like hot dogs."

When they left, Daisy took a glass of wine into Sam's room. She lay on his bed. "I never met a lasagna I didn't like," Garfield said. The room was odorless, sterile, without any indication that a little boy used it except for the pennants she'd hung on the wall. Sam seemed sometimes to be just a shadow, a small gray shadow that haunted her.

She tried to think of Sam's personality, who he was, who he had been before Alexander had died. Once, in the apartment in Georgetown, when they'd all still been together, Sam had stood on the dining room table and sung "I'm a Little Tea Pot" for them. He had bent his arms to form the handle and the spout and gave an exaggerated bow to "pour out." Alexander had applauded and had swung Sam into the air. "A real star," he'd said. "A singer and a scholar." But Daisy had found it effeminate, like the way he imitated the Nutcracker's sugar plum fairies.

Perhaps, she thought, if she'd had a daughter it would have been better, like Allison and Brandy. Alexander had been able to relate to Sam so easily. The two of them used to whisper and laugh together all the time. They used to imitate the Three Stooges, knocking each other on the head and falling on the floor.

Daisy fought an urge to pull the stickers of smiling faces off the headboard and throw them out.

Instead, she undressed and climbed under the Garfield sheets. She sniffed the pillow, thought she caught a whiff of toothpaste. She felt like a very bad person, thinking these things about Sam, wishing, almost, that he didn't exist at all, that none of the Porters did, thinking that she herself hadn't existed until the day she'd met Willie.

She fell asleep, and woke to the sound of the front door closing. Daisy jumped up and tried to dress quickly, knocking over the empty wineglass as she grabbed for her clothes. She ran out of the room half-dressed, barefoot, pants unzipped and only the lace camisole on top, her sweater clutched in her hands. She slammed the door closed just as Willie appeared in the hall. There was snow in his hair and beard.

He frowned when he saw her.

"You look like you were having a late afternoon tryst in there." He laughed nervously.

"What are you doing?" she said. "Spying on me? This is my house, you know."

Willie took two steps backward.

"I'm not—"

"What exactly do you think you're doing?" She threw the sweater at his feet, weakly. It landed at her feet, sprawled out, arms extended.

"Daisy," he said. His voice was low. "Is someone in there with you?"

"Yeah," she said. She banged on Sam's bedroom

door. "Better jump out the window," she said, "he's back. Don't forget your pants in there."

"Look," he said. "I'm sorry."

She looked into his eyes. Sam would be home tomorrow and she had to figure something out.

"I've got to do something," Daisy said.

"What?"

She climbed over her sweater and went into the kitchen. What? she thought as she poured a new glass of wine. When she walked into the living room, Willie was standing in the middle of the room. On the floor was a Christmas tree, still bundled, tied in red string.

Daisy knelt beside the tree and breathed in the smell of pine. She thought of the Porters, their majestic tree and the rituals they had for decorating it. Cal always hung the icicles, one by one, and Alexander placed the star on top, a chipped gold one with one point glued on. Mackenzie photographed it. One year she made a book full of the pictures of their trees from year to year. In one, Sam slept underneath it, nestled among the packages. Grammie always said, "What can we do with Daisy? Maybe she can just watch."

"I thought we needed a Christmas tree," Willie said.

"We do," Daisy said, unknotting the ropes.

"All right," Mackenzie said, "in no time you'll be back at home. Playing with Brandy. Seeing your mom. What else? Maybe you'll even be able to build a snowman."

The apartments along the road all looked the same, row after row of fake colonials. Mackenzie remembered the last apartment Daisy and Alexander had shared, a skinny townhouse in Georgetown, the bricks painted white and steep steps leading down to it. In the back was an English garden. "Built in 1890," Alexander had told her. He had pointed out the moldings around the ceilings, the wide-planked oak floors. "The ceilings are too low," Daisy had complained. "The floors slant."

In Boston, Mackenzie never saw her brother's apartment until after he had died. A policeman escorted her there to pack his things. The apartment had been recently restored. It had exposed brick walls and skylights. In the bedroom, the imprint of his body was still on the bed, the crease of his head in the pillow, the long shape of him in the blanket. The pillowcase had had black stains, like gunpowder. From the electricity, the policeman had explained.

"How do you know which one of these is yours?" Mackenzie said.

Sam shrugged.

Mackenzie looked at the directions she had taped to the visor above the windshield. The last ones Daisy had given her got her lost and so Mackenzie had thrown them away. For two days she had been calling Daisy and leaving messages on her answering machine. Finally, this morning, she'd reached her. Mackenzie had called from a phone booth at the Molly Pitcher rest stop on the New Jersey Turnpike. Daisy had whispered the directions into the phone and Mackenzie had to keep shouting, "What? What?" over the sounds of trucks passing. "Can't you speak up?" Mackenzie had said. "No," Daisy told her.

Mackenzie gestured toward a group of brick and wooden buildings.

"Does this look familiar?" she said.

Sam frowned, his eyes searching the apartment complex.

They drove around traffic circles planted with shrubs strung in red and green Christmas lights.

Sam pressed his face against the window. His breath made a small steamy spot on the glass. He started to point to something, then shook his head.

"Wait," Mackenzie said, backing up. She stopped under a street sign. "Pierce, right?" The streets were named after presidents. She thought of Daisy's whisper this morning, "Straight on Buchanan 'til Filmore, then right, then another right on Pierce."

Sam pointed to Daisy's pink Cadillac in the parking lot.

"I don't believe it," Mackenzie said.

She turned off the car. It smelled of french fries and dry heat.

"Well," she said.

Sam pulled his mittens on, tugged at the thumbs.

"Tonight I'll be all the way across the country," Mackenzie said, trying to explain. She felt by leaving him that she was losing Alexander all over again. "San Francisco. In California. But way up north. There aren't palm trees there. They have a lot of fog, like just before it rains. And big hills. I'll get Grandma and bring her home and then we'll all get together in Rhode Island for a special turkey dinner."

Sam looked away from her, out the window. The thumbs on his mittens stood at attention, empty.

"Jams puts apricots in the stuffing, and oranges. Maybe," she added, "we'll be there New Year's. One week from now."

He looked at her, finally, his face wrinkled as if he might cry. But he looked too as if he were expecting something from her.

"Hey," Mackenzie said, "maybe your mom will come too. We'll be in the old house. There's a lace tablecloth that my Grammie got for her wedding as a present and we'll put that on the table. And the family china."

Mackenzie imagined it all there, the dining room smelling of lemon wax, the silver polished, the ivory lace of the tablecloth forming delicate bells over the dark oak table. The pattern on the china was three salmon-colored flowers, off center, the edges trimmed in silver. One plate had a chip, like a bite had been taken from it. The chip got there one Thanksgiving when Alexander tried to spin the dish like a top. A few pieces had fine gray hairline cracks across them, from age and use.

In the rearview mirror Mackenzie watched Daisy wobble toward them in high-heeled white boots. Her arms were full of bags. She wore a white bunny fur coat, a piece of shocking pink knit showing a few inches below it.

"Here's your mommy," Mackenzie said.

Daisy's hair in the winter light looked very yellow.

They got out of the car and waited for her, Sam kicking the hard snow with his toes.

"It's so icy," Daisy said when she reached them.

She put all the bags on the roof of the car and opened her arms wide, kneeling.

"Come here, Mr. Sam Porter," she said.

He moved, almost in slow motion, into Daisy's embrace.

"Don't knock me over," she laughed.

Someone had thrown tinsel into the bare trees above them and Mackenzie watched as it sparkled and shimmered silver against the gray sky. They looked like some kind of high-tech icicles. She thought of real icicles, of breaking them off trees and eating them like lollipops.

"So," Daisy said.

She straightened and glanced back toward her condominium.

"Have I got a wonderful Christmas surprise for you," she said.

Something in her voice made Mackenzie flinch.

Daisy reached into one of the bags and pulled out a flat package wrapped in silver paper with metallic blue snowflakes.

"For me?" Mackenzie said.

She tore the paper off. It floated to the ground, the blue snowflakes settling against the pavement like neon snow.

"Airline tickets?" Mackenzie said.

"Yes," Daisy said. She laughed nervously. "For you and Sam to go together to San Francisco." She grabbed Mackenzie's arm. "They're business class," she said.

"But I have a reservation."

"This is better though. I mean, you wanted Sam with you for the holidays, right? And you'll all come back together. You and Sam and your mother. Maybe I can meet you in Rhode Island. I could use a little break." She knelt beside Sam again. "You're going to have a real adventure, Sam."

Sam crumpled the discarded paper into an awkward shape.

"But I don't know how long this will take," Mackenzie said.

Daisy stood again, rubbed a small spot off the cuff of her boot.

"Well, Mackenzie, if you don't want Sam with you just say so."

"It isn't that," Mackenzie said.

Sam looked up at her, eager. It was Alexander's face. And eyes.

Daisy glanced back over her shoulder, and Mackenzie followed her gaze. In the distance, a little girl moved across the parking lot, clutching a big box.

"Shit," Daisy said.

Then, "Look, I have some clothes for him in here. And a few presents. I wrapped a bottle of perfume for Cal. And a belt for Iris. I thought maybe you'd get to see Iris. It's leopard." She lifted a present from the bag. "This is for you. An engagement book," she said. "It's terrible the way I always tell. There's pictures by a famous photographer in it." Her eyes met Mackenzie's and held there. "Ansel Adams," she said.

Sam had spotted the little girl too now. He began to wave his arms to her.

"Sam," she called.

"It's really wonderful," Mackenzie said.

It was. But something was very wrong. She studied Daisy's face. A pulse beat, rapidly, below one eye.

The little girl stopped in front of them. She wore an old suede jacket with long fringe on the arms. She smelled of mothballs and old cigarettes.

"This is Brandy," Daisy said.

"My mother says are you coming to the party or not."

Sam pet her hair softly.

"I'll go over there now," Daisy said, "and discuss it with her. I'll walk you back."

"I want to see Sam open his present first," Brandy said.

He untied the ribbon and bow slowly.

"You don't have to be so neat," Daisy said. "Give it a good tear."

Sam gently lifted the tape from the paper and it fell open like a woman's coat.

"Wait," Brandy said. "See all the elves?"

She pointed to the wrapping paper, covered in busy elves, hammering and painting and stacking toys.

Sam smiled, traced an elf.

"Honey," Daisy said, "I'm going over there now. Come on."

"What's going on?" Mackenzie said. "What's the rush?"

Daisy smiled.

"No rush," she said.

Brandy helped Sam open the box and pull out a big stuffed bear.

"Watch," she said.

She squeezed the bear's nose and spoke close to his face.

"Hello, Sam," she said.

She let go of the nose.

"Hello, Sam," the bear said in Brandy's voice.

Sam's eyes widened.

"Merry Christmas," Brandy said into the bear's face.

"That's wonderful," Daisy said. "You can take it with you on the plane."

"Merry Christmas," the bear said. Then, "That's wonderful. You can—"

Brandy laughed.

"Why don't you give Brandy a big hug before you go?" Daisy said.

The two children wrapped their arms around each other and moved together in a waltz.

"Isn't that sweet?" Daisy said. "Now come give Mommy a hug good-bye."

The children kept dancing. Brandy hummed "The Blue Danube," softly and off key.

Mackenzie said, "Are you sure—"

"Absolutely. Yes. Yes."

A man and woman pulled up beside them in a brown Yugo.

"Thirty-seven miles to the gallon," the man said as he got out. "In town."

"I don't care," the woman said. "They're still Communists."

"Do you drink Stoli?" he said. "Don't tell me you don't because I know you do."

"Listen," Daisy said. She touched Mackenzie's arm. "I met a guy. He's really nice."

Mackenzie pulled her arm away. She thought of Alexander and Daisy together. The way he held her feet in his lap at night. And then she thought of Carmen Havana, sitting alone at a picnic in the woods, away from the rest of the family, making origami birds and trees out of colored paper.

"I just wanted you to know," Daisy said. "When Sam meets him, it'll be fine. They'll be crazy about each other."

What about Alexander? Mackenzie thought. She felt mixed up. They hadn't even really been together when he died. In fact, the last time she had spoken to him he'd told her he'd met someone interesting. "Her name is Lydia," he'd said. "She's a resident at Mass General. We've only had a few dates but I like her." "Take it slow, Alexander," Mackenzie had said. "You always jump in feet first." "Heart first," he'd laughed.

A piece of tinsel fell from the tree and floated down between them.

Daisy separated Sam and Brandy.

"Come on," she'd said. "Give Mommy a hug."

Brandy held the weather indicator Sam had given to her. The bonnet had turned pink.

"Snow," she read.

They got into the car.

"What an adventure, Sam," Daisy said.

She and Brandy waved as the car backed out.

Sam pressed the bear's nose, then released it. The hum of the car played back. And faraway voices.

CHAPTER FIFTEEN

"What about this wife of yours?" Ursula asked Jams.

They sat together in a new Mexican restaurant, on top of high stools, their food and drinks crowded onto the small round tiled table. It was happy hour, and their plates were heaped with cheese-soaked chips and soggy miniature tacos.

Jams's stool wobbled slightly, and he thought of rolling up a matchbook and sticking it under the short leg to balance it. Instead, he stirred his margarita with his finger.

Ursula's bruises were almost all gone now. He thought her face was one of those that would always look young, like a child's. Perhaps it was all those freckles, or the round Betty Boop eyes. Cal's face had lines around her eyes and mouth, and her hair was streaked with gray that she rinsed every month to a reddish brown. It was a face of character, whereas Ursula's was malleable. She could stretch it into a wide smile or pull it all forward into a frown, as if it were made of Silly Putty.

"Cal was always ahead of the times," Jams said. "Years ago, before anyone had even heard of Mexican food, she was making it. Burritos and guacamole. All of it."

"So," Ursula said, relaxing her face slightly, "she was a good cook."

She waited for him to answer, but he didn't say anything else.

What about this wife of yours? he thought. What about her?

Jams would never forget the first time he saw her. It was before he'd opened his own store in Rhode Island, while he was still learning the liquor business from his uncle in a store outside of Boston. He didn't really know liquor back then, and he'd get confused when people asked for wine suggestions, or when they wanted to know which brand of Scotch was best. His own father had owned hardware stores back in Pennsylvania and that's what Jams knew. Hardware. Bolts and screws and nails. But his brother had a wife and a family and it was only right that he stayed and took over the business. Moving to New England and starting a business with his uncle had seemed like an adventure. "I'd do it," his brother had said. "In a minute."

Cal had come in that first time with a thin pale man named Matthew. His hair was somewhere between red and blonde, but not clearly either color, and thinning in the front. He had very deepset eyes, sunken way into his head.

"We need a wine," Cal said to Jams.

Her hair was long and loose, full of natural waves, not cut or set into any real style. She reminded him of a colt—chestnut hair with a widow's peak, tall spindly legs, and a long face with big teeth.

"Something Spanish, maybe?" she'd said to Matthew.

"No," he said. "Not Spain."

Her eyes were a clear brown, with big flecks of yellow and green, like an abstract mosaic tile.

"All right," she said. "Not Spain."

She turned to Jams.

"What, then?" she asked him. "What non-Spanish wine can you recommend?"

He cleared his throat.

"Is it for meat or poultry?" he asked her.

She laughed. Around her neck she wore a single strand of pearls, the color of oyster shells.

"Red," Matthew said. "And inexpensive."

Jams looked down at him. The man was barely Cal's height and Jams stood well over six feet tall.

"Red. Inexpensive. Not Spanish," he said.

He handed them a simple bottle of French table wine from the sale rack.

Cal paid.

"He's leaving for a mission in Guatemala," she whispered at the cash register. "He wants me to marry him and go there too. To convert Indians. What do you think about that?"

She glanced at the name sewn onto the pocket of his shirt. It was someone else's shirt, a former employee who had left long ago.

"What should I do, Bob?"

"Well," Jams said, "it sounds like a noble cause."

She laughed again, showing all of her horse teeth.

He thought she was an outrageous woman, bold and unusual.

For a while, after they were married, Matthew sent her hand-woven blankets in vivid blues and purples from

Guatemala. And hand-carved birds, the national symbol there, a bird that died if it was kept in captivity. She kept these things in a box in her closet until one day, after one of their times at Cape Cod, she threw them all out, violently and tearfully, smashing the wooden birds.

Cal came back to the store a week or two later with a different man. This one had very black curly hair and eyes so dark that Jams couldn't distinguish the pupil from the iris. It was almost frightening to look into those eyes.

She didn't laugh so much this time. The man kept his hand on her arm and asked for a wine, a specific type and year. Jams fumbled around, looking for it. He wanted to ask her if she had decided to go to Guatemala or not. But he didn't get the chance.

Jams had had a girlfriend in Pennsylvania. Margaret Kildoyle. She was plump but pretty. He used to tell her she looked like Gene Tierney. She was a kind of star in their town, a champion baton twirler who won trophies statewide. She used to toss flaming batons into the air, two or three at a time, spinning in brilliant unison. She smelled, always, like lilacs, and had in her backyard a lilac grove where so many grew that they formed a kind of canopy over a small stone bench. Margaret and Jams used to sit for hours on that bench and kiss, the smell of lilacs all around them. Once she had asked him, "Don't you even want to put your hand under my sweater? Don't you want to touch me?" The answer had been no, but he thought that must be the worst insult to someone, to refuse. And so he had done it, sliding his hand over her soft flesh. She had leaned toward him and pulled off her sweater, unhooked her bra. "Finally," she'd said after they'd made love.

Then, later, she spoke vaguely of marriage and he'd wondered when he'd left if they were engaged somehow. She wrote to him weekly, talked about taking a train up to

Boston to get things settled. When he thought of her, he thought of those flaming batons and her softness under him in the grass, and the smell of lilacs. But that was all.

He had met a lot of women since he'd arrived in Massachusetts and had dated them once or twice, friends of his cousins and girls he had met at parties. But he felt unmoved by them all, until Cal walked into the store. She both frightened and aroused him. After that second time, he was afraid she'd gone off to teach the Indians and that would be that. He'd imagined Margaret arriving at South Station with her hope chest and trousseau, all white and plump and round-faced, and he was afraid he'd somehow have to marry her, that there was some code of honor involved here that he wasn't quite sure of.

But then Cal appeared again, just at closing time, with her friend Vivvie. Vivvie wore large hoop earrings in the shape of a coiling snake, and a cashmere sweater with no bra. Cal, he remembered, was dressed all in black, baggy men's trousers and pullover sweater with her pearls lying against her collarbone.

"We need champagne," Cal said. "Lots of it."

"And none of this domestic stuff," Vivvie said.

"My whole world is falling apart," Cal said.

"Guatemala?" he said, afraid she'd tell him she was leaving that very night.

She nodded.

"Tell her," Vivvie said, "that she doesn't need to marry a goddam priest."

"And Isaac is hitchhiking across the country," Cal said. "He wants to go all the way to Russia. To Alaska and the Bering Strait."

"Tell her if she wants adventure like she claims she does then she should go with him," Vivvie said. "Tell her she could be one hell of a poet."

"Vivvie here is going to London to study," Cal said. "Everyone is deserting me."

"The others are dropping like flies," Vivvie said. "Missy is actually marrying a dentist."

They both doubled over in a fit of giggles over this.

"An orthodontist, actually," Cal said.

He smiled awkwardly, completely enchanted.

Later, he went with them to Vivvie's apartment in Brookline, already stacked with packed boxes, and drank three bottles of good French champagne. They all passed out on the floor, on a Japanese mattress called a futon.

He wondered how long he'd been sitting quietly, lost in memory and breaking the nachos into tiny pieces on the tiled tabletop. Ursula had chewed off all of the lipstick on her full bottom lip and was drumming her fingers against her glass. Jams watched her fingers against the glass, short square nails polished in gloss. She had invited him here for drinks. "You know," she'd said, "it's Christmas Eve." He hadn't known at all.

Jams felt like he owed her something, some secret piece of news. She had told him over the months stories about her and her husband. In the car over here just tonight she had said, "You know, his sister told me once that he's got some kind of brain tumor that makes him violent." She had whispered the words, given him the secret like a gift.

"You know," Jams said, "Cal had this friend. Missy. She was a beauty. Long blonde hair. A perfect smile. Sort of like that model who's around these days—"

"Cheryl Tiegs?"

"No. This one married a big rock star."

"Jerry Hall?" Ursula leaned toward him, her face eager.

"Maybe," he said. "I don't know. Anyway, I always had a crush on Missy. A real crush."

"Christie Brinkley," Ursula said, smiling. "That's who she looked like. Right?"

Jams nodded. "That's the one," he said. He wondered if his secret hadn't been as interesting as Ursula's husband's brain tumor.

"I really did," he said. "She was a beauty and I had quite a crush on her."

He had never said that out loud and he felt a pang of guilt, as if Cal could hear. Or Grammie, who had always mistrusted him slightly. Once, at a party at Missy and Art's—he smiled at the memory. They always gave great parties, with themes. This particular one was a Hollywood theme, and Missy had written across their picture window in glitter, HOLLYWOOD, just like the sign that hung over the hills out there. There were palm trees everywhere, and a cardboard limousine pressed flat against one wall. Cal had gone as Hedda Hopper. She had worn a big floppy hat and carried a notepad and pen all night. He had dressed as Charlie Chaplin, and practiced walking and swinging a cane.

Missy had looked the most beautiful he had ever seen her. Weren't there still photographs around somewhere of her that night, dressed as Scarlett O'Hara, her waist pinched small, her walk a rustle of petticoats and ruffles? He had been hypnotized by her shoulders, bare with the flashing green of the dress beneath them. They were the color of pure cream.

Jams had followed her into the kitchen when she went to get more ice. She held a clear glass bowl, and dropped the ice cubes into it like precious crystals.

He had stood in front of her, big and silent, the derby hat and crayoned mustache making him feel both foolish and brave. He would never know what came over him then, if it had been too many vodka gimlets, or the way she tilted her face up to him, the blonde banana curls grazing her collarbones, and she said, "What?" with a lipsticked smile. Whatever caused it, at that moment he touched her bare shoulders lightly and pressed her against the refrigerator, like someone in a bad movie about suburban adultery. The glass bowl full of ice pressed against his chest when he kissed her and he felt the cold right through his shirt.

He remembered that she had tasted very sweet, like maraschino cherries. Her shoulders felt the way a child imagines clouds feel—soft and velvety. The thing he was remembering now, though, was that Missy had kissed him back, hard. She had tilted her head upward to meet his kiss and opened her mouth easily to let his tongue in. Or was that, he wondered, just a trick of memory? He had, after all, drunk five or six vodka gimlets. Cal even had to drive home that night, he'd had so much to drink. But still, it seemed he could recall the slightest trace of his crayoned mustache across her mouth.

"Well," Ursula said, "maybe you married the wrong girl."

"No," Jams said. "That's not it."

"Of course," she said.

Jams thought that Ursula was the type of woman who would eat a tunafish sandwich someone had made her even if she hated tuna, just not to disagree or cause trouble.

"I'm looking for an apartment, you know," she said. "Or a small house somewhere. I feel strong enough to go it alone."

"Really? That's great."

They ordered two more margaritas. Jumbo Goldens. He raised his glass.

"Congratulations," he said.

He felt envy, jealous that Ursula was able to leave. During the four months he had been there, she had seemed weak and frightened, always talking about her cruel husband. "The Monster," she called him. "Enough about him," she'd say after a long while, "what about you?" and she would look almost eager to hear another story of misery. On trips they all took, she used to always manage to sit beside him. She knew a lot of facts, about cranberry bogs and unsupported domes. If no one spoke to her, she would rattle them off, always starting with, "I guess you already know this but . . ."

"Do you know what else I'm doing?" she asked Jams.

Jams was thinking, "I can do it too. I can leave there. I'm not sick. My wife left me and my son died and my grandson won't talk but I am all right."

"I'm going on *Jeopardy*," Ursula said. "I'm flying out to California right after New Year's and I'm trying out."

"Really?" he said again.

He thought of her rattling things off to him on those bus trips. "I'm sure you already know this," she'd said once on the way to Fenway Park, "but isn't it funny that New York is the only state that ends with the letter *K*?" And damned if he hadn't missed the entire first inning going over all the state's names, trying to find another one that ended in *K*. She had been right.

Ursula held up three fingers.

"My New Year's resolutions," she said. "Find a place to live. Try out for *Jeopardy*. Stay away from The Monster."

She bent her head. Jams saw that it was the same orange color all the way through.

"The last is the hardest," she said. "His name is Jack, you know. I used to tutor him in college. History. I was always pretty good with facts. He was a big football player. All-state and everything." Even now, years later, saying this made her blush with pride. "I was a nobody and here was this big hunk of a guy, practically famous, and he liked me. We thought for sure he'd make the pros. Pittsburgh paid a lot of attention to him and we were so sure. I've got to get over that feeling of not being worthy enough for him. That's the thing."

Jams nodded.

Then he did something he had tried hard not to do for a long time. He thought of Cal, pushed her image to the front of his mind and forced himself to remember something out of the haze he had put her in.

Ursula was saying, "His hands are huge. He could kill me with those hands. But I remember them best the way they cradled a football."

He thought suddenly, clearly, of Cal's legs. Beautiful long legs, thin but taut with muscles. She used to ski when he'd first met her. Once he told her that her legs were better than Betty Grable's. During lovemaking, she'd wrap her legs around his waist and he could feel the muscles in her calves, flexing, clutching.

"You know," Ursula said, "he won't even watch the Super Bowl."

Jams tried to set the images out of focus now, but one remained. Cal's mouth. It had become set, firm and pushed downward slightly. My God, he thought, she's been so unhappy for so very long.

"She always wanted to be a writer," he said.

"What? Your wife?"

"A poet. People said she was good. Some old boyfriend of hers moved up to Montana and actually got to be quite well known. He writes about wolves and winter. Depressing stuff but you can see him in *The New York Times* now and then. He used to say she had talent. But you know, you have kids, a family, you get responsibilities."

Ursula nodded.

"It takes a special kind of person," she said.

"To me," he said, "poems are too vague. At least in a story, in a book, people say what they mean."

"Yes," she said, "I feel that way."

"My son dying," Jams said, "was the single most horrible thing in my life. My life ended too with that phone call. I stopped knowing who I was. I had that phone in my hand and this terrible news and I couldn't figure out why I was sitting in this living room in Rhode Island with this stranger. This stranger who was my wife."

They didn't talk on the way back.

Ursula drove slowly along the icy roads, bent over the wheel. It had snowed while they were inside the restaurant and the new snow settled on everything like a sugar glaze.

Jams felt emptied. Dry. He sat straight, his gloved hands folded in his lap, his insides feeling like dead autumn leaves. He thought of Mackenzie and Sam, the two people who were still his family, but they too seemed distant and remote, as far from him as his wife driving around out west somewhere, unreachable. He felt too old for this.

The car skidded in the parking lot.

Jams thought of reaching over and grabbing the steering wheel. But he didn't move.

Ursula smiled when they parked.

"I still remember that from driver's training," she said. "Turn into the skid."

She was proud of herself.

Jams reached over then and turned off the car, turned the key in the ignition, as if that action meant something. And then he took Ursula's round face in one of his gloved hands and kissed her. Close up, she smelled like a flowery perfume, like the junior prom, and her freckles blended together. There were so many of them that they actually blurred into her skin, giving it an orange glow.

The kiss did not wake him. It made him, instead, feel old and foolish, sitting in a baby-blue Volkswagen Rabbit and kissing a freckle-faced woman with orange hair. He sighed.

Ursula turned her face toward him, having shaped it into a smiling moon. She had taken, he supposed, the sigh for one of pleasure.

"Thank you," he said, and started to leave before he remembered they lived in the same place.

She took his arm and held it as support against the icy path. He thought of her on television, on *Jeopardy*, listing the buildings with the largest unsupported domes. "What are St. Peter's Basilica, the Capitol, the capitol buildings in Providence and Madison, Wisconsin?" She would win big and be happy.

In the elevator, Ursula pressed the buttons for their floors. His was first, and she wedged herself between the doors. They kept dinging and trying to close, but they would hit her arm, then slide back. She was, he thought, waiting for something and so he leaned over and kissed her again, this time pressing her against him. She was soft in all the places Cal was tight, waist, arms, hips. He thought again of Cal's legs, wrapped tight around him, calves straining, and this memory aroused him for just an instant. And in that instant he heard his own breath quicken. It was a moment, a second, of passion. His first in a long time. Then it passed and he freed his grip. Her freckles separated on her cheeks and he shoved her backward lightly so that the elevator door closed with a final, firm ding.

He looked down. In his hand he held a tube of lipstick, half a roll of Certs, and three pennies, all from her coat pocket.

CHAPTER SIXTEEN

Iris's flat was big, a sprawling long apartment with rooms opening onto each other. She had shared it with many different roommates, each of whom had left for a bigger apartment, or to get married, or for a better job in a new city. They all left something behind—a framed poster that said "Tanglewood 1982" over a black and brown piano, a lamp shaped like a goose, a batik rug from Jakarta. Iris's own things reflected the stages she'd been through. She had an oversized purple bean bag chair, a colorless couch, and a large crystal pyramid on a low table. Nothing went together, but it all fell into a lopsided harmony.

She compulsively dusted the apartment. She stood on chairs to reach the tops of the cupboards and the refrigerator. She ran a cloth over lamps and frames and then polished her crystal pyramid until it glistened.

Iris was dusting when the doorbell sounded, a long hesitant croak like an old man wheezing. When she looked out the window and down at the street, there was no one there.

Iris shook her head and climbed back onto the chair. It had been a strange week.

Yesterday she had received a letter addressed to Cal Porter, in care of Iris Bloom. Iris hadn't been sure what to do with it. She considered opening the letter. But wasn't that a federal offense? It did have her name on it, which seemed to make it all right, but there was that "in care of." Didn't that mean she should take care of it until she could hand it over to Cal? That posed a whole new problem. How was she supposed to give it to Cal? From what Iris understood, that whole family had fallen apart since Alexander died. Daisy had told her that Mr. Porter was in jail, or a hospital somewhere. Mackenzie had quit a good-paying job to do freelance stuff in New York. And Cal had up and disappeared. They had even rented the house out. The house being occupied by a different family really got to Iris. That house had become in Iris's mind a symbol of family, of a home. Like a Norman Rockwell painting come to life. If that was gone, what was left of anything?

Iris had even called the post office and asked them what to do with the letter.

"Open it. Keep it," the woman said. "Just don't mail it. At least not until after Christmas. We are up to our noses in mail here."

"Well, of course you are," Iris had said. "You're the post office."

The letter sat, unopened, in the hall on a mahogany secretary an old roommate had left behind. She had left several other antiques. An ornate clock that chimed loud and heavy every hour and a lamp with a green tasseled shade.

Iris's boyfriend had said to just leave the letter alone.

He was also her name therapist, and a stand-up comic. His own name was Lloyd Gray, which had caused him a lot of distress, since the meaning of Lloyd was gray. So, in essence, he was named Gray Gray.

Iris opened the window and shook out the dust rag. It was an old T-shirt of her last roommate's. CAMP BEVERLY HILLS, it said in fat pink letters.

"What a week," Iris said.

Just this morning Daisy had called and told her not to be surprised if Mackenzie and Sam came by.

"In fact," Daisy had said, "they probably will."

"Mackenzie and Sam? Here?"

"They'll be in town."

"Wait a minute," Iris had said, "last week you called me up and you were hysterical—"

"Upset," Daisy said.

"Whatever. You couldn't believe you were letting Mackenzie have Sam for the holidays."

And then the oddest thing had happened.

Iris had heard a man's voice, as clear as can be, say, "Daisy."

"I've got to go," Daisy had said then. "Have Sam call me if they do show up."

"A lot of good that would do," Iris said, "since he can't even talk."

But Daisy just whispered "Bye" and hung up.

So now what was she supposed to think? Maybe Sam was talking again.

Iris went into the hall to dust the banister.

Her flat was on the second floor. There was no door separating it from the stairs that led up to it. If she leaned over the banister, Iris could look right into the downstairs people's living room. And they could look up into hers.

She walked by the desk and Cal's letter caught her eye. She should have told Daisy about it. Maybe Mackenzie would take it if she did come here. Why Mackenzie Porter would ever come to her apartment was a big mystery to Iris. All she knew was that she had enough on her mind without worrying about the Porters' mail. She had wanted to buy Christmas decorations today, nice traditional ones. Snowmen and Santas. Then she had to figure out a way to get to Los Gatos to see Lloyd at that dinner club.

The antique clock struck two.

Iris wished she could figure out a way to turn those chimes off.

Then the doorbell rang again.

"What is going on today?" she said.

The front door opened.

Iris hung her head over the banister. She could see the oriental furniture in the downstairs people's living room, all black lacquer and floral screens.

"Hello," Iris called.

A woman walked in and stood, staring around the foyer. She hesitated, then walked into the living room. Almost immediately she turned back toward the stairs.

The woman's hair was a rich brown, woven with silver, and wavy. She had on a black cloth coat with a silk scarf the color of smoke. When she looked up, Iris couldn't believe it.

"Iris?" she said. "Is that you up there?"

Iris's mind filled with the smell of cinnamon and peppermint and pine, and she felt a rush of homey warmth. Her hand touched her hair. After so many colorings and bleachings, it had turned a washed-out brown, the color of dirty water.

"Yes," Iris said. "It's me."

Iris watched as Cal Porter climbed the stairs. Even though she saw her as Cal looked now, the loose hair and thick eyebrows and plain face, Iris imagined her in that living room, before a large tree with a fire popping beside her.

"What a day!" Iris said when Cal reached the top of the stairs. "What's next?"

Cal couldn't stop staring at Iris. She had to stop herself from saying what she was thinking. Iris looked normal. Her hair was long and layered, a sort of flat color of brown. She had on Levi's and a man's red and white striped Oxford shirt with the sleeves rolled up.

"And here I was," Iris said, "expecting Mackenzie."

At the sound of her daughter's name, Cal felt herself shiver.

"Mackenzie?" she repeated, as if perhaps she hadn't heard correctly.

These past few months on the road had allowed Cal to live in an unreal world, a world of Best Westerns and tourist attractions. The days were marked off by pins on a map, by bumper stickers in her suitcase: I VISITED THE LAUREY CAVERNS. HIKE THE CANYON. THIS CAR CLIMBED PIKES PEAK. Mackenzie wasn't a part of this world. She lived, instead, in a distant part of Cal's mind, where she floated safe, golden, and beautiful.

Suddenly Cal's unreal world was dissolving, and she was being forced back into reality. Mackenzie's face came to her, and her daughter looked worried, hurt, abandoned.

"Why would Mackenzie be here?" Cal asked. She tried to push away the image of her.

"That's what I'd like to know," Iris said. "Why don't you come in and sit down."

Cal's legs felt like lead weights were attached to them as she followed Iris into the living room. She sat on the couch. It was made of scratchy cotton, colorless and rough. She ran her hands over the fabric.

Iris half sat, half fell into the bright purple bean bag chair.

"Remnants," she said.

"What?"

Iris moved her head to face Cal and Cal caught sight of her ear. It was outlined from top to lobe with pearl stud earrings, like a jewel-encrusted shell.

"Remnants of my past," Iris said.

She patted the bean bag chair.

Cal nodded.

"What about Mackenzie?" she asked. Her stomach rolled.

"I don't know," Iris said.

The other ear, Cal saw, was bare.

"Daisy called this morning and said Mackenzie and Sam might come by. Apparently they're in San Francisco. Visiting."

Iris held up her hands, a motion of surrender.

"Sam's with her," Cal said.

She thought of Mackenzie, right after Alexander's funeral, holding Sam to her. "He looks just like Alexander," she'd said. "Doesn't he? Look at him." Sam had stood, stiff in her arms, silent, his eyes the color of a troubled ocean.

The day he had been born, Jams had said, "Spitting image, isn't he? No doubt whose father this boy's is."

Cal had refused to agree, had seen, instead, Daisy's thinness, her awkward gait. But here, with the California sunlight bouncing off a giant prism on a low table in front of her, Cal thought of Sam and saw, in him, Alexander. The eyes and chin and wheat-colored hair. The round cheeks that would, like Alexander's, grow angular as he grew older.

She stared into the large crystal, focused on the way the sun refracted off it, shooting tiny rainbows across the wooden floor.

"You know Daisy," Iris was saying. "No details and in a big rush."

Cal nodded—a small movement of her chin, really.

Before the funeral she had knelt in front of Sam in her dark green woolen dress, too warm for June but all she could think of to put on.

"Sam," she had said, "what was your daddy saying just before he stopped talking?"

The child, in a tight blue suit and an inappropriate bright red bow tie, had stared past her. His lips, she remembered, had been cracked and chapped.

"Answer me, Sam," she'd said. "What was he saying?"

When the boy didn't make a gesture toward her, she had taken him by the shoulders and shaken him.

"Goddam you," she'd said. "Talk!"

His shoulders had felt bony and small.

That information had seemed so vital at the time. Had Alexander been laughing when the lightning hit? Telling a story? It had been as if that last word, that last thought, would solve something, or somehow ease the loss.

"Enough," Jams had said, prying her fingers off Sam. "The boy has had enough."

"So have I," she'd said.

"Cal," Iris said. "Why are you here?"

Cal kept her gaze on the rainbows. A round spot on the floor was bleached from the sun and it framed the shots of color.

"In San Francisco?" she asked. Or in your apartment with you? she thought.

"Well, yes. I mean, people are worried about you."

Cal thought of herself, bumping along in Alexander's car, feeling like she was on some glorious journey. The states blending into each other. The smell of Alexander, strong when she'd begun, fading every day. Once, in

West Virginia, she'd found an old shirt of his in the trunk, and had plucked a strand of dirty blonde hair from it. The hair had shone in the daylight, shimmered with life. She'd found napkins with phone numbers written in his pointed way in the glove compartment, and three packets of condoms folded together, and a note on a scrap of paper: "Lydia is off Wednesday and Thursday." But none of it had affected her like that single strand of hair.

"I mean," Iris said, "they want to know that you're all right."

"I know."

Iris shifted uncomfortably on the chair.

When Alexander died, Iris had sent the Porters a fruit basket. All that day, trucks had delivered somber floral arrangements, lilies and mums with dark bows draped around the pots. Then a man appeared at the door with a huge watermelon. It had been carved into a basket and filled with small round balls of cantaloupe and honeydew, chunks of pineapple, and slices of oranges and grapefruit. Its edges were cut into perfect triangles. Nestled among the fruit were two or three orchids.

"This can't be for us," Mackenzie had said to the delivery man. She had held the heavy watermelon in her arms like a baby.

"Someone has died here," she said. "This seems to be for a party of some sort."

A tag hung off the watermelon handle.

ORCHIDS, it said, ARE EDIBLE! ANOTHER FUN FACT FROM FANNY'S FARM!

Once, Missy had had a theme party called Hawaiian Luau. She had roasted a baby pig with an apple in its mouth on a rotisserie in the backyard. Everyone who came got real floral leis and Art played Pineapple Princess on the ukulele. Missy had carved a watermelon and filled it with rum and melon balls. At the end of the night,

Missy, Vivvie, and Cal had sung "Tiny Bubbles" and cried. That's what Cal had thought of as Mackenzie stood rocking the watermelon basket from Iris Bloom. Later, after everyone was asleep, she'd eaten the orchids.

Suddenly, Iris jumped to her feet.

"How could I forget?" she said, slapping her forehead. "I have so much on my mind, I completely forgot."

Cal stood too.

Iris's eyes, she noticed, were the color of brandy.

She waited, standing, as Iris went into the hallway, then returned, holding a letter out to her.

"This is for you," Iris said. "It came yesterday and I had no idea what to do with it."

Cal took a deep breath before she opened it.

"I didn't want to open it," Iris was saying.

DEAR MISS PORTER, WE'RE HAPPY TO ACCEPT YOUR THREE POEMS—POINT JUDITH LIGHTHOUSE, IN THE DESERT, AND LAST THOUGHT . . .

"I even called the post office," Iris said.

Cal tried to read the rest of the letter, but her eyes kept returning to the first line, to the word "accept."

"I mean," Iris said, " 'in care of' is a very confusing phrase."

"My poems," Cal said. "*The San Francisco Review* accepted three of my poems."

"Poems?"

Cal sat back down. Read the letter again. MISS PORTER. She laughed. Wait until they find out she was a grandmother.

Iris sat too, beside her on the couch this time.

"Cal," she said again, "why are you here?"

Cal looked at her.

"I might stay here a while," she said. "Find an apartment. A job. I was thinking it would be nice to work in a bookstore. And take some courses. Maybe I'll even enroll in a program. There's a thought."

Her possibilities seemed limitless.

"But that's all sort of long range," Iris said.

"Yes," Cal said, nodding. "I see what you mean. Well, I think I'll drive out to Point Reyes tomorrow, for a day or two."

This last surprised even Cal herself. Once, years ago, when Vivvie had been a visiting professor at Berkeley, she had written to Cal about Point Reyes. Stretches of beaches, isolated except for lovers with bottles of wine, and rare birds. Vivvie had rented a cabin there after her divorce. Her husband had wanted to take their daughter, Karen, back to England to live with him. She had felt revived there, she'd told Cal. There's nothing there but you and the ocean and nature. You realize things.

"Bodega Bay," Iris laughed.

"What?"

"Bodega Bay. Tippi Hedron. *The Birds*. That's out by Point Reyes."

The movie came back to Cal slowly. A sleepy coastal town invaded by birds. She had dropped all the children off at a Beatles movie. *Help*? *A Hard Day's Night*? It was a rainy Saturday afternoon and she'd taken herself to see *The Birds*. Later, over pizza, Mackenzie had tried to explain how Paul's grandfather got kidnapped. But all Cal could think of were those birds, lining up on the telephone wires, planning to attack.

"When are you going?" Iris asked. "Tomorrow?"

Cal nodded.

"The thing is," Iris said, "if Mackenzie shows up, what should I tell her? To wait for you?"

The sun had shifted and the colors from the crystal lay across the couch now in fuzzy stripes.

Cal smoothed the letter on her lap, seeking energy from its words.

It is possible, she thought, to start a new life here.

"Yes," she said to Iris. "Ask her to wait."

CHAPTER SEVENTEEN

S am thought Fisherman's Wharf
smelled awful, like french
fries and fish. He was glad to finally go inside the museum called Believe It or Not. In the window there, the
fattest man in the world sat on a chair and ate pies. The
man was so fat that the chair looked tiny underneath him,
as if it were a child's. Sam wondered why it didn't snap in
two, and send the fat man tumbling to the ground.

The museum was full of amazing things. Aunt Mackenzie read the descriptions to Sam as they wandered
through the rooms. They stood in one of the shoes of the
world's tallest man, and watched a film of a man riding a
miniature bicycle. The bicycle itself was in the museum
and it was the perfect size for a GI Joe. They watched
another film of a man eating a car, piece by piece, the
bumpers and windshields and doors crunching loudly.

"Boys and girls," a voice in the film said, "don't try
this at home."

Sam watched the movie three times. He wondered about his mother's big pink Cadillac. Would it taste like cherries? Or watermelon? An X ray of the man's stomach showed pieces of rusty metal. The man had eaten a Peugeot and a Mercedes Benz, and the Mercedes's logo sat right inside his stomach.

The museum had two sounds. Music and slapping. The music, his aunt told him, was Handel's Water Music.

"Believe it or not," she said, "a man played that tune under water on a violin for sixty-two hours."

Sam didn't believe it. But then again, he had just watched a man eat a car and that didn't seem too believable at first.

The slapping came from a cardboard arm that stuck out of the wall and swung back and forth, slapping two cardboard faces.

"In Russia," his aunt said, "two men in a bar slapped each other in the face for thirty-eight hours."

Sam decided to believe it right away.

There was nothing in the museum about people disappearing and then reappearing. Mackenzie read him a card under a blonde doll sleeping. It said, "Mrs. Helen Jones was in a coma for fourteen years. In 1966 she opened her eyes, sat up, and asked her husband what he wanted for dinner." Mrs. Helen Jones gave Sam a little hope. A coma, in a way, was a little like disappearing. He tried to imagine his father walking in and asking his mother what was for dinner. Something seemed wrong there, though, and Sam couldn't really believe that would happen.

Outside, Sam watched the fat man eating pies. On one side of him were stacks and stacks of empty boxes, and on the other side were piles of pies. As they turned to leave, the fat man waved good-bye to Sam. His fingers were like fat white worms.

The street was lined with people selling things—T-shirts, jewelry, watercolors of the city. On the sidewalk, three black kids danced like robots to music playing from a big radio. People stopped and watched them and put money in a top hat. Down the street a man played the piano, drums, harmonica, and tambourine all at the same time. He shook maracas with his teeth.

Then Sam saw the man who wouldn't talk.

His face was painted white. He was dressed all in black. He came up to Sam and stopped, as if he'd banged his nose on a door. Then, slowly, he opened this imaginary door and stepped through, closing it behind him.

Sam kept waiting for the man to talk. But he didn't. He pretended to climb out a window, lasso a horse, and cut down a tree.

A crowd had gathered, all watching the man.

"Hey, mister," a teenaged girl said. "Can we talk?"

Everyone laughed.

Except Sam, who watched as the man slowly shook his head no.

Why, Sam wondered, hadn't this man disappeared?

Suddenly, a thought struck Sam. A thought so terrible it made him lose his breath and gasp for air. It was only his father who had disappeared when he stopped talking. This man, and Sam, and Helen Keller were all silent, and they just stayed put.

Mackenzie didn't understand why the gentle-faced mime had upset Sam so much. She remembered her mother telling them how frightened Alexander used to be of Santa Claus. Perhaps this was the same type of thing. Cal had said that Alexander used to refuse to sit on Santa's lap. He would hide his face as they passed Santa sitting on his golden throne at the Garden City Shopping Center. Maybe the mime's painted face had seemed ghostly to

Sam, in much the same way as Santa's cotton candy beard and eyebrows had seemed, as Alexander later had recalled, spooky and otherworldly.

The mime, realizing he was frightening the boy, had quickly blown up an orange balloon and twisted it into a dachshund for Sam. Then he made a yellow poodle for Mackenzie. But still Sam had stood, gulping air, pounding his thighs with tightened fists until Mackenzie led him away. She had planned on taking him for a cable car ride, and to Alioto's for dinner. Instead, they went right back to the hotel.

The balloon dogs sat deflating on the bureau. Sam lay on one of the beds, rolled into a ball with his eyes scrunched closed. Mackenzie had ordered them cheese-burgers from room service, but his remained untouched.

She dialed Information. They hadn't come here, after all, to sightsee. She had to find her mother.

"What city?" The voice was nasal and annoyed.

"Do you have a listing for a Cal Porter?" Mackenzie asked. "It would be a very new number."

"Our computers are updated daily. What city?"

The names of the cities around them stretched across Mackenzie's mind. Sausalito. Tiberon. Berkeley.

"San Francisco," she said.

"Sorry," the operator said. She spread the word out as if it were two words. Sor. Ry.

"How about in a different city? A Cal Porter?"

"*What* city?"

"I don't know," Mackenzie said.

"Well, ma'am, neither do I."

Jason would blame the operator's attitude on divesti-ture, Mackenzie thought as she hung up the phone. He argued constantly with the telephone company, refused to pay for calling 411. "Why should I pay thirty cents to get the phone number of someone who's just moved to town?

Or for a new restaurant? There's no other way to get those numbers.'' Every month he subtracted directory assistance charges from his bill. The totals, ninety cents, $2.10, kept growing.

Mackenzie leaned against her pillow. What was she supposed to do now? Comb the city's streets? Go to a detective? Her trip here seemed futile and for a moment she found herself wondering if her mother wanted to vanish. Mackenzie imagined a life in which her mother was just a faraway woman sending postcards.

"No," she said out loud.

She pushed the thoughts away. Everything would work out and they would all be home together again. Her mind drifted back to Jason. Lately he had been talking about buying a co-op together in the East Village. He knew the exact one he wanted. It had white walls and hardwood floors, a fireplace that didn't work, and a staircase that looked like it was straight from a Doris Day movie, curved and white, leading upward to a sleeping loft. "In the morning," he had told her, "you'll descend it like an angel."

He had wanted her to look at it before she'd left for California.

"After this is all settled," she'd said. "When everyone's back home again."

"You sound like a bad John Denver song," he'd told her.

He'd strummed his stomach like guitar strings.

Mackenzie picked up the telephone again.

Jason's phone rang, sounding distant and lost to her, New York seeming like another planet from here. She thought of leaving a message about that apartment. "It sounds," she wanted to say, "like the stairway to heaven." But she stopped herself. She couldn't really imagine doing it yet. The thought of marrying Jason now, the two of them in that apartment hanging his Avalon Ballroom posters and setting up her darkroom, seemed wrong. A betrayal, somehow, to her family. To herself.

His recording clicked off. The tone sounded.

"Well," she said, "we're here."

She tried to sound cheerful, but her voice came out hollow and sad, and she couldn't think of anything else to say.

Outside, the moon shone white and flat against the inky blue sky. It looked, Mackenzie thought, like the round pieces left over after paper has had holes punched in it. It was as if someone had pasted one of those circles in the sky.

Jason's answering machine buzzed once, then turned off.

CHAPTER EIGHTEEN

"**W**hy are you so jumpy about this party?" Willie said.

He lay in bed, smoking a cigarette and watching as Daisy dressed. She had put on three different outfits already, and discarded them all. She turned to him.

"I'm not jumpy," she said.

Willie focused on the wineglass on the bureau. It had a hot pink lipstick smear on the rim. Daisy kept refilling the glass, before it even got empty.

Willie smiled and stretched. She drinks too much, dresses like she should be working 14th Street in D.C., and I'm crazy about her. His wife, Zoe, had been wild too, but in a different way. She was a painter, and she used soft pale ripples of watercolor. Zoe drank like a sailor. Gin. She'd go on binges, days of drinking and crying, acting crazy. Once she'd cut off all of her hair on one of her binges. Her hair used to be so black that it seemed like it had a bluish tint to it, like a midnight sky. Another time, she'd cut his paintings to pieces with a putty knife, giant angry slashes across the canvases.

"What are you smiling about?" Daisy said. She had on parts of different outfits. White spandex pants. An electric blue dress. A feathered headband.

"I like crazy women," he said.

She pulled off the dress and put on a lime green tube top that shimmered like metal.

"Nice," he said.

"I'm not crazy," Daisy said. "I just don't want to go to this party."

"I thought Allison was your friend."

"It's going to be all these IBM types." She rolled her eyes. "Boring."

Willie smiled again.

He found her completely enchanting. She was strangely innocent, despite the bright pink rouge and lipstick. Zoe had had the same vulnerability streaked with toughness.

"Damn you," Daisy said, and threw a white bodysuit spotted with makeup at him. "Quit your smiling."

"I can't help it," he said. "I just realized something."

Her back was to him now. He watched her shoulder blades rotate, slide up and around as she lifted her arms to rub mousse in her hair. The mousse, he knew, was called Pizzazz, and left gold highlights in her hair.

"What?" she said. "Did a light bulb come on over your head or something?"

"More like a bolt of lightning," he said.

Her back twitched.

"What did that bolt of lightning tell you?" Her voice was lazy from the wine.

"It said, 'Willie Forrester, you are in love with Daisy Bloom, the Princess of Pink.' "

Her back stiffened and she let her arms drop to her

sides, leaving a mist of Stiff Stuff hairspray. Why hadn't she told him about Sam and Alexander? she thought.

"That's okay," he said. "You don't have to say 'I love you too.' I'll give you twenty-four hours and then begin my persuasion tactics."

She didn't answer.

"I'm joking," he said. "About the tactics."

The muscles on her back twitched again.

"Daisy," he said.

"I've tried telling you that I'm a terrible person, Willie. I tried to make you go away."

"And I told you that you're not a terrible person. I've slept around a lot myself. And I don't sit home at night and read Great Books. Big deal."

Her shoulder blades made half a revolution as she lifted her arms to her hair again.

"You'll see," she said.

"The Brie," Brad said when they arrived at the party, "is chilled. I'm so sorry."

His voice sounded bored. His face was pink and bland, except for his nose, which had large flaring nostrils like the openings to a cave.

"It's my fault," Allison said. "I thought cheese should be cold. You know."

"Yes," Brad said, staring down at her. "Like Kraft's Singles."

Willie and Daisy smiled nervously.

"That's a good one," Willie said.

Allison laughed, too late and too loud.

She wore a black and white plaid dress with huge shoulder pads that shifted independently of the rest of her skinny body.

"Where did you get that dress?" Daisy whispered as

they followed Brad into the dining room where a bar had been set up.

"It's a Norma Kamali," Allison said.

Daisy stumbled slightly, grabbed Allison's shoulder to steady herself. It felt, she thought, like a bag of marshmallows.

"Daisy, are you drunk?" Allison's eyes opened wide under her slate gray eye makeup.

"I'm in trouble," Daisy mumbled.

"What?"

But they were at the table now. It was lined with every type of liquor and mixer. Crystal bowls held twists of lemon, green olives, wedges of limes, cherries.

Two men drinking martinis stood in front of the bar. One of them had curly blonde hair, the color of Alexander's. He whistled as Daisy walked past him. She smiled, a slow deliberate smile that a man had once called delicious.

"I'll have whatever you're drinking," she said to him.

The other man was small and round, like a Weebel. He kept reaching into the bowl of olives and popping them into his mouth.

"We're having martinis," the round man said.

Daisy watched as Willie went back into the living room with Brad. She thought of the way he'd looked, his reflection in the mirror when he'd told her he loved her. Well, Daisy said to herself, you've really screwed this one up royally.

To the blonde man who was holding a martini out to her she said, "Haven't I seen you around IBM?"

"You're with them too?" he said. "I can't believe I've never seen you."

The round man frowned. "Are you a secretary?"

"No, darling," Daisy said. "I'm in sales."

"Name's Warren Metz," the blonde man said.

"Daisy." She gulped at her drink.

"Whoa, there," Warren said, laughing.

Daisy felt right then as if she were back at the Country Western Playhouse, having a stranger buy her a drink and Allison working on someone else at the bar. She could almost smell the beer and tobacco there. Those men used to make her feel better for a night, make her forget. With them, she'd felt like maybe she wasn't such a bad person after all. A chill came over her. She thought of all those mornings, or late nights, when those men left her alone in bed. She remembered how she'd felt then. Sometimes she'd hear Sam in the hall, and though she never went to see, she always imagined he was standing, sleepy and silent, watching the men leave.

Daisy closed her eyes for an instant and tried to imagine this blonde man—Winston?—doing the two-step with her, pressing her close.

When she opened her eyes, he was standing there in his gray pinstripe suit, his face as pale and bland as Brad's. His friend munched olives.

Daisy laughed.

"I bet you've never done the two-step in your life," she said.

"That's a good one," the friend said. "Two-step."

Allison came in the room and grabbed Daisy by the elbow.

"Come on," she said.

"Hey," Warren said, "I'll keep your spot warm."

Allison brought her into the bathroom and closed the door.

"I'm about to have a nervous breakdown," she said.

"Cold Brie," Daisy said. Her mouth felt numb. She leaned her head against the cold porcelain of the sink. "I'm drunk," she said. "Absolutely."

"It's not just the cheese," Allison said. "It's everything. I don't have the right music. I bought paper plates. Cute ones, I thought. With little snowmen. But Brad said they're tacky. He told me it's a good thing I'm so kooky. He loves women who can make him laugh."

"He's a horse's ass," Daisy said.

"No, he's not. Don't say that."

Daisy lifted her head. The shower curtain, a clear plastic one with penguins on it, seemed to jump at her.

"Fine," she said.

Allison opened the cabinet under the sink and took out the wooden box that used to sit on her coffee table. She lifted the lid and took out a joint.

"I'm about to have a nervous breakdown," she said again.

She lit the joint and sucked on it, then handed it to Daisy.

"Let's leave here," Daisy said. "Let's go to the Country Western Playhouse and pick up some real men. Everyone here looks like a dead fish."

"Count me out," Allison said. "I have struck gold with Brad. I want to be an IBM wife. Move to Maclean or Reston, to a big brick house with pillars in front." She moved her hands gently, like waves. "Maybe I'll even be able to get custody of Brandy."

Daisy inhaled on the joint again. She felt a buzz click on deep inside her head.

"I've been there," she said. "It's not worth it."

Someone knocked on the bathroom door.

"Excuse me," a woman's voice said, "but I've been waiting for quite some time."

Allison put the last of the joint back in the box, then hid the box in the cabinet again.

The woman waiting had her hair in a perfect French braid, with a red velvet bow. A Christmas tree pin on her blazer lapel blinked on and off.

"It's battery operated," she said.

Daisy and Allison laughed. They leaned against the wall and roared.

"Mommy," Brandy said from her room, "what's funny?"

"Oops," Allison said, and went down the hall to her.

Daisy poked her head in the living room.

"Face it," she heard Willie say, "the Giants' defense is unbeatable."

He saw her there and winked.

Daisy felt an ache in her chest. Why hadn't she just told him from the start? Now she was a liar on top of everything else. "I need a drink," she said out loud.

"Well, there you are," Warren said.

The bowl of olives was empty and his friend had started on the cherries.

"You know," the friend said, "I just can't place you in sales. You under Sullivan?"

"Sullivan," she said. "Right."

"So you're on the tenth floor."

Daisy poured herself some vodka. She filled the glass to the top, and when she lifted it, it sloshed everywhere, down her pants and shirt, onto the floor.

"You look drunk," the fat friend said.

Behind them, the woman with the blinking Christmas tree was talking to Brad.

"It's the wrong data base," she said. "Regardless."

"And you," Daisy said, trying to keep her hand steady, "look like a Weebel." But her words slurred so that it sounded like she said, "You look real blue."

"Well, I'm not," he said. "Not at all."

"I need some air," Daisy said.

She went out the kitchen door and leaned against the building. Her head was spinning. She tried to organize her thoughts. But all she could come up with was that Willie

235

was going to leave her. Across the courtyard, someone was having a party too. She watched as the guests lifted their glasses in a toast.

Warren's face, blurred, appeared in front of her.

"How about if I take you home?" he said.

Daisy thought about this. She imagined again that she was in a bar. Warren could take her home and they would get in bed and she'd let him release her from herself. She thought of all those times, the men above her, faceless, freeing her.

"Let me convince you," he said.

She wanted to tell him that wasn't necessary. Hadn't he bought her a drink? Hadn't they danced the two-step?

But he was already kissing her. His kisses were wet like a puppy's, and sour from gin. She let her mouth open, lazily, drunkenly. The pain was subsiding. The hell with Willie, she thought. The hell with Alexander.

Far away, a door slammed.

"What are you doing?" Willie said.

He grabbed Warren by the shoulders and pushed him away.

"I'm just—" Warren said.

"Not you," Willie said.

He faced Daisy.

"You," he said. "What are you doing?"

"Gee," Warren said, "I'm sorry."

Willie waved him away.

"Answer me," he said.

Daisy slid to the ground, felt the cold ground through her pants, the wetness of ice.

"Add liar to the list," she said.

As soon as she'd heard Willie's voice she had started to cry. She tried to wipe her face, but the tears fell too fast.

"What list?" he said.

She shrugged. "You know."

"There is no list."

He sat on the ground beside her.

"I've got a kid," she said. "I was married and I have a six-year-old son. The works. I screwed that all up too."

"You're divorced."

"I would have been but he went and got himself killed."

Her crying overtook her now. She had been trying, she realized, to get back at Alexander ever since that day he drove off and left her behind. She had done exactly what he and all the Porters had expected of her all along. And then he had died, and she had been haunted by him, as if the hold he'd had on her was stronger from the grave. It was as if she really expected him to be watching, to know. Suddenly, sitting here on the cold ground, Daisy realized that she'd never see him again. Never. There was no hold on her. She was, despite her loss and sadness, free.

"You know," she said, "I didn't screw it up. We were all wrong for each other, Alexander and me. I loved him for all the wrong reasons."

Willie put his arm around her.

"Is that locked room your son's?" he said.

She nodded.

"Is he in there?" Willie laughed.

She saw hurt in his eyes and had to look away.

"He's with his aunt. But he'll be back soon."

It took all of her energy to face him again.

"Do you want to leave?" she said.

"No," he said. "I want to stay."

CHAPTER NINETEEN

The sun was warm on her face. Cal opened her eyes and looked around, confused, sad. Her hand reached instinctively for Jams.

"Jams," she said softly.

She had expected to find herself beside him in their four-poster bed, the posts reaching upward like spires on a minaret. She had expected to look down and see the pale green and salmon pattern of the rug that had sat beside their bed for years. Raised flowers, one small bird in cornflower blue atop one of them.

She touched the unfamiliar wall beside her. Someone had stuck stars on it, metallic green and blue and red ones, the type schoolchildren got on their papers. Cal thought she could pick out Orion's belt, the arrow in Sagittarius. But that was all.

The windows were curtainless, the room empty except for the twin bed she'd slept on and bookshelves made of bricks and boards. The night before she had read the titles of the few books left behind. *Developmental Psychology. Abnormal Behavior. Walden Two.* She had studied a photograph that leaned against the books. In it, a young man with a flowing beard played a guitar while sitting cross-legged on the bed in this very room, the stars behind him.

Cal's hand trembled slightly as she pushed her hair from her face. She tried to imagine her ride to Point Reyes. She had called ahead and reserved a cabin. Her two days there, she thought, would give her strength. There would be whales in the distance, swimming off the coast. And cranes on the sand with her. She would have picnics on the beach, and collect shells and driftwood, the way she had when she was a child. If she found a sand dollar, she would paint it with colored chalk, the way she and Hope used to. Bright pink and turquoise.

Cal's mind lingered on the image of her sister. How was she? Cal wondered. She thought of Hope from long ago, before Ricardo Havana had come into her life, before any of it had happened and she and Cal had lived a safe childhood in that house. Cal remembered the way they would huddle together in bed, their bodies smelling of lilac talc, Hope's soft stomach pressed against Cal's back. "When we grow up," Hope would whisper, "let's be famous ladies." Her breath smelled of milk and Pepsodent. "All right," Cal would say. "Let's move to Paris or Argentina and dance in fancy slippers." Sometimes, before bedtime, they would practice dancing together, their bathrobes twirling taffeta dresses, their hair fastened by an imaginary jeweled tiara. Years later, Cal would watch her own children do the jitterbug together. "Look, Mommy," Mackenzie would say, "I'm Gidget." "I'm Moon Doggie," Alexander would say.

Cal heard voices outside the bedroom. She thought

again of her days ahead, in the cabin at Point Reyes. The sea there, she imagined, was full of abalone, their shells sparkling, bone and purple.

The night before, in a mood for celebration over her poems' acceptance, Cal had offered to buy Iris dinner.

"Name the spot," she'd said. After all this time alone, the idea of company had appealed to Cal. Even Iris Bloom's.

I made it, she'd thought. I am in San Francisco.

"We'll even have champagne," she'd added.

Iris had frowned, and Cal wondered if Iris drank. She had still been expecting some cult oddity to surface.

"That sounds great," Iris had said. "But I already have plans tonight."

"Oh." Cal had felt disappointed. She wanted, suddenly, to talk to someone. Or even to just listen. She could ask Iris Bloom why she'd dyed her hair purple, then sit back and listen to the story. The thought of another silent dinner distressed her.

"My boyfriend," Iris had said, "does a stand-up act in Los Gatos every Thursday. It's just a hobby, really. But he is such a riot. You should hear him." Iris had laughed at some remembered joke.

Cal had pictured herself at a restaurant. Linen tablecloths and candlelight. "Table for one," she'd say, and watch the San Francisco Bay below.

"I'm sure it's not your thing," Iris had added, "but you could come with me to see Lloyd. They serve great chicken wings there."

"Chicken wings," Cal had said. "Well, that sounds fine."

She had imagined a dinner of crab and a good white wine, but felt so tangled with emotion that she opted to be with Iris in her bar in Los Gatos instead.

"You know," Iris had said before they left, 'I'll never forget the way your house used to look at Christmas time.

It was like stepping into the pages of the *Saturday Evening Post*."

Cal had had to turn away from Iris. Her words hit her like a punch. My God, Cal thought, it was like that. There were white poinsettias on every table. Silver bells hung from the front door and tinkled musically when it opened.

"It really was lovely," Cal had said.

"Mrs. Porter, I was wondering something. Do you think you'd help me decorate my place? I mean, my family was never very big on traditional things like that. Last year I went to buy some decorations and I got overwhelmed. There was so much to choose from. Lights and little Santas and wreaths. I didn't end up buying anything."

Cal and Iris had gone shopping, and bought fresh boughs of pine tied with red ribbons. They strung red lights on Iris's avocado tree. Cal had gotten an urge, surrounded by the smell of fresh pine and the glow of Christmas lights, to call her family. But they were all scattered, distant. She wondered about Jams, all alone. Had he bothered to go up to the attic and bring down the boxes that were marked in green ink: *X-mas decorations*? In one were the stockings that they hung from the mantel on Christmas Eve. She thought of the droopy candy-cane-striped one with *Alexander* across the top, the letters stitched long ago, cramped together so they'd all fit. Mackenzie's had a big *M* on it in silver glitter.

"You need a Christmas stocking," Cal had told Iris. She gave her one of her own knee socks—an old one of Mackenzie's, actually—with a blue and white reindeer and snowflake pattern on it.

Then they had driven to Los Gatos.

COMEDY NITE, the sign outside said.

They ate spicy chicken wings, dipping them in blue cheese dressing, and drank Anchor Steam beer. Amateur comics came on, bathed in a too-bright spotlight. Cal had laughed at all of their jokes. A bald man who couldn't get dates. A divorced woman down on men and stewardesses. A Chicano telling Mexican jokes. She couldn't imagine actually standing up in front of a room full of strangers and talking about her own faults or infirmities.

Lloyd Gray was short and husky with a tuft of white hair amid a head of black curls.

"I am dull," he'd said in a monotone.

I left my family, Cal thought, pretending the spotlight was on her, the faces turned toward her.

"Even my name is dull."

Bad mother. Bad wife.

"Gray Gray."

Iris had touched Cal's hand lightly.

"Didn't I tell you?" she'd whispered. "He's a riot."

Lloyd had driven back into the city with them. His voice never wavered or rose. He *is* dull, Cal had thought.

Now Cal went into Iris's kitchen. Purple flowered wallpaper showed faintly through a coat of white paint. At the small round table, Iris sat with a woman so thin her bones poked at her skin, sharp and white. Her hair hung down like dried husks of corn to her shoulders.

"And," the woman was saying, "I'm allergic to dust."

Her eyes scanned the room for hidden lint.

Iris nodded and jotted something in a notebook.

"So," Iris said, "that's cats, smoke, and dust."

Cal cleared her throat, a habit Jams had that had always irritated her.

Iris and the woman looked up.

"Hi," Iris said.

"I'm going to get started," Cal said. After her dream, she felt the ocean beckoning to her, offering solace, answers. "I'm sorry to interrupt but I wanted to tell you good-bye."

"We're having a roommate interview," Iris said.

The woman extended a bony hand, like a skeleton reaching from the grave.

"I'm Judith."

Cal nodded, shook the hand that was offered. It was cold and damp.

"It's a nice sunny room," Cal said.

"Then why are you moving?"

Iris laughed. "She's just a guest."

Cal inhaled. The apartment smelled like Christmas. From the living room, she could see the red lights twinkle. She went in and sat on the couch. The prism swallowed the red glow and sent it back out, pink, magenta, purple. Cal wrote on the back of a postcard shaped like the state of Idaho. On the front it said FAMOUS POTATOES.

"Mackenzie," she wrote, "back on Sunday. Wait."

The pen hovered over the card. She should write more, but nothing else came to her.

At the top of the stairs, she handed it to Iris, who had joined her to say good-bye.

"In case Mackenzie comes," Cal said.

"I thought Iowa had potatoes."

"No," Cal said. "Idaho."

"All those I states," Iris said.

Cal smiled, anxious to get on her way.

"Thanks for helping me with the decorations," Iris said.

"It was fun," Cal said, although at night the simple act had haunted her. She had lay in bed, feeling guilty and vaguely homesick, imagining all the Christmases past. She had thought of herself and Hope in that house, and then of her own children, and had been unable to sleep. How, she had wondered, had she wound up in California with Iris Bloom stringing lights on an avocado tree? She had read *Abnormal Behavior*, case studies on schizophrenics and multiple personalities, until dawn. Below her, a drunk had shouted obscenities against Lyndon Johnson.

"I'll probably have to take Judith," Iris said. "She's totally macrobiotic."

Cal nodded. "Well."

She turned to go down the stairs.

"Wait," Iris said. "Lloyd would really like to do your name."

"Do my name?" Cal said. She imagined Lloyd, in his monotone, making jokes about her to a group of strangers.

"He changed my life," Iris said.

Cal looked down at the card Iris had handed her. Pale gray background with dark gray print. LLOYD GRAY. NAME THERAPIST.

"Uncover your true self through your name," Iris said. "Iris is the goddess of rainbows, you know. Lloyd says there may be something in your name. Cal. And here you are in California."

"It's Caroline," Cal said. The name seemed unfamiliar on her lips.

"Oh," Iris said, disappointed.

CHAPTER TWENTY

Jason sat in the empty apartment. He imagined the wayang puppets that Mackenzie had bought in Indonesia hanging on one wall, his own Avalon Ballroom posters on another. There was a small room off the kitchen, what the realtor, Mindy, had referred to as a junior bedroom. Mackenzie, he thought, could use it as a darkroom. The building itself had a great doorway, which screamed to be photographed. The edges were bordered with a pineapple motif. "Pineapples," Mindy had told him, "mean welcome."

"Jason?"

He turned without getting up. Mindy stood in the doorway. She had very black hair, held back by a red and white bow. The bottom left lens of her glasses had a big rhinestone *M*.

"I didn't even hear you," he said.

She touched his arm with the tips of her bright red fingertips. He had only met her twice, and each time she had been perfectly color coordinated. He wondered if she did her nails every night to match the next day's outfit. Mackenzie's were short and square, covered in a clear gloss.

"The apartment gets you, doesn't it?" she said. She had a disconcerting air of familiarity. "And how about this view?"

She craned her neck, stood on tiptoe.

"I think," Mindy said, "yes, that's the World Trade Center off to the right."

Jason had lived his entire childhood, right up until he had left for college, in a suburb outside of Chicago. He hardly remembered the neighborhood, a blur of split-level homes and manicured lawns. The air, he recalled, was the cleanest air he'd ever smelled. Crisp. In his bedroom he'd hung a mobile of spaceships, and had followed each rocket's launching with an intense fascination. He used to write to Cape Canaveral. "Please," he'd said, "let me be an astronaut." But by junior high, he'd replaced the rockets with black light posters. His parents wouldn't allow him to get the black light that turned them into neon, and so they hung, pale, on his walls.

It was a neighborhood that people left. Families moved out all the time, to better neighborhoods or cities on one of the coasts, Boston, Seattle, Savannah. Only the Fines stayed. And the Adlers, their next-door neighbors, whose father drank and never got promoted or transferred. Jason's parents moved to Sarasota, Florida, after the children had all left home. They lived in another split-level house, this one smaller, and painted turquoise. It sat right on the ninth hole of a golf course. At least once a month, a stray golf ball shattered the glass on the sliding glass door that led to their patio.

The Adler's son, Steve, who had been Jason's best friend growing up, lived on East 88th Street now, and invited Jason to wine and cheese parties, and Trivial Pursuit tournaments. Adler kept intricate notes on all the tournament players, lists of questions that had stumped them, and their weakest and strongest categories. "Been brushing up on that science?" he always asked Jason. As teenagers they had hitchhiked to New York to hear the Beatles play at Shea Stadium. They had been fifteen years old, and, unable to get tickets, had sat in the parking lot to listen. "The fucking Beatles," Adler had said, over and over, in amazement. When John Lennon had died, Adler called Jason and cried.

Sometimes, Jason asked Adler what he remembered about their neighborhood. "It was dull," he'd said, "but a good place to grow up. I guess."

"I've got to be honest with you, Jason," Mindy said. "This place is a real steal. It will be scooped up quickly. If not sooner."

Jason remembered sitting in the parking lot of Shea Stadium, the Beatles's singing barely heard above the crowd's screams, and thinking that New York City was the best place on earth.

"Hey," Mindy said. She snapped her fingers. A loud click. "Where are you?"

"Shea Stadium."

"Right," she said. "The Yankees?"

Adler would say she'd have to brush up on her orange category. Sports and leisure.

Jason stood. The kitchen floor was covered with large black and white squares. The Formica that lined the countertops was pink. "Very sort of art deco-ish," Mindy had said. He wondered if Mackenzie would like that. She talked so much, and so fondly of her family's house, recalling everything in great detail. "How can you not remember what your family's kitchen looked like?" she had said, exasperated. "You lived there your whole life." He pictured, faintly, daisies or mums on the wallpaper, big and yellow, opened wide. But that seemed more like a house he'd seen in a movie once. Or a television show. "That was either our kitchen wallpaper," he'd said, "or the Cleavers'. I can't remember which." The Porters' dining room walls were painted a clay red, with white borders. "How can you not remember?" she'd said.

"Yes," Mindy said, following his gaze. "The kitchen is fabulous." She did a few quick tap steps, her red cowboy boots Shuffling off to Buffalo across the big squares, a happy housewife with shining floors.

"You know what, Mindy?" Jason said. "I've got to walk around and think about it some."

Her smile didn't falter for a second. "Of course," she said. "Absolutely."

He was thinking that he had to buy it. He had to live here with Mackenzie, have her perfume in the air, the smell of photography chemicals faint behind it, the bathroom full of her powders and lotions, their square white bottles trimmed in silver, lining every shelf. He was thinking how he'd remember forever that the kitchen walls were stark white against the pink countertops.

Mindy looked at her watch, a slow and deliberate gesture.

"I've got a couple coming to look at it in about twenty minutes," she said. "If they want to take it . . ." Her voice trailed off and she gave a helpless shrug.

He was thinking that Mackenzie would be furious if he bought it without talking to her first.

"You can let yourself out?" Mindy said. "I'm going to just sit here and wait for them."

On the stairway, a small boy pushed a fire truck back and forth, bored. Inside, a round head with a fireman's hat sat at the wheel, featureless and bodyless.

"Zoom," the boy said. "Zoom."

"Got to get that fire out," Jason said. If he lived here, he thought, he'd see the boy every day.

"Fire?" the boy said.

Jason pointed to the truck.

"There's no fire," the boy said. "It's just a toy."

Jason walked around the block, pretending this was his neighborhood. Here's where we'd buy the paper, he thought. Here's where we'd come for milk when we ran out. He looked at all the doorways in the buildings he passed. When he talked to Mackenzie he would give her every detail, every smell, every great doorway.

He wondered if there really was a couple coming to look at the place. Or perhaps Mindy was using some sales techniques she'd learned in real estate class. Always make them think someone else wants it too. When he'd moved out to LA with Amanda he'd had to buy a car. After so many years in Manhattan, cars had seemed strange to him, the act of driving ridiculous. The car salesmen had bantered and joked with him, avoiding his questions, changing prices and deals. Finally, tired of all the games, he'd bought a green Dodge Dart, square and plain like someone's old uncle's car, bought it only because the salesman had had no bargaining points with it. It was ugly and had no extras, not even a radio. It was exactly what it seemed. Amanda had refused to ride in it with him. "Honestly, Jason," she had said when he drove it home, "why do you do these things to me?" She'd given him a red Ferrari matchbox car the next day.

Except for his time with Amanda, he'd lived in New York City for almost ten years. Like his neighborhood near Chicago, it had never seemed like home to him, but rather just where he lived. A place. Since Mackenzie had moved here, though, it was full of personality and meaning to him. The streets and corners were suddenly familiar and dear. It was true he could be totally immune to his environment, sit inside for days working without even lifting his shades, then walk outside to discover there had been a snowstorm, or to his complete surprise find that spring had arrived, or that the building next door was gone. But with Mackenzie, he was constantly aware of his surroundings. He'd found a row of wooden houses with small plots of lawns, a touch of suburbia off Sixth Avenue. The smells of cardamom and coriander pulled him into the Indian grocery on Lexington. Every doorway was beautiful. He felt like he had a home.

She has to move into that apartment with me.

As a child, immersed in Gemini and Apollo space programs, he'd been convinced there would be men on the moon sometime soon. He'd imagined cities there, shiny and silver. "Be serious," his father used to say. When Neil Armstrong walked on the moon, Jason had been sure anything was possible.

Maybe she'll really do it, he thought.

He was in front of the building again. The pineapples carved above the door were delicate scalloped ovals. Welcome.

Inside, the little boy and his truck were gone. Jason smelled chocolate, brownies, or a cake baking.

Mindy sat alone on the windowsill, looking out in the direction of the World Trade Center. Her jacket puffed out around her like a gentle red parachute.

"Back already?" she said when he came in.

"I want it," he said. "Call that couple and tell them not to come."

She smiled. Her lipstick was fading, and as if she was aware of that, she touched her mouth lightly. "This is fantastic, Jason," she said. "The apartment is so you."

He wanted her to go now. Already, the apartment felt like it was his and Mackenzie's, and the realtor seemed an intruder. He wanted to fill the apartment with things for Mackenzie, corny things. A cross-stitched sampler that said Home Sweet Home. Towels embossed with His and Hers. A geranium in a pot.

"Call the other couple, okay?" he said.

"Oh. I have a feeling they won't show," Mindy said. "Do you want to come back to my office and fill out the preliminary papers?"

"Sure," he said. "In a minute."

"I'll meet you there?" she said.

He nodded.

He wanted Mackenzie there with him, and Mozart playing in the background. He wanted Mindy gone.

"I guess you want to let it sink in," she said.

He nodded again.

When she finally left, he stood in the middle of the empty living room and closed his eyes. Already the details of the apartment were clear to him. The kitchen floor, the painted border around this room. He heard the violins of a Mozart concerto rising, rising around him.

When Mackenzie was in junior high, she used to have a black and white poster of Paul Newman taped to her bedroom wall. In the poster, his eyes were in color. A vivid blue. She would sit for hours in her room, gazing at those eyes. She remembered the first time her mother saw it, the way she was startled by the blueness of Paul Newman's eyes.

She had laughed at first, then, running her fingers around the poster's edges, had turned to Mackenzie, angry.

"This isn't taped up here, is it?"

Mackenzie had laughed, not used to seeing her mother so angry.

"How else would it stay up there? Magic?"

She had laughed when she said it. Cal usually joined in with a joke, but this time she hadn't.

"You are going to ruin these walls. The tape will pull the paint off. Don't you care about anything? I'm tired of all of this. Of no one caring about anything."

Mackenzie had refused to take the poster down. Years later, the outline of it was still marked off on the wall by yellowed squares of tape, a perfect poster-shaped outline.

She remembered this as Sam sorted through posters in a store on Union Street. He stood at a bin of old movie stills, and stared into the soulful eyes of Bette Davis, Vivien Leigh, and Humphrey Bogart as if they knew something that he needed to know too. Watching him, Mackenzie thought of those blue Paul Newman eyes staring down at her. A girlfriend, she remembered, used to say before she undressed, "Cover your baby blues, Paul."

The door opened and a woman walked in quickly. Her head was bent and Mackenzie glimpsed a wavy crown of chestnut. For an instant, she thought it was her mother. But then the woman looked in her direction and she saw that the face was too wide, the eyes too green.

Sometimes, after Alexander died, Mackenzie would see a man pass her and she would think, for a fast moment, by his gait, or the color of his hair, that it was her brother. She wanted to reach for him, stop him. Alexander is alive, she'd think, until the man moved closer. Then she would see that he was a taller man, or fatter, that his eyes were not Alexander's at all. And Mackenzie would have to admit to herself that Alexander would not ever be seen again, coming out of a restaurant, or holding a pretty girl's hand.

Since she'd been in San Francisco, she had scanned every crowd for her mother, knowing that someone with Cal's hair or walk could indeed be Cal herself. Mackenzie had a fear that she would really pass her mother on the street, and Cal would ignore her, refuse to talk. She imagined screaming to her, "Mom, it's me. It's Mackenzie," and Cal just continuing to walk, disappearing over one of the city's dropping hills, or into the fog.

Sam held a black and white poster of Charlie Chaplin in his hands. His face was pressed close to it, as if Charlie Chaplin were whispering very softly to him.

What is he thinking? Mackenzie wondered. She sometimes had the urge to shake the boy. Talk, she wanted to shout at him. But she knew that he wouldn't respond, but instead would turn his face from hers. It would be like her brother turning away. With Sam, she found herself pretending he was Alexander and they were both children together again. In the fantasy she could keep him safe. And then Sam would do something uniquely Sam and again Mackenzie would have to remind herself that Alexander was dead.

That had happened on the cable cars this morning. She and Sam had ridden them over and over, up and down the hills, zigzagging the city. It was what Alexander would do, the same thing, again and again. Every time they reached the end of a run, Sam got right back on the next car. He stood in the open doorway and let the wind blow through his hair, his mouth opened.

In Chinatown, a woman got on with a pair of twin daughters, and Sam had made a face behind their back, a face that looked, to Mackenzie, very much like Daisy. And she had had to remind herself that Alexander was dead, they were not children again.

"Enough," she had said. "I'm hungry."

Sam was disappointed and at Sears, where she ordered him a large order of sourdough french toast, he refused to eat.

"This is a very special treat," she'd said, feeling guilty for making him get off the cable car.

She wished she could crawl into his head, even for a few minutes. Here he was, far from Daisy, but not seeming homesick or sad at all. He seemed, instead, like he was waiting for something, always.

Sam still held the Charlie Chaplin poster.

"Do you want this?" she asked him.

He nodded.

Earlier, she had tried to buy him a souvenir in an attempt to befriend him again. A metal cable car, painted a brick red with yellow trim. But he had refused it, still angry at her.

"Do you know who Charlie Chaplin was?" Mackenzie asked him after they had left the store.

Sam smiled. He clutched the rolled poster and swung it like a cane as he walked, bowlegged ahead of her.

"Where did you learn that?" she laughed.

For a split second then, the way he looked at her, Mackenzie was sure he was going to answer her. That he was going to talk right out loud.

"Sam," she said, her voice only slightly more than a whisper, "who taught you to walk like Charlie Chaplin?"

She kneeled in front of him, remembering how Alexander had once pretended to eat his shoe, copying Charlie Chaplin, and Mackenzie had run to their mother screaming that Alexander was eating leather. Cal had sat on the floor and laughed uncontrollably while Mackenzie had watched in horror.

"Sam," she said again.

But the moment had passed and she knew he was not going to speak. He looked past her, down the steeply sloping hill that seemed to disappear into the water below. She had promised to take him down the crookedest street in the world.

"Come on," she said, "I think you're ready for Lombard Street."

*   *   *

The last thing Mackenzie wanted to do was go to Iris Bloom's. Once, when Alexander and Daisy were dating, Mackenzie had gone with him to the Blooms' house. It had smelled like food, an overwhelming odor of barbecue sauce, Fritos, and french fries. Mrs. Bloom had given her a glass of milk with a smudge of salmon lipstick on the rim. "The furniture," Mrs. Bloom had told her, "is contemporary Danish." Iris had sat beside Mackenzie on the aqua couch, and had stared into her eyes. "Is your hair dyed?" she'd asked her finally. "No," Mackenzie had said. The couch, she remembered, had low cushions and blonde wood trim. Iris had kept staring. "I believe you," she'd said after a while, as if Mackenzie had passed some sort of test. Iris had shown her some turquoise and silver jewelry then, triangular earrings and a bracelet and ring that some boy had given her. He had a strange name, like Stick. Or Stone. He had bought the jewelry in New Mexico. "Someday," Iris had whispered to her, "I'm going west."

Sitting there at the Blooms', Mackenzie had kept thinking about Emma Matlock. Every summer, when school ended, Alexander and Mackenzie took the train to New York and spent a weekend with Emma at her mother's apartment. The lobby of the building had marble floors, and chandeliers that sparkled like glass rainbows. From the Matlocks' windows, they could look down on the Hudson River and all the lights of the city. Emma always took Mackenzie on a shopping spree, to Saks and Bergdorf's, then to Rumplemeyer's for ice cream in silver bowls.

The walls of the Matlocks' apartment were covered with masks from all over the world. "Africa. Java. Japan," Mrs. Matlock would say, her voice soft like Emma's, as she pointed to the different masks. Years later, as Mackenzie had watched the news and had seen, over and over, where John Lennon had been shot, she'd recognized the

Matlocks' building in the background. She had called Alexander. "That's Emma's building," she'd said. "I know," he'd told her. "So what?"

That day at the Blooms', she'd thought of the quietness of Emma's apartment, and the damp, junglelike smell from all the exotic plants that filled it.

"How can you go out with someone like Daisy Bloom?" she'd asked her brother as they drove home.

The top on the Mustang was down, and she had breathed in the clean autumn air.

Alexander had slammed on the brakes, had stopped the car right in the middle of the street.

"Don't you ever ask me that again," he'd said.

At Iris Bloom's apartment in San Francisco, Mackenzie expected to find the same stale food smell, the same furniture. She was surprised when Iris opened the door, dressed normally except for one ear laden with stud earrings from top to bottom.

"Your hair," Mackenzie said.

Iris laughed.

"That's just what your mother said."

When, Mackenzie wondered, had her mother seen Iris? She was certain Iris had not been to Alexander's funeral. She had, Mackenzie remembered, sent a fruit basket, a large carved watermelon as if they were having a luau instead of a burial.

"Now, Sam," Iris was saying, "tell me all about your adventures. I understand your Aunt Mackenzie whisked you off to Rhode Island."

They followed Iris into the living room. There, behind an avocado tree draped with red lights, hung one of Mackenzie's own socks.

Iris chattered to Sam about his name.

"Samson," she said, "means sun. Like sunshine. Isn't that lovely?"

Sam shrugged as he stared into a large pyramid-shaped crystal.

"Of course, I know your name is just Sam, not Samson, but it's something to think about."

"That's my sock," Mackenzie said.

Alexander had given her those knee socks one Christmas. Blue and white with reindeer and snowflakes. One of the reindeer had had a red rhinestone nose that fell off long ago.

"It is?" Iris said. "I thought it was your mother's."

Mackenzie sunk into the bright purple bean bag chair, exhausted. She wanted, more than anything now, to crawl into her own bed in the house in Rhode Island, with stenciled flowers on the headboard and the smell of winter and Christmas everywhere, and to sleep. When she awoke, Alexander would be there and her father would be well and Cal would stroke her head and tell her it had all been a bad dream. Like Dorothy in *The Wizard of Oz*. She would look up and point to them all and say, "You were there and you were there and it's so good to be home."

The fact that Cal had been to Iris Bloom's seemed preposterous. But there was Mackenzie's sock, and Iris was holding out a postcard.

"She left this for you," Iris said.

FAMOUS POTATOES.

"Idaho," Mackenzie said.

"Actually," Iris said, "she's up at Point Reyes. To reflect."

"She's had three months to reflect," Mackenzie said.

She looked at the cryptic message.

"Mackenzie, back on Sunday. Wait."

"Is this it?"

"Yes."

Mackenzie tried to call to mind one of the images of

her mother that had filled her these past months, but instead remembered her sitting alone on the beach at Cape Cod. It was late, the stars so plentiful it seemed like they could be plucked from the sky, picked like fruit from a low-hanging bough. The tide had rushed in, wrapped around her ankles. Mackenzie had wanted to call to her, had been gripped with fear as Cal stared out, not at the sea, but beyond. Suddenly, her mother had turned and, seeing Mackenzie, had waved and walked to her. What she felt now was like that fear that her mother would not come back to her.

"My mother and I used to stay up and watch the late movies together after everyone else went to bed," Mackenzie said. If she said it out loud, it made it more real than the other memory. "She knows every line from some of those. Like *Stella Dallas*. And *Dark Victory* with Bette Davis. 'Prognosis negative, right, doctor?' " In recalling those nights now, Mackenzie wondered if her mother had been looking beyond her too as they sat together.

"Do you want your sock back?" Iris asked.

Somehow, her mother relinquishing that sock so easily to Iris Bloom disturbed Mackenzie, even though she herself had left it at home, tucked carelessly in a drawer, its mate long gone, eaten by the dryer or lost somewhere. The red rhinestone nose, she remembered, had sparkled so in the box.

What Christmas was that? Before Sam was born, when Alexander had lived in New York.

With a jolt, Mackenzie realized that this Christmas had passed unnoticed. She and Sam had spent it riding cable cars and taking a taxi down Lombard Street, his eyes growing wider at every jagged corner. He had squeezed her hand, afraid, she supposed, of dropping into the Bay that glittered below them. The radio in the cab had played Christmas music, Burl Ives and Perry

Como. Thirty-six hours of cheer, the disc jockey had promised. For dinner they'd eaten in Chinatown. Sam had picked out a pair of Chinese slippers with pink and turquoise flowers embroidered on the toe for Brandy. Outside, in the distant sky, someone sent off fireworks, thick clouds of chalky red and blue exploding beneath a half-moon.

"No," Mackenzie said. "I don't want the sock. It used to have one reindeer with a sparkly red nose."

"Rudolph," Iris said.

Just a year ago, Mackenzie thought, she and Alexander had sat together under the Christmas tree and talked about every ornament that hung above them, the decorations a history of their childhood, and their mother's childhood. They had searched, as they did every year, for the apple ornaments. They were red and slightly misshapen, the paint chipped and the white ink across them faded. But the names were still legible. HOPE. CAL. It had been a ritual every year, to find those ornaments. Last year, as Alexander had reached deep into the tree's branches for one of those apples, pine needles had showered down onto him. When Mackenzie brushed them away, she had seen strands of silver in her brother's hair. She had held her hand there, slightly above him, the silver and dark blonde dusted with pine, for a moment, frozen.

CHAPTER TWENTY-ONE

Cal sat on the beach at Point Reyes, behind a dune covered with scratchy brown grass. The wind whistled like a chorus of men singing to her. She held her thick hair in one hand to keep it out of her face. There was sand in her mouth and in the picnic food she'd brought with her. She wiped some off the Monterey jack cheese.

Alexander had been the only person who knew she was a fraud, she thought.

Not long before he died, she'd met him in Boston for lunch, at an outdoor cafe in Fanueil Hall. The Flower Garden, it was called. But there had been no garden. Just a view of a nearby greenhouse, with pots of tulips and lilies and daffodils in front.

Cal had arrived there early, and sat amid the Saturday afternoon tourists, feeling like a foreigner herself. She had watched as Alexander approached, and had been struck by his manliness, his adultness. He had had his hair cut short, and it looked blonder that way, the top slightly bristled. She had remembered, watching him come toward her, the crew cuts he'd had as a child, sitting in the barber's chair, scowling. She'd felt, suddenly, very old and tired.

Alexander had studied the wine list with great interest.

"What do you say, Mom?" he'd asked her, and pointed to a wine.

It was as if he'd gone from a teenager to a man overnight. All of his years with Daisy seemed remote then. The girl had always seemed an unpleasant intrusion, interrupting the family and keeping Alexander away. Now, here he was, back again, and Cal had been taken by surprise, not only at the sight of him as he tasted the wine and flirted with the waitress, but also at herself. Her children were grown, she'd realized, and her life had become endless nights of playing cribbage and staring into the darkness as she lay in bed beside Jams, feeling empty. At least when the children were small, they had kept her occupied, busy.

They'd had almost the entire bottle of wine before Alexander had brought up the subject. He'd talked first about the summer class he was teaching—"On that all time favorite trio, Hemingway, Faulkner, and Fitzgerald," he'd laughed. He'd told her that he wanted to take Sam to the Cape. "You have good memories from there?" she'd asked, needing to hear that he had been a happy child, that she had done something right.

That was when he'd said it.

"You know, I always felt while I was growing up that you'd rather be someplace else than where you were." He'd looked at his glass of wine instead of at her. "I mean, you did all the right things for us. More than what would be expected. But somehow I always felt it wasn't what you wanted to be doing. Like you wished you could disappear from us and reappear someplace else."

They had both stared at his wine, swirling in the glass, making a red web.

"Remember when we all went to the Ice Capades?" he'd said.

"Mackenzie's birthday."

"I remember Mackenzie asked you if you could have any one thing there, what would it be. She said she'd like the ladies' blue sparkling suit and white skates. You said—"

"The freedom." Cal lifted her head, thought of that lovely black-haired woman dressed in glittering blue, a blue that twinkled like stars in the spotlight and ice. That woman had stood alone on the clean ice, her skates scratching as she swooped around and her hair blowing in the gentle breeze. And then she had lifted one leg, and held her arms above her head as she turned, faster and faster, a swirl of shiny, sparkling blue.

"The skater's freedom," Alexander said, and looked up.

"Did Mackenzie think that too? That I was distant?"

Alexander laughed. "Mackenzie thinks that you are the greatest mother that ever lived."

"And you think otherwise."

"I know that you love us," he'd said quickly.

She'd tried to act casual. Inside, though, she was shaking. She had been found out, exposed.

"Nowadays, everyone wonders about these things," she'd said. She'd tried to pour more wine and it splattered on the tablecloth. "Should I have children? Be a working mother? Can I have it all?"

"I always sensed a distance," Alexander had said.

Their eyes met. In that instant she'd known that she could tell him everything. She had thought too of Guatemala, of the bird that can't live in captivity.

But she'd only smiled at him, waved her hand between them as if she were erasing a blackboard.

"Are you saying I was a bad mother? Like Cinderella's?"

"That was her stepmother."

"All right. Like Cinderella's *step*mother."

He'd smiled too, but hesitatingly.

"You were," he'd said, "the model mother. Brownie leader, PTA chairman, gourmet cook—"

"Enough," Cal had said. "Enough."

Now she found herself wishing she had told him the truth that day. For years, she should have said, I planned escapes. From your father, that house, all of it.

She remembered how, when she had been pregnant with Alexander, she had felt the trap closing, snapping shut on her. Missy had been pregnant too. She would show Cal charts of her baby's movements. "He's very nocturnal," she'd told Cal proudly. Missy used to call her every day, with questions. Do you have nausea? Fatigue? Cravings? While Cal, for months, denied it all. No, no, no, she'd told Missy. I have nothing.

The night she went into labor, she had sat and watched Ted Mack's Amateur Hour, pretending for as long as she could that there was no pain, no baby. Her mother and Jams had packed her overnight bag, a round, pale blue Samsonite filled with new nightgowns. Coral silk trimmed in lace, a blue flannel with tiny pink flowers, a yellow with a matching robe. All with color coordinated slippers. "Let's go," Jams had kept saying as her mother held up *New Yorkers*, their covers flashing in front of Cal. Children sledding. A teapot on lace. "Have you read this one?" her mother asked each time. "There's a good Cheever."

All the while, Cal had ignored them both. She'd concentrated instead on the dancing dogs on the television. Poodles with tutus and party hats. Until finally she'd had to go.

In the hospital she'd shared a room with a woman named Connie. They'd sat in bed, both in new nightgowns. Connie reading movie magazines, sharing the stars' secrets with Cal, who stared straight ahead at the spotted green hospital wall, the *New Yorkers* stacked beside her.

"What are you naming him?" Connie asked her every day as they each fed their sons.

Cal never answered. She would stare at this little pink baby, count his fingers and toes, and wait for her maternal instinct to come, the way Connie's had and Missy's had. "I watch her all night," Missy had told her. "I watch her breathe. And say her name. Kathy. Kathy. Kathy. Like a song. You'll see what I mean soon enough." But she didn't.

"Here we are," Connie had said their last morning there. "Two nameless babies."

Cal had looked down at her sleeping son. He was bald, which meant, according to Missy, that he would be blonde. Vivvie had sent a bottle of champagne from Persia. At the bottom of the card she'd written in Arabic, the lines unfamiliar and complex.

"He's Alexander," Cal had said.

"Great." Connie had told her. "I'll name mine Alexander too. I've been thinking of Cary. Like Cary Grant. But this is better. Alexander the Great. An emperor, right? A ruler?"

What had happened to all of them? Cal wondered. To Missy and Kathy and the other Alexander? She herself had gone home and watched Alexander sleep, repeated his name like a litany, waited for rapture. He had been right, her adult son. She had wanted to be someplace else, someone else. The skater in shining blue. The mistress of a Portuguese fisherman. And the more she wanted it, the more she'd baked and thrown birthday parties and invited other mothers over for coffee. Look at me, she'd been saying, I want to be here. I do.

The sky was darker. The clouds tumbled across it, low and gray. Her chest felt heavy as she watched the storm approach. Alexander's death, she thought with horror, has freed me. The guilt she'd felt all her life rose in her and filled her until she thought she might burst. And then, as if she did burst, she cried like she had never cried before, in loud, heavy sobs. And the tears that had seemed a part of her for so long left her. Left her, finally.

It rained all night. Cal heard it, dancing on the roof, against the windows. She lay in her bed in the cabin and imagined the rain waltzing, at first lightly, then shifting to a noisy tango. When the pounding became frantic, she gave up on sleep and went to make a cup of tea. She sat on the couch that smelled of the woods and of mothballs. Cal thought of her children, dancing along with go-go dancers on TV. The dancers hung in suspended cages, and did dances called the jerk, the swim, the watusi.

Cal wondered what time it was. She imagined Mackenzie, just a few hours away in San Francisco. Had she been to Iris's yet and read the note? It hadn't been until she got here that Cal realized she had not even signed it with Love, Mom. Or signed it at all. She thought again of her children dancing, their arms flailing. Mackenzie's hair, long and blonde, falling in her face as she moved. Alexander would tease her, call her The Thing, a furry creature from a television show. At the end of one dance, the swim, Mackenzie and Alexander would hold their noses and slowly sink to the floor, like swimmers, imitating the miniskirted caged dancers in their white go-go boots.

A yellow-gray light filled the window. Dawn. She wished it were forty years earlier, and she was sitting in Vivvie's apartment in Boston, leaning against the overstuffed pillows covered in brightly striped Haitian cotton. What did they used to talk about then, hour after hour? Men, usually. Films. Poetry. They would create scenarios —a trek together across the Himalayas. Or to the Taj Mahal, the monument to love.

"We have to be extraordinary," Vivvie used to say. "There's too damned much ordinariness in the world already."

They'd giggle about friends' weddings.

"How tired are you of hearing about color schemes and china patterns?" they'd ask each other. Their closets filled with taffeta and crinoline bridesmaid's dresses in shades called huckleberry, indigo, and saffron.

How had she gone from extraordinary to ordinary so quickly? Cal wondered. It seemed she rose from Vivvie's bright pillows and incense-filled apartment and had gone directly to her own country club wedding, whose details sometimes blurred with those of other weddings where she'd been a bridesmaid. The chicken breasts stuffed with wild rice, the string beans almondine and pale sorbets. Hope stood in a sea-foam-green ruffled gown. In all of the photographs, Cal looked stunned, out of place in the layers of white satin and lace. A child whose name she could no longer remember held her train, daintily, between pudgy fingers.

The ceiling in the cabin began to leak in three places, the raindrops falling through in syncopated time. Do Re Mi. Do Re Mi. Cal put pots and pans under the leaks, the musical drops sounding tinny, Caribbean.

She and Vivvie hardly spoke anymore. It was not that they were any less close, but their lives rotated around such different worlds. When they did talk, it was still like it used to be. Cal would hear Vivvie smoking on the other end, inhaling sharply.

Cal had to look up Vivvie's phone number, it had

been so long since she'd called her. She imagined her in her Vermont house as the phone rang. It was, Cal knew, littered casually with items from all over the world. Rugs and paintings and dusty vases.

A man answered, his voice muddled and British.

"Yes," he said, as if answering a question. "Yes."

"Yes," Cal said too. Then, "Is Vivvie there?"

There was movement, bed springs creaking and the phone scraping.

"Hello. Hello," Vivvie said loudly. She was a traveler, and was used to calls at all hours, from people who didn't stop to think about time zones before they called her.

"It's me," Cal said.

"Where are you?"

"Point Reyes," she said. "You told me once it was purifying here."

"Did I?" Vivvie laughed. "So is the Ganges, some people say."

A new leak started, somewhere close to Cal.

"You've left him," Vivvie said. It was what she always said.

"Yes."

"Not for a Portuguese fisherman? Or was he Italian?"

"Portuguese."

"And you're what? Miserable?"

"I was wondering," Cal said, "whatever became of Missy."

"Missy? She moved to LA, I think. Or San Diego."

"And her daughter? Kathy?"

"I don't have any idea. There were two daughters, weren't there? Wasn't there a Kim?"

Cal listened to Vivvie inhale on a cigarette.

"Who answered the phone?" Cal asked.

Vivvie laughed. "Are we avoiding the issue here?"

"There is no issue," Cal said. "I don't even miss him," she added softly.

"I miss you," Vivvie said. "I miss our grand notions. So few of my students have them. They want to make money. Work for a Fortune 500 company. Buy a Porsche. They think literature and art are a waste of time. A curse. Worse than locusts."

Cal looked for the new leak.

"Did you hear about Isaac?" Vivvie asked.

"Isaac? No." Cal thought of him, naked, stretched out beside her, his skin like yellow marble.

"He killed himself. Up in Montana or Wyoming. Wherever he lived."

Cal waited, for sadness or regret, but felt neither. She had an image of him dipping shreds of pita bread into putty-colored humus and feeding it slowly to her.

"How did he do it?" she asked Vivvie.

"How gruesome. I don't know the details."

"You know," Cal said. "Alexander had drinks with him once. He called to tell me he'd had to entertain a moody minor poet from Montana."

"Did you tell him you knew that minor poet intimately?"

"No."

Cal thought of her own poems, imagined them in print, her name below them. She thought of the rhythms of them, the flow. Isaac had accused her of many things—of being fearful, sheltered, and the writer of overly romantic poetry. "You don't face up to things," he had said once. "You run from harsh realities." She couldn't help but wonder how he had faced up to the harsh reality of his death. Had he put a gun to his head? Hung a noose? There had been times when she had contemplated suicide, thought it might be easier than facing the dullness of her life every day, easier than realizing that she was not even a little extraordinary.

"Actually," Vivvie said. "I think it was pills."

"Pills," Cal said. She thought of all the things, the common everyday things that brought death. Pills and childbirth and bolts of lightning.

"What next?" Vivvie was asking.

For a moment, Cal felt confused. Next? After what?

"You mean since I left Jams?" she said.

"Yes. Of course."

"Life," Cal said.

"I'm going to stay out here," Cal said. "In San Francisco."

She heard Jams's breath, slow and even. She imagined it traveling across the miles of the country, through the telephone wires, to her.

"I thought so," he said, "when I got your postcard."

In that instant, she faltered. Behind her, cars sped south, toward San Francisco, Carmel, San Diego. He knows me so well, she thought. What am I doing? Since Alexander had died, Cal had been consumed by the wasted parts of her life. It had forced her to face the things she had tried to hide from.

But now, standing at this pay phone on a California highway, her husband's voice, which had lately seemed irritating, sounded soothing and comforting in its familiarity. She thought of his arms around her, and she moved against the phone booth as if that would move her closer to him.

"Your voice," he said, "it sounds so good."

"Yours too." At first, when she had called Jams at home, she had been startled when an unfamiliar woman had answered the phone, telling her that Jams no longer lived there. She'd given Cal his number at Oakdale and Cal had felt relieved that he was being taken care of, helped.

"There have been times before," Jams said, "when I thought I was losing you. One summer at the Cape. You actually went away for a day or two."

"I remember." Forty years, she thought, is a very long time. She had, after all, spent her life with this man. She wanted to tell him that their time together wasn't really bad. That it was something in her that had made it worse. She could still recall happy times, she thought.

"One night," she said, "we walked together on the beach. The moonlight was so bright it cast a white glow on everything. The ocean reflected in it like jewels."

This time it was his turn to say it. "I remember."

She thought of how that night they'd made love in the sand, in that incredible moonlight, and for a time she'd thought everything would be all right. Her life, and their life together. They'd rolled, gently, into the water, and she'd watched his body move on top of hers through a film of saltwater, the waves licking them, foamy and cool. Later, back in the crowded rented cottage, with the sounds of everyone breathing all around them, he'd combed the sand from her hair, and licked the salt from her body.

"Perhaps," Jams was saying, "you should have left a long time ago."

"Or you should have tried harder to keep me."

But she knew as she said it that it wasn't in him to keep her. No matter how many moments of love she could recall, they didn't add up to enough. They were just flashes over the years.

"Sometimes," Jams said, "I find myself thinking I should call Alexander. I think, I haven't talked to my son in a very long while."

"I don't let myself think," she said.

"The detective told me that there was probably no pain. That it was all over very quickly."

Cal thought, Yes, it was over too quickly. All of it. The way he was taken, in a split second.

"Sam was here," Jams continued. "With Mackenzie."

"Did he say anything?"

"No. But, Cal, he looks so much like Alexander that it hurt to look at him."

The image of her son as a small boy came rushing to her. Memories she'd fought all these months. She had, over the years, punished herself for her ambivalence about her life, had felt recently that losing Alexander was perhaps her ultimate punishment. But she knew as she stood here with the Pacific Ocean somewhere behind her and the smell of redwoods in the air, that despite that ambivalence, ultimately she had loved her children, and had done the best she could do with them.

"Jams," she said. Her voice was choked with tears. "I loved him. You know that, don't you?"

"Yes," he said. "Of course."

Again, his breathing filled the silence. Cal pressed her head against the cool metal of the phone. Before she'd called him, she had taken all the silly souvenirs that she'd accumulated over this trip and had thrown them away, emptying the trunk completely. In San Francisco she would sell the car.

"I thought," she said finally, "that I'd open a bookstore in the city. Maybe have a little coffee shop in it too. Have poetry readings there. And good books. And espresso."

"You would like that," he said.

"Maybe I'll call it Porter's."

"Cal's," he said.

"I gave myself that nickname, you know."

"No," he said, "you never told me."

"I was ten. I thought Caroline was such an ordinary name. I never felt like a Caroline. One day I read in a book about a young girl named Cal. She had a magical horse and together they rode around the world and had adventures.''

She hesitated. ''The horse's name was Alexander,'' she said. ''I announced at breakfast the next day that I wanted to be called Cal. My mother said she'd do no such thing. Caroline, she said, was a perfectly good name. But eventually they came around to my way of thinking.''

''You never told me,'' he said again.

''Well.''

''The renters,'' he said, ''at the house. They want to buy it.''

She nodded. This was it.

''They have,'' Jams said, ''two little girls.''

She thought of two girls growing up there, carving their names in a beam in the attic, their growth being marked off on the doorframe of the master bedroom.

''Tell them where our names are,'' she said, ''mine and Hope's. Tell them not to paint over those names.''

''I will,'' he said. ''Cal?''

''Yes?''

''Cal,'' he said, ''did you ever love me at all?''

She felt like he was an old friend, someone she'd known for a long time, a long time ago. Then she thought again of that night on the beach, and the way he'd looked in the moonlight.

''Yes,'' she said. ''I did.''

Hope looked out the window, then at her watch.

''Five more minutes, John-Glenn,'' she said.

She used the window for a mirror, put on more lipstick, fluffed her hair. She had on her wedding suit, white wool with gold buttons. A Chanel suit her mother had bought her long ago.

''I'm leaving these,'' John-Glenn said.

Hope turned.

He stood in the living room, surrounded by his butterflies, stacks of them, layer after layer of velvet colors, their wings spread and tacked.

"Leaving them?" she said.

His whole life had been spent with these butterflies. Catching them, labeling them, affixing them to the boards. He had files on all of them. Once he had told her he was going to go to Indonesia where the world's biggest butterflies lived. He had saved pennies for months, filled empty mayonnaise and Ragu jars with pennies.

"They're all dead," he said.

"But they've always been dead."

He shrugged. "I don't want them."

"All right," she said, and she looked out the window again.

In her suitcase, wrapped in tissue, she had all the framed photographs from the mantel. Alexander and Grammie, frozen forever in life, captured in short instants —at Christmas, in a Little League game, sitting in a favorite chair.

"Tell me again," John-Glenn said.

Hope hesitated. All these years she told him Ricardo was dead. Now, here they were, ready to go off with him on his Caribbean tour. You have haunted me like a ghost, Ricardo had told her yesterday morning in his hotel room. She had run her fingers over his hairy body, the hair thick and black and curly. Since you left, she'd told him, I've felt like a ghost. His mouth tasted the same as always, of cigars and strong coffee. He still wore a lime-scented cologne. She had been afraid lying there with him, that when he left her again, she would truly fade away.

All of her life she'd been the odd one, shadowed by a strong mother and a sister, beautiful and smart. She had been, always, the most alive with Ricardo. Come with me on this tour, he'd said. His hand had drawn small circles on her stomach as he talked. The islands' names sounded magical. Barbados and Antigua and Curaçao. She'd imagined palm trees and drinks served in coconuts. Giant seashells, delicate and pink and perfectly shaped, each elaborate curve holding the ocean inside.

"Well," Hope said to John-Glenn, "there was a plane crash and they thought Ricardo had been killed—"

"But really it was someone else. Right?"

When she'd come home yesterday and had told John-Glenn the news, he'd wanted to write to the children of singers who had died in plane crashes. Maybe your father is alive too, he wanted to tell them. Check with the authorities. He'd shown her a list. Buddy Holly. Ricky Nelson. Jim Croce. She'd felt guilty then for the lie.

"Did John Lennon die in a plane crash?" John-Glenn asked her. He stood beside her at the window, both of them looking out at the snowy parking lot. The sun reflected on the snow like tinsel on a Christmas tree.

"No," she said.

"Did Paul McCartney?"

"Paul McCartney's alive."

"He is?"

Hope remembered something once, Alexander trying to play a record backwards. "I Am a Walrus"? Somewhere it said that Paul was dead.

"Maybe not," she said. "I can't remember."

John-Glenn glanced back at the butterflies. A note he laid on top said—"FOR SAM." Hope touched him, rested her hand on his. They stood like that, gazing out, waiting, long after it grew dark, after the bright lights flashed on in the mall parking lot. Above them, the moon was a milky white sliver. Neither of them spoke. They just kept waiting.

In her mind, Hope said the names of the islands again. Barbados. Antigua. Curaçao. She imagined a balmy night, Ricardo Havana and the Hoochie-Coo's on stage, and Ricardo looking right at her as he sang. "Say, it's only a paper moon, sailing over a cardboard sea. But it wouldn't be make believe if you believed in me."

Jams had a lot to do. He had to talk to Patty and her husband about buying the house. He had to pack his things and call his brother in Pennsylvania. The hardware business was what he knew and what he was going back to. Nuts, bolts, two-by-fours. Jams could see himself already in one of the Porter Hardware Stores, could smell the scent of sawdust and new wood.

One more thing to do first, though.

Ursula's new house was small and painted dark green. It sat in a circle of houses around a tiny pond, covered with ice that shone black-blue in the night.

She came to the door wearing new jeans and a V-neck sweater, the same orange as her hair. She was barefoot, and her toenails were round, painted the color of cranberries.

"Hi," she said.

The house had all the smells of newness—floor wax and fresh paint. Unpacked boxes were pushed into one corner. On the coffee table were a bottle of wine and two glasses.

"Nice place," Jams said, uncertain of what else to say.

He felt awkward around her. And old, embarrassed by the memory of their kisses.

She motioned toward the couch, and he sat, watching as she poured the wine. A California chardonnay. He imagined Cal out there, sipping the same wine.

"So you're leaving the hospital too," she said.

"I'm going back to Pennsylvania. Out of retirement and into the old family business. I never knew too much about liquor anyway."

She nodded.

He thought she looked sad. He tilted her face up.

"Hey, there," he said.

"I was just getting to know you," she said.

Her perfume was sweet and heavy, like honey.

"I'm an old guy," he said.

As he said it, he thought of himself in a singles bar, surrounded by other wifeless men, buying white wine spritzers for women who took Chinese cooking classes and Club Med vacations.

"I haven't been alone for over thirty years," he said.

"She's really not coming back? I mean, I know women her age who go to find themselves for a while. But they come back."

He wanted to say that Cal had found herself long ago. But he just shrugged.

"I'm going to LA, like I told you," she said.

Jams realized he still held her chin cupped in his hand. He found himself wondering what her body was like, all plump and white with orange freckles everywhere. So opposite of Cal, of what he'd known for so long.

"The game show," he said.

She nodded, her face sinking deeper into his hand.

"You'll win."

"Oh," she said. "I don't know."

"No. You will."

Her freckles were mesmerizing.

"If I connected these dots," he said, tracing the freckles along one cheek, "what would I find? The shape of Florida? A hitchhiker's thumb?"

She put her hand on top of his as he moved along her face.

"You'd find," she said, "a broken heart."

He was surprised, later, to learn that she was forty.

That's okay, he thought. Then he had stopped thinking about it, and lost himself in her whiteness. She was soft everywhere, like a cloud, like angels' hair. He couldn't even remember the last time he'd made love. An image of Cal came to him only once, when he first entered Ursula. In it, Cal was flushed and smiling, her head turned away from him.

"There are trains to Philly," he said afterward.

Her bed was narrow, the light beside it a peach-colored frosted ballerina. "I could pick you up at the station and you could spend the weekend."

In the dim light, her freckles disappeared, or blended together completely. Her breasts were large and white, and he held one lightly in his hand.

"Yes," she said. "We'll go to see the Liberty Bell."

Jams laughed. He was beginning to lighten, to feel less blurred and more even again, like he was landing from a long way away. He didn't want to be alone. He didn't want to sit in that bar he'd imagined or buy those women drinks. He would go to Pennsylvania and work in the store and have Ursula come on weekends. She would tell him facts he'd never known. Tonight, in bed, she'd asked him if he knew the three state capitals with president's names in them. She would fill him with facts.

"You know," he said, sitting up, "I came here to return something to you."

"Return something?"

He groped on the floor for his pants, reached into a pocket.

"Here."

He dropped her lipstick, and the Certs, and the three pennies onto the bed.

She examined the lipstick.

"Cantaloupe," she said. "That's mine."

"I took them from your pocket the other night."

"You stole them."

He wanted to turn off the light. She was sitting up too, and the sheets had fallen from her, and he wanted to lose himself inside her again. He reached for the light, but she stopped him, climbed on top of him, and held his wrists. Her freckles made patterns on her chest.

"But you brought them back," she said.

"Yes."

"And we'll go to see the Liberty Bell."

"Yes."

His mind was filling again with her whiteness.

"Jackson, Mississippi," she said. "Jefferson City, Missouri. Lincoln, Nebraska."

CHAPTER TWENTY-TWO

M ackenzie had imagined that she and her mother would rush into each other's arms when they finally met up. She would, she had thought, bury her head against Cal and say, "Let's go home, Mom." But instead they stood awkwardly, mother and daughter, in the Cafe Trieste, while around them people read newspapers, the pink section of the *Chronicle* scattered around like crepe paper at a party. The smell of coffee hung in the air, surrounded them.

The night before, Jason had told her that he'd gone ahead and bought the co-op. Come back, he'd said. She had screamed at him, cried. "You are so selfish," she'd said. "What about my family?" "What about us?" he was saying when she'd slammed the phone down.

Cal smiled at her, tentatively. She indicated a wooden chair, always the perfect hostess.

"I was having a café au lait," Cal said. Her hair was

too long, and was streaked with gray. She had it pulled back, fastened it with a fat barrette, like a schoolgirl would have done.

Mackenzie ordered an espresso, but when it came she concentrated on shredding the lemon peel rather than drinking the coffee.

Beside them, a gray-haired man wearing a lime-green beret held a woman's hand. The woman wore a necklace made of shark's teeth, and a long purple dress.

"But I love you," he said.

"But I can't stay," she said.

"But I love you."

"But I can't stay."

Over and over.

And then, out of somewhere deep within her, Mackenzie wailed, a low cry of unbearable sadness.

"Mom," she said, "why did Alexander die?"

It wasn't what she had thought to say. She had felt her mission was to bring her mother back home. But sitting here she felt no need greater than the need to hug her brother. And her arms ached from the emptiness. Mackenzie bent her head, rested it on the table, and sobbed.

Cal, seeing her daughter there, felt the emptiness too. Her life, everything that had come before, was over. She had left it. She reached for her daughter, tried to bring her close despite the distance of the table between them, and was able only to clutch at Mackenzie's arms.

It was a long time before Mackenzie lifted her head. The tears made her eyes blaze turquoise, like the Caribbean.

"I. Want. To. Go. Home." Her voice was choppy from tears.

Cal shook her head sadly.

"We have to get on with our lives," she said softly. Mackenzie thought, What have I done to get on with my own?

Earlier that morning, Daisy had called her at the hotel. "Bring Sam back," she'd said. "It's time we got on with our lives." Everyone was moving forward, Mackenzie thought, except for her. She was frozen in time with Alexander, who would never be able to get on with his life. "Remember that guy I told you about?" Daisy had said shyly. "We're getting married. Put Sam on. Let me tell him." Sam had listened, frowning, his foot swaying, back and forth, faster and faster.

Mackenzie had wondered what they had told him about Alexander. That he was visiting the angels? Or sleeping in heaven? Those were the things she had heard as a child.

"Sam," Mackenzie had said when Daisy hung up. "Do you understand that your daddy can't come back?"

The little boy had shaken his head, slowly. And his mouth had moved as if words were there, ready to spill out at any time.

Cal still held Mackenzie's arms, tight.

"I want you to understand something," she was saying.

"No."

"I'm staying here, Mackenzie. I drove around all these months, running from myself. I have to stop. I have to face things. So do you.'"

"What about Dad?"

"We've talked. He understands. I'm not saying any of this is easy, Mackenzie."

She looked at her mother.

"Mom," she said, "what about me?"

Cal dropped her arms.

"I don't know," she said.

Mackenzie walked through the unfamiliar streets to pick up Sam at Iris's. She walked, crying, stopping to get her bearings, then quickly losing them again.

Remember our special Porter dinners? she had said to her mother. Remember our Christmas trees? Remember us? Her mother had said, "We all remember." Or maybe she'd said "We'll always remember." Mackenzie wasn't even sure which.

She hugged herself against the wind. She was perched on top of a hill that dipped straight down. A VW kept rolling backwards, trying to make it up. The Golden Gate Bridge stretched, orange, across the bay, then disappeared into the fog.

The VW rolled back again.

What do you call a pregnant elephant on roller skates? Alexander had asked her. A Volkswagen! He'd taught her elephant jokes and how to play "Heart and Soul" on the piano and the French verse of the Beatles song "Michelle."

She closed her eyes and pictured herself with Alexander. They were children again, in the living room at home, watching the *Ed Sullivan Show*. The Z in Zenith across the bottom of the television was a jagged lightning bolt. The Beatles were on. Alexander had written out the French words on index cards so that they could sing along with John, Paul, George, and Ringo. His arm was draped around her shoulder.

"My seester," he whispered in a terrible French accent. "Je t'aime."

"Let's have a big hand," Ed Sullivan said, "for the Beatles."

No one else in the world had that memory but her.

When Mackenzie opened her eyes, the fog was lifting slowly from the bridge, like a film in slow motion.

The VW reached the top, chugging, then disappeared up the next hill, a small fat dot. She looked again across the bridge. The burnished hills of Sausalito and Tiberon were beginning to peek out.

*   *   *

Things were happening that Sam didn't understand.

His grandmother was here, in San Francisco, somewhere between all these hills and the bridges and water and wet misty clouds. Aunt Mackenzie had told him that his grandmother had driven across the country all by herself. The United States stretched across his mind, big and bumpy. He thought of the cactus he'd seen on that postcard, the way the branches looked like arms, waving good-bye.

"While you're with Iris," Mackenzie had told him, "I'm going to get Grandma Cal and she's going to come home with us. Home to Rhode Island."

But the way his aunt had said it made Sam think it wasn't really true. It hadn't even sounded like she believed it, and Sam had thought of Rhode Island, the way it looked on maps his father used to show him, just a tiny speck with Providence floating in the Atlantic. He could hardly imagine his grandmother in San Francisco. She belonged, instead, by the big window in the front room of her house, gazing out. Her eyes, he thought, sometimes seemed like they were looking very far away, at something very distant.

He didn't understand why his Aunt Mackenzie had yelled at Jason last night. Or why she'd slammed the phone down hard, then sat and listened to it ring without picking it up, even though she had to know it was him calling back. Sam had counted ten rings before it stopped. At home, he and his mother sat and *waited* for the phone to ring, and if it finally did, Daisy practically pounced on it. Usually, though, they just sat and waited. Sometimes, Daisy would call the telephone company and tell them to check for trouble on the line. She would never, never just let it ring like Mackenzie had. Besides, Sam thought she liked Jason. They had held hands while they walked down that street full of Indian restaurants, the street that smelled like a foreign country must smell. He thought they were in love and would get married, that Mackenzie would wear a long white gown, like Brandy's Barbie doll, with tiny ballerina slippers and a veil that floated like clouds around her. But now she was mad at Jason and Sam wasn't so sure they would get married after all.

And then, this morning, his mother had called and told him that *she* was getting married to a man named Willie.

"Sam," she'd said, "I was too excited to wait for you to get home before I told you. You're going to love Willie. He paints great big pictures. He can help you with your drawings. And he can play lots of songs on the guitar." Then she'd added, "He's got a big beard." Like that would make it all right.

"So what?" Sam had screamed in his mind. "What if Daddy comes back and you are married to a man named Willie?" He'd scrunched his eyes shut, pretended he was in a seashell, on a beach. Then he'd tried to imagine his father's face. Lately, his father's face had started to grow fuzzy, no matter how hard he tried to remember it exactly. Just like he mixed up his father's stories with the ones in books, he had started to mix up his father's face with the way he looked in pictures. After he'd hung up the telephone this morning, he'd only been able to think of his father the way he looked on Aunt Hope's mantel—in uniform, swinging a bat, in a Little League game.

Then, just when Sam was thinking that even the *memory* of his father was disappearing, Mackenzie had said, "Sam, do you understand that your daddy can't ever come back?"

No, Sam had thought, I don't understand.

Now, after a day with Aunt Iris, playing checkers over and over and polishing her crystal pyramid, she was telling him the same thing.

"I know," she said, "that Willie can't replace your daddy. But he'll be kind and fun in a different way. A new way."

She bent beside the pyramid.

"Sam," she said, "as sad and terrible as it may be, your real daddy is gone. He's left this world of ours." Her voice was soft and sweet. "He can't come back anymore."

Sam thought of his father. He thought of Helen Keller and the man on the street who couldn't talk. He thought of Atlantis and how it disappeared and never was found again.

When Mackenzie came to get him, he was staring in the bathroom mirror. Waiting to vanish.

Mackenzie and Sam walked from Iris's down Union Street to the hotel.

She had picked him up and talked to Iris, her tone light and almost cheerful, even though her eyes were red and puffy from crying. Outside the apartment, Mackenzie had held Sam's hand tight as she leaned against the building, as if she could somehow get strength from the stucco wall. Sam had focused on the man wearing the red bandana who sat in the doorway. His sign said: STOP LBJ. Later, a few blocks away, Mackenzie had said softly, "Grandma's not coming home after all." That was all she said. She didn't let go of Sam's hand.

Every few minutes he poked himself with his free hand, pinched his flesh, pressed his nails hard into his palm. Mackenzie stared straight ahead as they walked. She felt numb, the way she had been right after Alexander died, after she'd realized that her brother was never coming back again.

The people on Union Street pushed past them. Laughter trickled out of an open window, and music. Huey

Lewis and the News. *The Heart of Rock and Roll is Still Beating.*

Mackenzie tried to imagine going back to Rhode Island. She thought of the seashore, the smell of clam chowder. She thought of that woman, Patty, living in the house, moving easily through the mostly empty rooms. Her mother, Mackenzie thought, had seemed girlish in the cafe this morning—the way she touched her hair, the new light in her eyes.

Sam tugged at his aunt's hand.

"What?" she said. She looked down at him and was, again, struck by the blueness of his eyes, by the fact that this little boy was part of Alexander.

He led her into a store. Harry's Haberdashery. It smelled of mothballs and potatoes. Hats were crammed onto every available space—the tops of counters, stacked on racks, hanging on hooks.

Sam stood, confused for a moment, in the center of the tiny store. He grabbed the flesh on his arm, below his shoulders, and squeezed, hard.

"Sam," Mackenzie said.

A sales clerk sat perched on a stool in the corner. His belly was big and round, stretched tight across his T-shirt. The shirt said KILL 'EM ALL AND LET GOD SORT 'EM OUT. His hair hung in a flat ponytail, woven with leather.

"You okay, kid?" he said.

Sam looked around, took in all the hats. Then he began to put them on. A tall silk top hat. A straw boater. A dusty gray fedora, a white Panama, a Brooklyn Dodgers cap. One on top of the other. He turned very slowly, one hand held high to catch any that might topple off, and faced the store's triple mirror. His image looked back at him from every angle. Sam traced the shape of his face with one finger, as if its tip held a magic potion that he was anointing himself with. The places he touched softened and he smiled, a slow, unsure smile. He reached up, and placed one last hat on the lopsided stack he already wore. A blue sombrero, heavily beaded and braided and fringed. His mouth opened, then closed quickly.

"Hey," the salesman said.

For an instant, Sam's eyes grew round and flat. Then they refocused and settled on the image of himself wearing all those silly hats. He pointed his finger at the reflection, opened his mouth, and laughed. Right out loud. At first, the laugh was tinny and cracked, like the laugh of an old man. But as it grew louder and stronger, it turned into the laugh, the uncontrollable giggle, of a little boy.

Mackenzie kneeled down beside him.

"Sam," she said.

He laughed even harder, his finger still pointing to his own reflection in the mirror, the sombrero's fringe bouncing and dancing along with him. And then Mackenzie began to laugh too. She put her arms around his shoulders and laughed with him.

The salesman said he'd never heard anyone laugh so hard before. He began to put new combinations of hats on Sam. A black Stetson. A bowler. A fishing hat with dangling bait. Sam laughed even more.

Mackenzie stood back and watched him, listened to the sound of his voice. She imagined him back in Maryland. Playing with Brandy. Riding in Daisy's big pink car. He would get used to this man, Willie. They would eat breakfast together, play softball. She thought of her mother, how she looked stronger and younger in that cafe this morning. Mackenzie looked away from Sam, out the window. She felt again a sharp pain of loss and desperation. Sam was going to be all right in time. Her mother was going to live here, write poems, open a bookstore, probably find a lover. Jams had told her that her mother wasn't going to come back. He had said it with such certainty. Everyone was going to get through this.

Her eyes settled on a pay phone at the back of the store. Mackenzie went to it and dialed Jason's number. Maybe Kyle O'Day was in that new apartment now, swishing her long red braid, popping her bubble gum. Maybe he had changed his mind about Mackenzie. He might not ask her again.

Please be there, she thought as the telephone rang. She imagined the wires carrying her energy to him, imagined the way they had shuddered with electricity and killed Alexander. Perhaps now they could save her.

"Hello," he said.

She took a deep breath.

"Hello," he said again.

"It's me," she said. She squeezed the cord hard in her hands.

"Mackenzie," Jason said, "come home."